A Plain Disappearance

A Plain Disappearance

An Appleseed Creek Mystery

Amanda Flower

Nashville, Tennessee

Printed in the United States of America

978-1-4336-7699-4

Published by B&H Publishing Group,
Nashville, Tennessee

Dewey Decimal Classification: F
Subject Heading: ROMANTIC SUSPENSE NOVELS \ AMISH—FICTION \ MYSTERY FICTION

Publisher's Note: The characters and events in this book are fictional, and any resemblance to actual persons or events is coincidental.

1 2 3 4 5 6 7 8 • 17 16 15 14 13

For Meredith and Hayden
and in memory of Puddleglum

Acknowledgments

Special thanks to my agent and friend, Nicole Resciniti. You are a shooting star to the top. Thank you for allowing me to hitch a ride.

Always thanks to my editors, Julie Gwinn and Julie Carobini, for pushing me and helping me see how to make each book better than the last. Also, thanks to the rest of the B&H team. You are my personal dream team.

Thank you to Suzy Schroeder-Green, who answers my tireless technology questions and whose answers help both Chloe and me look smarter on the job. And appreciation to the Ursuline College community for encouraging one of its librarians to moonlight as a mystery author, and for finding the academic twists in my novels amusing.

Always love and gratitude to my mom, Pamela Flower, who reads every word of everything I write.

And finally, I want to thank my heavenly Father for my dreams and for the people around me who help them come true.

Chapter One

Steam rose from Sparky's nose and mouth into the frigid late December air as he shook his bridle and pulled the sleigh over a small hill. The sleigh owner's grandson, Timothy Troyer, sat in the driver seat, wearing a thick wool coat, black knit cap, and navy scarf wrapped about his neck. He held the reins with a light but firm touch, and he looked every bit the part of a young Amish man out for a sleigh ride—even though he'd left the Amish way years before.

Did that mean I was the Amish girl to complete the picturesque scene? I pulled the wool blanket up closer to my face and chuckled to myself. Beneath it I wore a purple and gray ski jacket and flannel-lined jeans. A pink and purple Fair Isle stocking cap, complete with pompom, covered my shoulder-length, straight red hair, and tortoise shell-patterned framed sunglasses protected my hazel eyes from the sun's glare off of the snow. *Not exactly Amish attire.*

Timothy cut his bright blue eyes to me, and a smile played on the corners of his mouth. "What's so funny?"

I burrowed deeper under the heavy wool blankets wrapped around me cocoon-style. "I was just thinking that this was unlike any first date that I've ever been on."

Amusement lit his eyes. "Have you had many first dates?"

"A few," I teased.

"Really. And what did you do on these dates?"

I thought for a minute. "Went to the movies or out for coffee. Once a date took me putt-putt golfing."

"Putt-putt golfing?" He laughed. "And how am I doing in comparison to that?"

"Not bad. The putt-putt guy didn't ask me out on a second date when I beat him twice in a row."

He winked at me. "I'm glad to hear it."

Ahead of us a weathered barn came into view through a stand of pine trees. The trees stood well over twenty feet high in a straight line perhaps to protect the barn from the wind and rain flying across the fields. If their purpose was to shelter the barn from Ohio's dramatic change in seasons, nature won that battle. What remained of the old building consisted of grayish-white weathered boards, the structure's edges and shape barely discernible in the falling snow until Sparky and the sleigh cleared the stand of trees.

Timothy pulled back on the reins. "Whoa!"

The horse came to a stop.

I released my hold on the blanket. "Why are we stopping?"

"I thought it might be nice to stretch our legs. The hardest part of the winter for me is being stuck indoors."

I tilted my chin. "You don't exactly have a desk job." Timothy was a sought-after carpenter in Knox County and he'd parlayed his business into being a general contractor. Unlike me, he never sat still. As the Director of Computer Services at Harshberger College, I spent most of my time sitting at a desk in front of a computer screen. I inhaled the cold air, and it stung the inside of my nose. "A walk sounds nice."

Timothy hopped out of the sleigh and whistled. His black-and-brown, mixed-breed dog, Mabel, snuffled from her spot under the bench seat but made no move to leave the warmth of the sleigh. Her body curved around the warm brick that Grandfather Zook—the sleigh's owner—had placed inside before we left the Troyer farm. "Come on, girl," Timothy said.

The reluctant dog whimpered.

Timothy placed his hands on his hips—a pose his mother made on a daily basis when she dealt with her seven-year-old son, Thomas. I stifled another chuckle.

Mabel woofed softly, but finally she wriggled out of her place. The dog jumped into the snow, and a cloud of white flew into the air and covered her entire body with a fine dust.

I stood, about to jump from the sleigh myself.

"Wait!" Timothy ran toward me.

I glanced around in search of any danger that may have caused Timothy's outburst. All I saw was the old forgotten barn, the pine trees, and the white fields. "What? What's wrong?"

He beamed at me and extended his hand. "Let me help you."

My face grew hot, but I placed my gloved hand into Timothy's and jumped lightly to the ground. To my pleasure, when I found my footing, he didn't release my hand. Despite the leather gloves that kept our skin from touching, a charge passed between us—something I first had noticed when I met Timothy five months ago after moving to Appleseed Creek, Ohio, from Cleveland.

Despite Mabel's grumbling about leaving the warmth of her blankets in the sleigh, she leaped over a snow-covered stump and rolled onto her back, lavishing herself in the feeling of white powder against her fluffy body.

Timothy blew out a mock sigh. "It's going to take me an hour to brush all of the knots out of her coat."

I smiled. Snow fell all around us, as if Timothy, Mabel, and I moved forward inside a snow globe shaken by a giant's hand. I could almost hear the tinkling notes of the music box.

I pointed to the barn. "Whose farm is this?"

Timothy squinted against the snow's glare. "This is the old Gundy place."

"Gundy? I don't think I've heard that name before."

Timothy brushed away the snow gathering on his coat sleeve. "They moved to Colorado six or seven years ago."

"They didn't sell their property before they moved?"

"Not as far as I know."

I took in the crooked window shutters and gaping hole in the roof of the barn. "It is pretty in a sad, abandoned sort of way," I said. "Becky should come here sometime with her paints and try to capture its loveliness before it falls to the ground."

Becky was Timothy's nineteen-year-old sister, my housemate, and an aspiring artist. Her brother had left the Amish in search of a different kind of Christian faith, but she left the Amish way to pursue her art—a pursuit put on hold by a terrible auto-buggy accident. The collision left an Amish bishop dead and Becky with a criminal record.

Timothy grabbed my other hand and turned me toward him. "I'm glad you like it, but I didn't bring you here just to see the old barn. I brought you here to give you your Christmas gift."

I frowned. "I thought we agreed to exchange them with your family tomorrow on Christmas Eve. I didn't bring mine for you."

He smiled. "I wanted to give you something without the entire family watching." He removed a small black box with a bright red bow on top from his coat pocket.

My breath caught. It was too soon. I wasn't ready for what he was about to ask me. He placed the box into my hand, and by its long rectangular shape I realized it wasn't a ring box at all. Disappointment replaced the sudden rush of fear that had coursed through my body.

"Open it," Timothy whispered. His voice sounded so much like Mr. Green's did when he watched his children, Tanisha, my best friend, and her young brother open one of their presents Christmas morning, I felt a rush of homesickness for the family that took me in when my father walked away from me. For Mr. Green the joy of Christmas was truly in the giving. I wasn't the least bit surprised that Timothy was the same way.

I opened the box. Inside on a bed of baby blue velvet laid a delicate silver necklace with two small charms on it. One of the charms was a computer mouse, the other a hammer. I glanced up at Timothy.

He removed the necklace from the box. "Don't you see? These things can be side by side."

He didn't need to explain. Timothy was the hammer, and I the computer mouse. It was such a thoughtful and creative gift, that it brought tears to my eyes. Embarrassment surfaced, too. Timothy bought me this lovely gift and I had a new ratchet set wrapped for him under my Christmas tree. How romantic was that? I suppressed a groan.

"Let me put it on you." Timothy stepped behind me and hung the necklace around my throat. He tucked the clasp under the collar of my ski coat, his calloused fingers brushing the nape of my neck, raising goose bumps on my skin. He moved back around to face me.

I kept the charms out on top of my scarf and rolled them back and forth between my fingers. "How did you find these?"

"Google." He laughed. "Actually, I found them with Becky's help."

Although Becky left her Amish family much more recently than Timothy had, she was already a whiz at searching and shopping online. Before long she would become better at it than me—and I worked with computers for a living.

"Thank you. I love it. It's the most thoughtful gift I've ever received."

Timothy leaned forward, and I closed my eyes. Nothing happened. I opened them again and I blushed. Timothy was staring at Mabel. She was hunched low to the ground as if prepared to spring into action. A growl escaped from deep within her throat.

I tucked my silver necklace from sight under my coat. "I've never heard her make that sound before."

Timothy placed his hand on the dog's fluffy head. "Neither have I."

Mabel's growls became louder and more ferocious.

I scanned the white landscape. "Do you think a wild animal is out here? Like a bear or a coyote?"

Timothy shook his head. "I've never seen a bear in Knox County and a coyote is too skittish to hang around us with Mabel's scent in the air."

"What—"

My next question was cut off as Mabel launched from her frozen position, running full tilt for the barn. Without a word, Timothy and I ran after her.

We drew closer, the barn much larger than I had first thought. In its prime, it could have housed horses, cows, and other large livestock. We reached the barn and icicles the size of baseball bats hung from eaves twenty feet above us. Mabel had already rounded the far corner of the weathered structure.

We followed her, and I hoped that she wouldn't run too far, or worse, come across the bear I worried about. As we jogged around the corner, we stopped short to avoid tripping over Mabel who, in a hunched position, stared at an object half-buried in the snow.

We peered over her at the mound of black and navy cloth. On closer inspection, it was much more than cloth that had caught Mabel's attention—a bluish, fine-boned hand stuck out of the snow, reaching for us.

Chapter Two

Timothy knelt on the ground beside the buried body. He shoveled snow away with his gloved hands, revealing a girl's head and neck. The black bonnet confirmed what I thought the moment we saw the hand: She was Amish and young. Her face was like a porcelain doll's—flawless skin and fine-boned much like the hand. It was lovely except for the otherworldly bluish tint to it. Timothy placed a finger to her neck. I knew what he would say even before he opened his mouth. No one that blue could still be here on earth.

Timothy dropped his hand to his side and sat back on his feet. "She's dead."

I removed my cell phone from deep in my parka's inner pocket and dialed a number with which I was all too familiar.

Chief Rose answered on the first ring. "What is it, Humphrey? Did you run into Fanning and Buckley?" She asked this in her typically terse fashion.

I closed my eyes. Curt Fanning and Brock Buckley, a couple of local thugs, had spent the last few months harassing me and the entire Troyer family. Could they have had something to do with the Amish girl's death? I winced from the stab of a headache coming on.

In the background, I heard laughter, conversation, and Christmas music playing. Was the Appleseed Creek Chief of Police at a holiday party? I found it startling to think Chief Rose had a life outside of her job, which she seemed to live, breathe, and eat. At least until I heard the background music playing through my phone.

"Are you still there?" she asked.

I removed my Fair Isle hat and pressed the phone closer to my ear. "Yes. I'm still here. We have a problem, and it doesn't involve Curt and Brock. At least, I don't think it does."

"I'm not going to like this, am I? Whatever this is, it's going to cause me to leave this party, isn't it?"

"I'm afraid so."

"Where are you?" Sharpness in her voice replaced the sarcasm.

"Um." I lowered the phone just a tad. "Timothy, where are we?"

He stood and held out his hand for the phone. I gave it to him and listened while he described our location and the sad discovery.

Mabel's growling stopped. She walked over to me and leaned against my leg with a whimper. I dug my fingers into the curly fur on the top of her head. "You did good, girl."

I turned my eyes away from the girl's face then. She was so young—just a teenager—a life cut short. I swallowed the lump in my throat.

Timothy handed the phone back to me. "It's going to take Greta and her officers a little while to reach us. Also, depending on the location, the sheriff and some deputies may have to be rounded up too. I don't know if this property falls within the limits of Appleseed Creek."

I couldn't look at the blue face, so I concentrated on the hand. "Do you know her?"

Timothy grimaced. "*Ya*," he said, using the Pennsylvania Dutch word. He was more likely to pepper his English speech with his first language when he was around his family or when he was upset. At this moment, it was the latter.

"Who is she?"

He walked over to stand next to Mabel and me. "Katie Lambright."

Katie Lambright. I rolled the name around in my head. I didn't remember meeting a Katie since moving to the county, but my stomach dropped. I did know a Lambright. Anna Lambright was Timothy's thirteen-year-old sister, Ruth's, best friend. I prayed I was wrong. "Is she related to Anna?"

He turned to me, tears in his eyes. "Katie was Anna's older sister."

Ruth and Anna had only recently been allowed to see each other again. The bishop and the deacon had punished the Troyer family for continuing contact with Timothy and Becky, who left the Amish way, by forbidding Anna to interact with Ruth. The separation had hurt Ruth deeply and almost ruined their friendship. However, when the bishop changed his mind and saw there was no harm in the Troyers interacting with their English children, Ruth's father had relented.

This tragedy could sever their friendship again—especially since Timothy and I were the ones to discover Katie's body.

Timothy strode around the corner of the barn.

Mabel and I hurried after him. "What are you doing?"

He slowed just long enough to glance at us over his shoulder. "I want to take a look around before Greta arrives."

The barn door stood halfway open and hung awkwardly from its hinges. A drift of snow four feet high blocked the doorway. Undeterred, Timothy stepped into the snow drift and sunk up to his thighs. He turned his head. "Mabel, stay."

The brown and black dog sat with a whine.

Timothy's steps broke a path into the barn that I was able to follow. The drift was deep but not long. It extended perhaps four feet into the huge expanse of the barn.

Inside the barn was dark, but the gaping hole in the roof worked as a sky light. We stood and let our eyes adjust. The items inside of the barn were what I expected to find: piles of old boards, rusty nails sticking out of the pillars, and grungy wagon wheels. Nothing was of any interest or relation to Katie Lambright, who lay dead on the other side of the barn wall.

Light from the hole in the roof reflected off the metal surface at the back of the building. Without discussion, Timothy and I moved toward the reflection.

The source of the light was a rearview car mirror sticking out of a blue milk crate. The crate was half-covered with an enormous blue tarp. Timothy pulled back the tarp, revealing dozens, maybe hundreds, of automobile parts from steering wheels to spark plugs. Ten tire irons were piled in a stack. "Looks like someone used this old barn for extra storage."

"Is that allowed?"

He shook his head. "Not without the permission of the owner."

"Who is somewhere in Colorado."

"Right."

"Maybe all this belonged to the Gundys."

Timothy shook his head. "They're Amish."

The sound of snowmobiles broke into the tranquil quiet of the frozen farmland. Chief Rose and her posse were coming.

Timothy turned. "We'd better step outside. Greta won't like it if she finds us in here."

"She'll know we were. We can't really hide all the tracks we made in the snow."

Timothy shoved his hands into his pockets. "You're right."

I scanned the car parts one last time because I knew Chief Rose would never allow me to snoop in the barn after she arrived. I gasped and stared at one of the mirrors.

Timothy touched my arm. "Chloe, what is it?"

Silver duct tape covered every inch of it except for the mirror itself. The duct taping had been a careful job, free of bumps or creases. Only one mechanic in Knox County, perhaps in the entire state of Ohio, used duct tape as a fix-all for automobiles and everything else: Uncle Billy from Uncle Billy's Budget Autos.

"What is it?" Timothy asked a second time.

I pulled a smaller tarp off of another crate, dozens of new shiny rolls of duct tape inside. "Duct tape."

Timothy picked up the duct-taped mirror. "It could just mean that this is Billy's stuff. It doesn't mean he has anything to do with . . . with Katie outside." He set it back inside of the crate.

Although Timothy made sense, something told me that Billy might have a larger role in this than either of us wanted to believe.

The noise outside grew louder now. I followed Timothy out of the barn as three snowmobiles pulled up about twenty yards from Sparky and the sleigh. The horse whinnied and kicked the ground as if to complain about the noise. Mabel was less discreet and barked at the intruders. The chief and her officers cut their engines.

Timothy grabbed Mabel by the collar and pulled her back toward the sleigh and agitated horse.

Chief Rose removed her helmet and her short poodle curls sprang perfectly into place. Had I removed my stocking cap, my straight hair would have stuck up in all directions as if I had been electrocuted. She hopped off her snowmobile and set the helmet on the seat, the other two officers following suit. As there were only three Appleseed Creek police officers, our discovery brought out the entire department.

Chief Rose stomped over to me, her peculiar peridot-colored eyes flashing. "For crying out loud, Humphrey, can't I even have Christmas off?"

I gave her a weak smile. "I guess not."

She pointed her thumb at the barn. "Is the body in there? I thought you said it was outside."

"It is. It's behind the farthest corner of the building."

She reached into her coat pocket and removed a navy stocking cap, placed it on her head, and pulled it down over her ears. "Then you and Troyer must have a really good reason for being inside of the barn."

I buried my hands deep inside my pockets. "We took a look around."

"I hope you're not up to your old tricks, Humphrey." She watched Timothy as he covered Sparky with a green horse blanket and tucked Mabel back into the sleigh. The dog would be asleep within seconds.

I tilted my chin. "What tricks are those?"

"Snooping. I don't need the extra headache." She rested her hand on her gun belt. "Did you touch anything in there?"

"No." I hadn't. Timothy had. I knew she would ask him the same question, and he wouldn't lie.

Timothy strode over to us.

A smile spread across the police chief's face. "So, Troyer, you were taking Humphrey out for an old Amish sleigh ride. How cute."

Timothy didn't rise to the chief's bait. "Do you want to see where we found her?"

Chief Rose whistled at the two officers, and they came running. "Riley, you stay here and keep watch."

Riley, a middle-aged man with a goatee, snapped his gum. "Watch what? There's nothing for miles."

She narrowed her eyes to forest-green-lined slits. The chief seemed to wear a different color of eyeliner every day. Was the new shade in honor of Christmas?

Riley snapped his gum. "I'll stand watch, Chief."

She nodded. "Nottingham, come with us."

Nottingham knew better than to argue with Chief Rose. He was the youngest of the officers, maybe around my own age of twenty-four.

I let Timothy lead the way, not eager to see Katie's body again.

"Don't walk in any of the existing tracks," Chief Rose said.

"The only tracks here are Timothy's and mine," I said.

She turned her gaze on me. "Humor me."

We gave the tracks a wide berth. As we rounded the last corner to where Katie lay, my eyes zeroed in on her blue hand reaching out from the snow drift. The first time I saw it I didn't know the victim's name. Now that I knew the potential impact Katie's death had on the Troyer family, the sight seemed that much more terrible, that much more gruesome. I swallowed, and stopped fifty feet away. "I'll stay back here."

Timothy squeezed my shoulder before he walked on with the two police officers. Despite the distance, I could hear their conversation clearly in the stillness of the winter air.

Chief Rose crouched a few feet from the body and examined the scene. "Nottingham, take photos."

The young officer removed a SLR camera from its case slung over his shoulder. Carefully, he moved around the body. In the silence, the *snap-snap* of the camera's shutter sounded like the *crack-crack* of a handgun.

"Will the sheriff be coming out?" Timothy asked.

"Nah." The police chief straightened her legs to standing. "This is still within Appleseed Creek's village limits, even if just barely. The Knox County sheriff will be happy to leave this mess in my hands. I'll give him a heads-up, of course." She peered at the baseball-bat-sized icicles hanging menacingly from the barn's eaves. Then she dropped her gaze, removing a collapsible trowel from her utility belt and unfolding it. She inched around Katie's head and carefully removed snow that surrounded her bonnet.

I crept closer to them as Chief Rose worked.

"Nottingham, get a shot of this." She pointed to a depression in the bonnet's frame. She continued to dig about Katie's head and revealed large pieces of ice frozen to the ground and to the girl's cloak. She looked up again. Then, I saw it—an empty space between the icicles. It stuck out like a missing tooth.

"Did the icicle kill her?" I asked, feeling oddly hopeful. If Katie's death was accidental maybe there would be no impact on the Troyers.

Chief Rose ignored my question. "Nottingham, how long before the coroner arrives?"

Nottingham pushed up his parka sleeve and checked his watch. "It will be another thirty minutes."

She grimaced. "Let's call it forty-five. He's always late, even on a good day, and two days before Christmas is not a good day."

Christmas. The word struck me like a blow. The Lambright family would be notified that their daughter died close to the holiday. From now on, this day would always hold a bitter taste for them.

Chief Rose stood. "We might as well record your statements while we wait. Humphrey, you're up first." She walked away from the barn out of earshot of Timothy and Nottingham, as the officer continued to snap photos of the barn, the snow, the icicles, and of Katie.

I worried my lip. Timothy gave me the briefest of nods and his grim smile buoyed me somehow to follow Chief Rose. The necklace he had given me rested against my skin.

The chief cleared her throat. "I hope you can answer a few questions after you and Troyer stop mooning over each other."

Heat rushed to my cheeks. I gritted my teeth, determined not to reply in kind. "Ask away."

"Tell me what happened from the beginning. Start by telling me why you were here. With luck, you and Troyer's stories will match."

"They will," I snapped.

Mischief glinted in her eyes. "That's good to hear."

I went on to tell her everything that had happened since Timothy and I left his family's farm with Sparky and the sleigh. When it came to the part of finding the car parts in the barn, I paused.

Her gaze sharpened. "What is it?"

I swallowed. "One of the mirrors is covered in silver duct tape. It struck me as odd." She could draw her own conclusions.

She understood immediately. "Sounds like I should talk to Uncle Billy."

I shouldn't be surprised the police chief came to the same conclusion. No doubt she was smart and very good at her job. Little happened in Appleseed Creek that Chief Rose didn't know about.

"I know another thing about this case, Humphrey."

"What's that?" I asked, unsure that I wanted to hear the answer.

She squared her peridot-colored gaze on me. "You are the common denominator in every murder case on my books."

I bit the inside of my lip because . . . she was right.

Chapter Three

After the coroner and Chief Rose's officer loaded Katie's body onto the sled attached to the back of a snowmobile, the chief waved us over to Grandfather Zook's sleigh. "I have a favor to ask, Troyer."

Timothy's brow shot up.

"You know the Lambright family, don't you?" she asked.

Timothy nodded. "They are my parents' close neighbors. My sister Ruth is good friends with the youngest daughter in the family."

She cocked her head. "What can you tell me about the family?"

"There are four children, Katie and Anna—Ruth's friend and the youngest—and two much older stepbrothers. The girls' mother died six years ago. A year after her death, Jeb Lambright married his new wife, Sally, who was a widow and had the two boys."

My brow shot up. I didn't know this about the family. In fact, the only thing I knew about them was Ruth's friendship with Anna, who I had met a few times while visiting the Troyer farm.

The chief noted everything Timothy said, her expression tense, sobering. "I'd like you to come with me to notify the family. I think it would be good if there was someone Amish—or with an Amish connection—along with me." As if ten years passed in a breath, the police chief aged before our eyes, the heaviness of her duty weighing on her narrow shoulders. "I never know if an Amish family will be willing to talk to me. Perhaps they will be more likely with you along."

Timothy nodded. "I'll go with you."

Was this the right decision? The Lambright family would associate him with Katie's death. They would associate the Troyers with Katie's death, which meant they would associate Ruth with the death. But I held my tongue.

"We should arrive there about the same time, so I'll meet you at your family farm. I need to take the snowmobile back to my cruiser."

"I'll be waiting," Timothy promised.

The snowmobiles fired up as Timothy helped me into the sleigh. Hours had passed since he had given me the necklace. The sun hung high in the sky, and rays made the surface of the snow sparkle like the ground was covered by a blanket of diamonds. My breath caught by the beauty of it. How could such a tragic place also be so beautiful at the same time? It wasn't fair or right.

Timothy took my hand. "Beauty lives on."

I stared at him in surprise. How did he know what I was thinking?

He smiled. "Every thought travels across your face just like those cute freckles across your nose."

Mabel whimpered from her place under the seat. I knew how she felt. The ride back to the Troyer farm was somber, each of us lost in our own thoughts. As much as I wanted to tell Timothy it wasn't a good idea for him to deliver the terrible news to Katie's parents, I knew it was no use talking him out of it. In some way he felt responsible for Katie now, just like I did.

As promised, Chief Rose waited for Timothy at the end of the family's driveway. She nodded to us from the warmth of her cruiser. Seven-year-old Thomas ran to meet us as Timothy parked the sleigh behind the barn, his bright blue mittens tethered to his black wool coat with a piece of yarn flying behind him like wings. I couldn't help but smile at the image. Thomas was a mini replica of his older brother with silky white-blond hair and bright blue eyes. All five of the Troyer children had the same light coloring like their mother.

Thomas's eyes were the size of tennis balls. "Timothy, why are the police here? Are you going to the pokey?"

I covered my mouth, knowing that Thomas must have learned this new English slang word from his grandfather. Ever since he learned the word "perp" from Chief Rose in November, Grandfather Zook had peppered me for similar English vernacular. He thought such words were a riot. His son-in-law didn't find them nearly as amusing.

Timothy hopped out of the sleigh and tweaked his younger brother on the nose. "I will tell you when I get home. I need to go with Chief Rose for a bit." He handed Thomas the reins. "Drive Sparky into the barn."

"But—"

"Go on now. Chloe doesn't know how to drive the horse. She needs your help."

The seven-year-old cocked his head. "I've been driving Sparky since I was six," he said proudly. "Chloe, you should really know how to drive a horse by your age."

I patted the wooden bench. "Then, why don't you teach me?"

He puffed out his chest, scrambled up into the sleigh, and took the reins.

I placed a hand over his to stop him from flicking the reins, and glanced at Timothy. No doubt, worry etched across my face. "Timothy?"

He gave me a reassuring nod. "I'll be fine." He smacked the side of the sleigh. "Teach her everything I taught you, *kinner.*" He turned and walked back down the long driveway to Chief Rose and the waiting cruiser.

I released my hold on Thomas's hands, and he urged Sparky on. The horse headed straight for the barn.

Thomas pulled back on the reins, hard. "Sparky, *nee.* We have to give Chloe a driving lesson."

The horse ignored his commands and continued plodding toward the barn. As we rounded the corner of the whitewashed building, a large wagon came into view. Two young Amish men I'd never seen before were loading the wagon with crates of wooden objects fitting them around pieces of Amish-made furniture. The young men looked to be somewhere in their twenties, and they were clean shaven, meaning unmarried. The blond draft horses in front of the wagon kicked the ground, creating a deep rut into the frozen earth.

Sparky blew hot air through his nose and pulled the sleigh farther away from the wagon as if he had no desire to approach horses twice his size. He stopped a few yards away and shook his bridle. Thomas grumbled at the animal in Pennsylvania Dutch, but the horse refused to take one more step.

The boy sighed. "Sparky never listens to me."

I bumped his shoulder. "It's not you. Sparky is tired. Timothy and I had him out a lot longer than planned."

He examined my face with his sky blue eyes. "Why?"

Time to change the subject. I gestured toward the wagon. "Who are those two guys over there?"

Thomas cranked his neck. "Nathan Garner and Caleb King. They buy Amish stuff from *Grossdaddi* and sell it to *Englischers.*"

My eyebrows shot up. "They buy Amish stuff?"

"*Ya.*"

"What stuff?"

He stood and jumped from the sleigh without answering my question. I followed while Mabel opted to stay put.

As I approached the wagon, the two young men ignored me. The one on the ground said something to the other in Pennsylvania Dutch. I couldn't understand the words, but I recognized the sharp, irritated tone. The young man on the wagon shot the other a dirty look. The air temperature dropped several degrees as they glared at each other.

A middle-aged Amish man with a dark brown beard slowed his pace to match Grandfather Zook, who shuffled forward on his metal braces. The man handed Grandfather Zook an envelope.

"*Danki.*" Grandfather Zook said. "*Frehlicher Grischtdaag*, Levi." He had wished the man a Merry Christmas.

"*Danki.*" Levi replied and switched to English. "Your wares will bring a good price at the warehouse."

Grandfather Zook grinned.

"Let's go *buwe*," he said to the young men, calling them *boys*. "We have one more stop before heading back to the warehouse." He pulled up short when he saw me, and then tipped his felt hat. A dimple showed in his right cheek when he smiled. "*Gude Mariye.*"

"Good morning," I replied. "I'm Chloe."

His dimple grew. "*Ya.* I thought you might be. Joseph talks about you often."

Grandfather Zook took a few more shaky steps onto the uneven frozen ground. I hurried to his side in case he stumbled. "'Course I talk about Chloe. She's a *gut* girl."

I blushed.

Nathan and Caleb, although I still didn't know them apart, finished loading the wagon and secured the gate at the end. The young men climbed into the back and wedged themselves into uncomfortable-looking spots between the hard-edged furniture, but as far away from each other as possible.

"You will have to forgive my son Nathan and his friend Caleb," Levi said. "They are in an awful fight over a girl."

Grandfather Zook chuckled. "That's what will always break a friendship in half. Best thing to happen would be for the girl to choose neither."

I glanced back at Nathan and Caleb. They mutually scowled at Grandfather Zook's idea. Now that I knew Nathan was Levi's son, I could pick him out in the pair. Like his father, he had dark, wavy hair sticking out from under his black felt hat. I couldn't see Caleb's hair color under his black stocking cap, but the tightness of the hat made his sharp cheekbones even more pronounced.

Levi climbed into the driver seat of the wagon. Carefully he backed the blond team away from the barn. Thomas peeked out to watch as Levi masterfully turned the horses to face down the long driveway.

Thomas tugged on my sleeve and whispered, "I'm going to make Sparky listen to me like that someday."

Levi waved as he drove the team away, but Nathan and Caleb ignored us and each other.

Grandfather Zook shook his head. "Boys are crazy when it comes to their young ladies."

I arched an eyebrow at Grandfather Zook. He laughed, which morphed into a dry cough. I supported his elbow. "You shouldn't be out here in this cold."

"Fiddlesticks," the elderly Amish man said. Yet he allowed me to lead him back into the barn.

The front corner served as Mr. Troyer's workshop, and Grandfather Zook eased himself onto a stool. "Thomas, go unhitch Sparky and bring him into his stall."

The boy ran out of the barn.

"Does he need help?" I asked.

The elderly man shook his head. "*Nee*, and he will likely be offended if you offer it. He wants to do everything Timothy can."

I bit my lip. Did that mean Thomas would leave the Amish like Timothy had?

Grandfather Zook pointed one of his braces at me. "I know what you are thinking. Thomas will make his choice when it is his time. He will follow *Gotte*'s way for his life, whatever that might be." He then picked up a hand chisel and a rectangular block of wood from the workbench.

Thomas led Sparky into the barn and opened his stall door. The horse walked right in. "Sparky, I'm very disappointed in you."

I covered my mouth. Thomas sounded so much like his mother when she was reprimanding him.

Grandfather Zook began to whittle at the piece of wood. "What is wrong, Thomas?"

A tear rolled down Thomas's cheek, and his forehead bunched in frustration. "I'm supposed to give Chloe a driving lesson, and Sparky won't listen."

Grandfather Zook snorted. "You can't tell Old Spark anything when his mind is made up. That's why he never made it very far as a racehorse. He wouldn't listen to the trainer."

Sparky lowered his ears as if he understood everything his master said.

Grandfather Zook struggled to his feet and adjusted his metal braces onto each arm. He suffered polio as a child, and the titanium braces helped support his crooked legs. "Don't you make that face at me," he told the horse. "You know it's the truth." He turned to Thomas. "*Grankinner*, Old Spark's been out for a long time and he is cold and tired." He shot a curious look at me, then, "You can give Chloe a driving lesson on another day."

Thomas pouted.

I bumped his shoulder. "It's lunchtime anyway, Thomas. You don't want to miss your mom's cooking because of me, do you?"

His face cleared. "*Nee*. She's making meatloaf sandwiches."

Grandfather Zook poked his young grandson with the end of one of his braces. "You'd better hurry up then, or your *daed*'s going to eat your portion. He's been working hard since the sun was up and is mighty hungry."

Thomas's eyes went wide, and he dashed from the barn.

Grandfather Zook shook his head. "One of these days that *kinner* will learn to walk from place to place."

I smiled, then glanced at the wood and chisel on Grandfather's workbench. "What are you making?"

"Napkin holders." He pointed to eight of them lined up on the workbench. Each completed napkin holder had an Amish scene chiseled into the front of it—a quilt, a horse and buggy, and a one-room schoolhouse.

I stepped closer to them and ran my fingers along their glossy surfaces. Grandfather Zook had sanded even the deepest crevice smooth. "I didn't know that you made these."

"From where do you think Timothy gets it?" He dug the chisel into the outline of a leaf. "Do you think I sit in my rocking chair all day and eat my daughter's meatloaf sandwiches?" His mischievous grin took the bite out of his words.

"Kind of," I teased back.

He snorted. "I make these and other small Amish kitchen utensils, like paper towel holders, wooden spoons, and letter holders to sell to Garner Dutch Furniture Warehouse. That's Levi's business. He is the man you just met. They come every two months or so to pick up more projects. They put them up for sale in their warehouse, and when they sell, we split the money. It helps the family and keeps my hands busy."

"So you sell them on consignment."

Grandfather Zook knit his bushy eyebrows together. "I don't know that *Englischer* word."

"It just means what you described."

"Consignment," he said, as if tasting the word. "I must use this in conversation with my son-in-law. It always riles him up when I add an *Englischer* word in my speech." He began sanding the wood, which would be the front of another napkin holder. "When you two took Old Spark out this morning, Timothy said that you'd only be gone for an hour or two. That has long passed."

I perched on an empty wooden stool. "I know. We were held up."

His silver, bushy eyebrows shot up, and my face grew hot. I swallowed. "Timothy and I were, um, delayed. He took me to the Gundy barn."

He nodded. "A nice spot."

"Yes. It was nice until . . ."

He raised his chin and examined my face. "Something bad has happened."

"Yes," I whispered. "We found Katie Lambright there."

"Katie? She's a quiet girl. Was she there by herself?"

"Yes and she—she was dead."

Grandfather Zook's chisel clattered to the floor. He started to struggle out of his seat to reach it.

I hopped off my seat to collect the chisel, and placed it on the workbench. "Timothy left with Chief Rose to tell the Lambrights about Katie."

"She is Anna's sister," he whispered. Like me, Grandfather Zook knew immediately the ramification Katie's death could have on the Troyer family, especially thirteen-year-old Ruth.

Tears threatened at the corner of my eyes. "I don't know how to tell Ruth."

Grandfather Zook picked up the chisel again. "If Timothy and the lady police officer are going over to the Lambright farm to tell the family, then Ruth already knows. She is there visiting Anna."

I wrapped my arms around my body against the cold. *Poor Ruth.*

Chapter Four

Grandfather Zook struggled to his feet. "Let's go inside. It's too cold out here for my old bones, and a hot meal will do us both some good."

I took his arm and helped him inch along the beaten-down, snowy path to the Troyer home. Knowing that I didn't have the responsibility of telling Ruth about the death of her best friend's sister didn't make me feel any better. If anything, it made me feel worse, realizing that Ruth would be there to see the devastating impact such a message would have on the Lambright family.

I helped Grandfather Zook over the threshold and into the house. He grunted. "It's been a bad winter. I'll be happy when all of this snow and ice melts. It will be much easier to move around then."

I kicked the snow from my boots just outside the back door, then left them in the mudroom and followed Grandfather Zook into Mrs. Troyer's warm kitchen, inhaling the sweet scent of caramel corn. Fresh caramel-coated corn cooled on waxed paper next to a stack of red and green tins that sat on the kitchen counter. When the popcorn cooled, Mrs. Troyer and her daughters will pack it into tins to give as Christmas gifts to friends and family. The Amish exchanged gifts just like the English, but the gifts were simpler and homemade. I resisted the urge to snatch a piece of the hot corn from the waxed paper. I'd done that when Mrs. Troyer made her first batch earlier in the week and burned my fingertips.

"Where's Timothy?" Mrs. Troyer asked.

Grandfather Zook sat in the paddle-backed chair at the far end of the table. His daughter placed a stoneware mug of hot coffee in front of him.

Before I could answer, Mr. Troyer stepped into the kitchen from the living room. "Chloe, why did Timothy leave in a police car?"

I bit my lip.

Mrs. Troyer dropped the tea towel from her hands. "What has happened? Is Timothy in trouble?"

Timothy had been in trouble with the law right after he left the Amish, before he found his way again in the Mennonite church in Appleseed Creek. I picked up the towel and handed it to her. "Timothy's not in trouble."

"But something has happened." Mr. Troyer sat down at the head of the long kitchen table. Backless pine benches, which could seat four adults, sat on either side of the matching table.

I nodded. "Yes." I took a seat myself on one of the benches, relieved that Thomas and the youngest Troyer, four-year-old Naomi, were not in the room as I told them about Katie's death.

Mrs. Troyer lowered herself onto the bench next to me. "What happened? Had she lost her way?"

I straightened a fork that lay in front of me on the table. "We don't know, but Chief Rose believes an icicle knocked her on the head."

Mr. Troyer's dark eyebrows knit together like a piece of shaggy wool. "An icicle?"

"There are giant ones hanging from the eaves of the barn. One was missing right above where we found Katie," I said.

"Icicles are dangerous. If they are big enough, they can knock a man out," Grandfather Zook said. "What a terrible shame. She was such a sweet girl."

Mrs. Troyer reached into her black apron pocket and removed an embroidered handkerchief. "What would Katie Lambright be doing there all alone?"

I shook my head. They assumed she was alone when she died, but I wasn't convinced of that yet.

Mrs. Troyer held the handkerchief to her chest. "The police think Timothy knows something about what happened to Katie? Is that why they took him away?"

I placed a reassuring hand on her arm. "No. Chief Rose asked Timothy to go with her to notify the family. She thought it would be easier with someone they knew there."

Mr. Troyer's face was like stone. "That is *gut* of my son to share the burden. The Lambright family needs the support of our community."

"Ruth is there now," the mother of five said. "Simon, you should go and fetch her."

He shook his head. "Timothy will be home soon. He will know to bring Ruth with him. The family needs their privacy today."

"You're right." Mrs. Troyer jumped up. "I'll make them a care basket. Ruth and I can take it over tomorrow." She covered her mouth, then lowered her hand. "On Christmas Eve."

The back door opened and Naomi and Becky's laughter floated into the kitchen from the mudroom. It was nice to hear Becky laughing with her youngest sister. Before Bishop Hooley said that it was allowable for the Troyers to interact with their English children, tension buzzed through the house any time Timothy, Becky, or even I entered the property. It had been difficult for Mr. Troyer to reconcile himself with obeying his church and loving his children who chose a different way of life.

Although twenty-seven now, Timothy had left the church in his late teens, and as far as I could tell, his relationship with his family had hardly changed. When Becky left during this past summer, everything was different. I could not help believing it was because she was a daughter—not a son. The auto-buggy collision she was in shortly after she left home had only made matters worse. The district's beloved Bishop Glick was killed, and even though the accident wasn't her fault, Becky was sentenced to probation and community service—both of which would not end until after the first of next year.

Becky held short boughs from an evergreen tree, and Naomi carried a bouquet of Christmas holly cut from the bush in their mother's garden. Even without a Christmas tree and twinkle lights, the Amish home was prepared for the holiday.

Finding us all in the kitchen, Becky pulled up short. "What has happened?"

I was startled by how much she had changed since meeting her months ago on my first day in Appleseed Creek. The look of innocence had faded from her eyes, and a new appearance of maturity and understanding took its place. She was still the sweet, beautiful girl I first met, but an expression of sadness told that she knew all was not right with the world and that bad things happened to good people—even her family.

Mrs. Troyer helped her youngest daughter out of her wool coat and mittens. "Naomi, go upstairs and choose a basket from the closet. We are making a Christmas gift for the Lambrights."

"Any basket?" the four-year-old asked in English. When I first met Naomi, she knew few English words, but she had learned so much in a short time. Since I don't speak Pennsylvania Dutch, the Troyers spoke in English whenever I visited.

Her mother smiled. "*Ya*, you pick."

She ran from the room.

Becky wore a guarded expression as she placed the evergreen boughs into a bushel basket by the threshold to the living room. "Why are you making a basket for the Lambrights?"

"Timothy and Chloe found Katie by an old barn." Mr. Troyer paused. "She was dead."

Becky's mouth fell open. "Dead? How can that be?"

I told her Chief Rose's theory about the icicle, and as I did, the sweet smell of caramel emanating from the kitchen made me nauseous.

Becky's eyes shined with unshed tears. "What was she doing there?"

A very good question.

Mr. Troyer folded his arm across him chest. "There is no point asking why now."

"But—"

Mrs. Troyer stood. "Becky, help me choose items for the basket. Should we send some of my blackberry jam?"

"*Mamm,* we can do that later. I want to know what happened."

Mr. Troyer's brow was hooded, but Grandfather Zook spoke up. "You can't have all the answers now. The best way you can help the Lambright family is to make a basket that shows them we care and stand by them during this time."

If either of her parents had said the same thing, Becky would have argued with them, but since the advice came from her grandfather, she sprang into action and started to open pantry doors, seeking homemade treats to tuck into the Lambright care basket.

Mr. Troyer tapped his fork on the table. "Let's eat supper first. Even at a time like this, I must return to the barn and tend the cows."

Mrs. Troyer placed her jar of blackberry jam back on its shelf. "*Ya*, your *daed* is right. We must continue the work *Gott* has given us. Help me put together that last of the sandwiches. We will finish the basket after supper." She gave a shuddered sigh.

A few minutes later Naomi and Thomas entered the room and sat on either side of me on the pine bench as their mother placed the platter of meatloaf sandwiches in the middle of the table. A tiny triangle of construction paper dangled from Thomas's shirt. I plucked it off. "What's this from?"

He smiled brightly and leaned close. "Naomi and I are making a Christmas garland of paper for the railing. Teacher had us make one for the schoolhouse, and *Maam* said I could teach Naomi how to make it. By the time she starts school, she will be the very best at cutting construction paper."

"You're a good big brother."

He shrugged and reached for a sandwich, but his mother swatted his hand. "Wait until *Daed* blesses the food."

The child retracted his hand with a frown.

Mr. Troyer bowed his head and gave the blessing. ". . . And may you comfort Katie Lambright's family during this difficult time. Amen."

Grandfather Zook murmured, "Amen," and selected a sandwich from the platter.

Thomas scowled. "You took the biggest one."

Grandfather winked. "I'm old. When you are as old as me you can have the biggest one."

Thomas placed two sandwiches on his plate.

"Thomas Troyer," his mother said, "You will never be able to eat all of that."

He scrunched up his face. "I will. I'm growing big and strong like Timothy."

"Where is Timothy?" Naomi whispered.

I took one of Thomas's sandwiches and moved it to my plate. "He will be here—"

The front door of the Troyer's farmhouse slammed shut, the sound of it echoing through the wall followed by the staccato sound of footsteps running upstairs. The footsteps stopped and another door slammed.

Naomi leaned close to me. "Is Ruth mad?"

I wrapped my arm around her. "I don't think she is mad."

Timothy entered the kitchen, his face ashen and drawn. "Have a seat, my grandson." Grandfather Zook patted the bench closest to him.

Timothy fell into the seat without greeting anyone. He appeared so stricken by his visit to the Lambright farm I wanted to take his hand, but I knew that the family frowned on this. They knew that Timothy was "courting" me, but the Amish did not approve of public displays of affection.

Mr. Troyer pushed away his plate. "Son, tell us what has happened."

Mrs. Troyer placed a kettle onto the stovetop. "Thomas, go upstairs and play with Naomi."

The boy frowned. "But I haven't eaten yet, and I'm starving."

Thomas's father glowered at his youngest son. "Thomas, your *mamm* asked you to go upstairs."

Mrs. Troyer nodded to the young boy. "You and Naomi can take your suppers upstairs and eat in your room."

Thomas's eyes went wide. "We can eat upstairs?"

Naomi's blue eyes were identical to her brother's and grew just as wide.

"*Ya*," their mother said. "This one time. Now, go before I change my mind."

The children scrambled off the bench and grabbed their plates and glasses of fresh milk before scurrying from the room.

Mrs. Troyer set a white mug of coffee in front of her oldest son. "Timothy, please tell us what happened."

Timothy looked to me.

"I've told them about . . ." I paused. "Our discovery."

He nodded. "Telling the Lambrights was as hard as I thought it would be. They didn't believe us at first, and Jeb Lambright refused to answer any of the police chief's questions about Katie. Anna crumbled to the floor like her legs were broken sticks. Ruth helped her to her bedroom before we left. She had wanted to stay with Anna, but Jeb told me to take her home."

The handkerchief was in Mrs. Troyer's hands again. "And Sally? How is she?"

Timothy made a face.

"Do they need help with the farm?" Grandfather Zook asked.

Mr. Troyer set his coffee mug on the pine table. "I'm sure the sons will come in and help with the farm while the family deals with this tragedy."

Timothy's brow crinkled. "I don't know. I got the impression that Jeb didn't care much for his two stepsons."

Becky's hands shook. "We're making a gift basket for them."

Timothy grimaced. "Don't be surprised if they don't accept it."

His sister's forehead bunched. "Why wouldn't they?"

Timothy shook his head, refusing to say anything more about it. He rubbed his naked chin, as if searching for the Amish beard that would be there if he had been baptized into the church and married a nice Amish girl. "Deacon Sutter showed up just as we left."

Grandfather Zook wrinkled his nose. "How did he know about it so soon?"

"I don't know that he did, but I'm sure he saw the police car drive by his place on the way to the Lambright farm."

"Did he see you?" Mrs. Troyer's voice was tight.

Timothy grimaced. "*Ya*. That much I know. He definitely saw me."

I wanted to ask Timothy so many questions about the visit. Why did he make that face when his mother asked about Sally? What did the deacon say to him and Chief Rose? Ever since Bishop Hooley sided with the Troyers about whether or not they could see their English children, the deacon had made his distaste for the family perfectly clear. For Deacon Sutter, the district's battle lines were drawn.

Grandfather Zook frowned. "We can only pray now." He bowed his head. "Dear Lord, we pray for comfort and protection over the Lambright family during their time of loss, a loss made even more painful because of the time of year. Please show them Your love and care."

When the prayer was over, Mr. Troyer picked up his coffee mug. "Let's not speak of it. It is time to eat and go about our day."

I stared at the heavy-looking meatloaf sandwich on my plate. In that moment, it was as appealing as a brick. However, I didn't want to offend Timothy's mother, so I forced myself to take a bite. At that moment, I thought of how blue Katie's hand had been sticking out of the snow, and the bite lodged in my throat.

Chapter Five

As we were about to leave, Becky hugged Thomas good-bye so tightly the boy yelped. "Becky, you will see me tomorrow. It will be Christmas Eve." He lowered his voice. "Did you bring me a gift?"

She tousled his towhead. "Maybe."

His mouth fell open.

I frowned. How would the Lambrights' Christmas be this year? The first Christmas after my mother died was the worst of my life. It was also the time when my father introduced me to his new girlfriend Sabrina. The memory tumbled inside my mind, so I said my good-byes to the Troyer family and went outside, needing to be alone.

After a few minutes, the door of the farmhouse's screened-in front porch slapped back against its wooden frame. Timothy removed his black stocking cap from his coat pocket and pulled it onto his head. "Are you okay?"

I nodded even though I wasn't sure that was true. "Why did you make a face when your mother asked about Sally Lambright's reaction?"

Timothy frowned. "Because it wasn't good."

I dug my gloves out of my pockets. "She cried?"

Mabel barked and galloped down the driveway from the barn. She must have been snoozing inside of Grandfather Zook's sleigh until she heard Timothy's voice. Mrs. Troyer didn't allow animals into her house. Even though Mabel was a big, shaggy dog, the size of a golden retriever or collie, she leaped into Timothy's arms. He caught her and hugged her before landing on all four paws on the ground.

"Timothy?" I asked. "What did Sally do?"

"It's not what she did. It's what she *said*."

"What was that?"

He sighed. "She said that Katie had this coming. That she brought this on herself."

My stomach tightened. "What did she mean?"

"Not sure, exactly. Greta asked her to explain, but that was all she would say. The chief believes that Anna will be the easiest to talk to, to find out what Katie was up to in her final days. She couldn't ask her then because Jeb kicked us off his property. Besides, Anna was hysterical at the moment. We could hear her wailing all the way from her bedroom on the second floor." Timothy stood there in the silence. Then he glanced back at the house. "It always takes Becky so long to say good-bye to the family."

"You know it's hard for her to leave."

"She could go back to the Amish and stay forever," Timothy said.

I frowned, but decided not to argue with Timothy. I knew he secretly wished his sister would return to the Amish and marry his best friend, Aaron, who was Timothy's age, but obviously in love with Becky, eight years his junior. "You can't even guess why Sally would say something so awful about Katie."

He shook his head. "That was the one and only thing she said the entire time. I did get an earful from Jeb. I think it was a mistake for me to be there when Greta told them. It only made it worse."

"Why?"

"Jeb said that it was runaway Amish like me that lead to these kinds of tragedies. If I hadn't left the Amish way, others wouldn't follow. He said that I was the example and the reason Becky left."

I touched his sleeve. "That's not true."

He shook his head. "It is to some extent. My sister would never have been brave enough to leave home if I hadn't already done it myself and turned out all right. Most of the Amish in our district stay Amish. Before she left home, she didn't know of any other fallen away Amish except for me."

"Becky left for herself."

"But I gave her the idea." His voice was thick with emotion.

I turned the conversation back to Katie. "Jeb thinks Katie left the Amish?"

"That was the impression I got. He didn't elaborate and completely ignored Greta's questions. I thought she was going to spit nails, she was so mad."

The police chief didn't like to be ignored. I knew that. "But Katie was in Amish dress. There was nothing about her that indicated she left the Amish way of life."

"Maybe she had just left before she died."

"Had she been missing? Did the family notice that she was gone?"

"Jeb wouldn't say."

I sighed. "Someone has to know."

"Do you plan to find out whom that someone is?" Timothy asked as Becky stepped into the yard.

She held a tin of caramel corn. I wasn't surprised. Rarely, did we leave the Troyer farm without a care package.

I looked him straight in the eye. "Yes. And you will help me."

THE DRIVE TO THE house Becky and I lived in was quiet as each of us, Mabel included, was preoccupied with our own thoughts. Most likely, Mabel contemplated when she would have an opportunity for her next nap. Timothy, Becky, and my own thoughts were much darker.

Temporarily, Becky and I rented the home of the Quills, an elderly couple who wintered in Florida. Unlike the Troyer house, which had been in the family for several generations and sat a quarter-mile back from the road, the Quills' two-story, brick home was only two car-lengths from the county road. Beneath the snow, perfectly manicured bushes sat shaped into spirals and balls. The Christmas tree that Timothy, Becky, and I chose from the farm in town was framed by the front window, its lights blinking on and off.

The home was similar to the house I grew up in Shaker Heights before my mother died, except that house had another floor and more square footage. It also had the same artificial perfection of the Quills' place. I liked the Troyer farmhouse better. Becky, however, did not. She loved everything about our rental—from the remote control that operated the gas fireplace to the professional kitchen appliances. If I heard her pontificate one more time about how wonderful the six-burner gas stove was, I might choke.

Becky's lawyer, Tyler Hart, had helped us find this new place to live when circumstances forced Becky and me into an unexpected move. With little time to find another place, and with few rentals available in the town of Appleseed Creek, the Quills' offer was the best option we had. When the Quills returned in April, Becky and I would have to find yet another new home, and I hoped for something more permanent that would suit us both. I was tired of moving. Still, even though the Quills' house was three miles from my job at the college, it was closer to Becky's. In good weather she could walk or ride her bike to Young's Family Kitchen where she waitressed.

Timothy parked his pickup behind my VW Bug in the Quills' driveway. Several extra inches of snow had accumulated on the Bug since we had left early that morning for the Troyer farm. Would we ever see green grass again? After Christmas, I would be ready for spring and summer to return; however, I'd lived in Ohio my entire life and knew we hadn't even entered the deepest part of winter.

Becky hopped out of the truck. "I didn't know it was so late. Carol will be here to pick me up for work in five minutes."

Carol, a middle-aged woman, worked in Young's pie shop. She was one of the few English people who worked at Young's on a permanent basis. Owner Ellie Young claimed she couldn't turn Carol away because she had some of the best pie recipes in the county—if not in the entire state of Ohio—trapped in her head.

Becky flew through the front door of the house just as Carol pulled into our driveway. I stepped out of the truck at a much slower pace as Carol powered down her window.

I waved. "Becky's run—"

Before I finished my sentence, Becky ran back outside with her Amish uniform—a dress and apron—slung over her arm, and jumped into Carol's car.

Timothy laughed. "I think that lecture Ellie gave Becky about being late for work scared her straight."

As we entered the house, my yowling Siamese cat, Gigabyte, greeted us. I removed my coat and scratched Gig under the chin, but he was not appeased and batted my hand away.

Because he was headed to work at Young's as well, Timothy didn't remove his coat. In addition to the restaurant, with its small Amish gift shop and bakery, the Young's owned a flea market consisting of three open-air pavilions behind the main building.

Timothy was the head contractor on a project to enclose those pavilions so the flea market could be open all year round.

"Do you have to go straight to Young's?" I asked. It seemed odd that I didn't have to go to work myself. The college was closed for winter break, with only a skeleton crew on campus. I stopped by the campus occasionally during break to check on the systems and servers, but beyond that, had no commitments.

A small smiled played on the corners of Timothy's lips. "No."

I steadied my gaze on him. "I'd like to go to Uncle Billy's. Will you go with me?"

Timothy grinned at me. "I was just waiting for you ask."

I laughed. "How did you know that I would?"

"I think I know you pretty well by now, Chloe Humphrey. I know you won't rest until you talk to Billy." He helped me back into my winter coat. "And neither will I."

Chapter Six

Snow buried the graveyard of auto parts in front of Billy's property, and ice clung to the sign that read, *Uncle Billy's Bud.* The rest of the sign—*get Autos*—had been destroyed in a storm over a decade before.

Mabel barked as Timothy's pickup came to a stop. For once, the dog was wide awake and willingly exited the truck after I climbed out. My boots sank into the freshly fallen snow until they reached the hard-packed layer underneath. Two sets of tire tracks carved up the lawn that served as a parking lot, and half-a-dozen pairs of footprints dotted the ground. One set of footprints wove through the graveyard, and there was evidence of digging in the snow. A quarter of a red sedan hood was visible, the only lump in the auto graveyard unearthed.

Timothy pulled on his gloves, so that they covered his wrists. "Greta and her officers have already searched the place."

"It would have surprised me if she hadn't been through here." I took another step toward the shop itself and my foot caught as I tripped over something buried under the snow. Timothy caught me by the elbow, keeping me from tumbling to the ground.

The day had reached late afternoon. We had maybe an hour before sunset. Timothy lifted a hand to block the sun's glare off the snow. "I'm surprised that Billy hasn't come outside yet."

"Do you think Chief Rose arrested him?"

His brow furrowed. "I don't know. Greta wouldn't make an arrest without being positive the person was guilty. She's too careful to rush anything, and it's only been seven hours since we found Katie. Could the case be wrapped up that quickly?"

"He was using the barn as a storehouse without permission."

Timothy's eyes flashed. "That doesn't mean he killed anyone."

I pulled on his sleeve. "I know he's your friend."

Timothy marched toward the office and knocked on the door like a cop. *Thwack, thwack, thwack.* Had Chief Rose taught him to knock on a door like that?

No answer. He tried the doorknob, but it was locked. "I know another way inside." He walked around the side of the building, as Mabel barked and followed. I fell into line after her. "Watch your step." He said over one shoulder. "Who knows what's buried under the snow."

Did Billy have so much junk on his property to scare people off? If so, a very effective away to discourage visitors from coming too close.

The back of the shop had one entry and two garage doors. One of the garage doors hung crookedly from its bearings. Timothy kicked the snow out of the way, revealing a gap between the bottom of the door and the frozen ground. "There. Billy showed it to me one time when he locked himself out of the shop. He couldn't fit through it, but he knew that I could."

The space looked like it couldn't fit much more than a small dog. It certainly would not have been enough space for Billy, who tipped the scale at three hundred pounds, to crawl under.

Timothy squatted next to the small opening. "It looks like the garage dropped since I crawled under there last summer."

"It could be the snow pack making the ground higher."

He moved more snow away with his gloved hand. "Either way, I don't think I can fit."

I squatted next to him. "You might not fit, but I can."

He swiveled a look at me. "You'll be covered with snow."

"So what? You were about to do the same thing." I sat back on my haunches. "Chief Rose won't like it if we go inside there, though."

Timothy hand shoveled away more snow. "Greta has already been here."

"But—"

"Chloe, I have to see inside of the shop. Billy might not be answering the door because he's upset or maybe there's a clue to where he's gone. I need to talk to him. He's my friend."

"Okay. Then help me squeeze through." I lay on my stomach and looked into the dark of the shop, unable to see an inch in front of my face. "Do you have a flashlight?"

Timothy handed me a tiny flashlight connected to his key ring. It wasn't much, but at least I could see there was plenty of room for me to wiggle through two stacks of worn tires. "I can fit."

Timothy placed a hand on my shoulder. "Be careful. There are lots of sharp objects in Billy's shop."

"I'll be careful." I stuck my head and shoulders through the opening. It was a tight squeeze, but I made it and slid on my stomach across the oil-stained concrete floor. The smell of gasoline burned the inside of my nose. I rolled over and bumped the edge of a metal shelf, and an oil can fell to the dusty floor with a bang.

I yelped.

Thankfully the can didn't explode.

"Are you okay?" Timothy asked.

I steadied my pounding heart. "I'm fine. Meet me at the front door." I struggled to my feet and dusted off the front of my ski coat. My hand came away smelling like motor oil and caked with dirt. I glanced at my coat. It would need permanent retirement after this little excursion.

The only light in the garage came through the opening under the broken garage door. I shone the key chain flashlight in front me, its light making monstrous shadows on the walls. I took a few tentative steps toward a lightbulb and chain hanging from the ceiling. When I pulled down on the chain, dim yellow light washed over the room.

A circa-1990 sedan was on the lift, its undercarriage exposed. I moved the flashlight's beam over the underside of the car. No duct tape anywhere. Apparently Billy only used the stuff for cosmetic fixes. Good to know. I didn't know much about cars, but something told me duct tape on a car engine was not a good idea.

Timothy banged on the front door.

"Coming!"

His knock sounded distant and I doubted he could hear me. He was outside, in front of the living quarters, which was an aluminum-sided mobile home that Billy had welded to the garage itself.

I wove through the crowded shop and knocked over a coffee can of bolts sitting on a stool. Not surprisingly, Billy was not the most organized shop owner in the world. I found the wooden door that led into the mobile home and switched on the main light switch, bathing the shop in garish yellow light. The door leading into the home was unlocked and it opened into the kitchen.

Billy kept his home as neat as his shop. The sink was full of dirty dishes with unidentifiable remnants of food clinging to them, and as I stepped on the floor, my boots stuck to something. A small, two-person Formica table was tucked into the corner of the room with a couple of folding chairs sitting on either side of it and a bowl of decaying cereal on top of it. A mug of coffee dregs sat next to the dried-out cereal bowl. My shoulders drooped. Is this how Timothy's friend lived?

Timothy banged on the front door again and called my name.

"I'm coming. Hold your horses," I added under my breath.

I picked my way through the living room, an unmade sleeper sofa. It sagged close to the floor. To my surprise the front door had not one, but *three* dead bolts. I unlocked each one and threw open the door.

Timothy scowled at me. "What took so long?"

"I had a little trouble reaching you. This place is an obstacle course. Do you think it looked this bad when the police were here?"

"I'm sure it did. I've been in here a few times to talk to Billy about cars. He's not a neatnick. That's for sure."

"Timothy, Billy's not here." I knew that to be true the moment I stepped into the trailer. The mobile home was tiny and had only three rooms: the eat-in kitchen, living/bedroom, and a tiny bathroom. I hadn't checked the bathroom closely, but the door stood open. Considering, Billy's mammoth size, had he been in there, I would have seen him.

Timothy wasn't convinced. "Stay here. Let me take a look around."

The serious expression on his face alarmed me. "Why should I stay here? I've already seen most of the place on my way to the front door." I swallowed. "You don't think you will find something back here, do you?"

Timothy squeezed my shoulder. "Greta probably would have already found it."

"Then what could we find that she missed?"

He shrugged and moved toward the kitchen, picking up the spoon that stuck out of the murky cereal. "I don't think Billy has been here for a while. I would even say a couple of days."

I glanced around. "I wish I could ask Chief Rose what she found here."

"Oh, I suspect that she will talk to you about it. You know she thinks of you as the Amish whisperer." His voice teased.

I rolled my eyes and scanned the room for anything that could give me a clue to where the car repairman may have gone. I stepped over a brake pedal lying in the middle of the kitchen floor. "It's like he left in a hurry."

"That's what I think too. The question remains, why did he leave?"

"Because of Katie Lambright?"

"That's what Greta will think." Timothy set the plate of half-eaten food back on the table. "Where did he go?"

I lifted my boot from the linoleum floor and it made that disgusting sticking sound again. "Maybe Billy being gone is unrelated to the Gundy barn and Katie. Maybe he's visiting family for Christmas?"

"Billy doesn't have any family."

"How do you know that?"

"He told me once. His parents are dead, and he's divorced."

I blinked. "Billy had been married?"

"That's what he said. I never asked him much about it and he never offered." His tone was regretful, as if he wished he had asked. I certainly wished that he had.

"Do you think Billy is involved with what happened to Katie? What's your gut feeling?"

"My gut tells me no. I can't even guess why he would have a reason to hurt Katie Lambright. I doubt the two ever met. They had nothing in common and no reason to cross each other's path."

"But Appleseed Creek is so small. They must know each other."

He shook his head. "Amish girls like Katie wouldn't have any interaction with *Englisch* men like Billy. Had her family owned a business in town, it may have been possible, but the Lambrights only have the farm."

It was hard for me to believe that in a place as tiny as Appleseed Creek Katie and Billy hadn't laid eyes on each other. "Didn't you say a lot of young Amish men come and see Billy during *rumspringa* about a car? Maybe Katie met him that way through a male friend."

"You're reaching."

I bit my lip. Of course, I was reaching. None of this made sense. What could the pretty Amish girl and the eccentric car repairman have in common?

"That's what I did, and I know others who did as well, but if you are implying that Katie Lambright was talking to Billy about a car, I highly doubt that happened. I've never heard about an Amish girl coming and talking to him."

I didn't know much about the Lambrights. Ruth's friend, Anna, was the only one of the clan I had met before. She was a soft-spoken, sweet girl with big brown eyes. "How well do you know the Lambright family?"

Timothy thought for a moment. "As well as any of our neighbors, I suppose. Jeb only married his second wife a few years back after I had already left the Amish church, so even though her sons were closer to my age than Jeb's two daughters, I hardly know them. Come to think of it, I don't think they ever lived on the Lambright farm. They were already married themselves."

"What's the father like?"

"Jeb was always very strict with the girls." He grimaced. "He's also a strong supporter of Deacon Sutter. If he had his way, the Amish district would have no interaction with the *Englisch* community in Appleseed Creek. *Daed* said Jeb was vocal with his hope that Deacon Sutter would be chosen as bishop after Bishop Glick died. He wasn't happy when Bishop Hooley took his place, although he would never question who the Lord chose."

"If he's so strict, I'm surprised he let Anna see Ruth at all, considering . . ."

Timothy gave me a half-smile. "Considering Becky, you, and I visit my parents so often." He exhaled, glancing around the tight quarters. "I think the only reason that he does is because he and *Daed* are old friends. They were in school together and are close—at least they were until *Grossdaddi* moved here. Jeb didn't approve of *Grossdaddi's* Lancaster influence on our family. I'm sure he looks to that for the reason that Becky and I both left the Amish way."

"Does Grandfather Zook know this?"

"If I know, I'm sure he does." He grinned. "But I imagine that he doesn't much care what Jeb Lambright thinks."

Grandfather Zook moved to Appleseed Creek from Lancaster, Pennsylvania, four years ago when Mrs. Troyer was pregnant with Naomi. His daughter had a string of miscarriages and he wanted to be here to support her in case the baby was lost again. After Naomi was born healthy and happy, he never went back to Lancaster. Instead, he found that the quiet pace of Knox County suited him.

Timothy sighed. "With that said, this will be the last straw. I would be surprised if Anna says three words to Ruth the next time she sees my sister."

"If her father's not around, why wouldn't she speak to Ruth?"

"She'd be too afraid to because he would be so angry with her."

I mulled this over. "Are you saying Jeb Lambright would hurt his girls?"

"No, no, I didn't mean that. He has a temper. That's all. After visiting the farm earlier today, I know his wife does too." Timothy moved back through the living/bedroom, then he checked the bathroom. I let him do that on his own. If the living room and kitchen were this bad, I shivered to think what the bathroom was like. Timothy's face was grim when he stepped out. "His toothbrush is gone. He left in a hurry, but he took the essentials."

"You assume he brushes his teeth." I waved my arms around the room. "Look at this place."

Timothy gave a half-hearted smile at my joke.

I folded my arms over my filthy coat. I couldn't wait to go home and take a shower. "How are we going to find him?"

Timothy's brow shot up. "Find him?"

I gave him a look.

He sighed. "I guess we can start by talking to Greta."

I smiled.

Timothy buttoned his wool coat. "I figured you would try to find him—whether or not I helped."

My smile turned into a grin. "Like you said, Mr. Troyer, you know me well."

Chapter Seven

I called the Appleseed Creek police chief from the cab of Timothy's truck. The snow glowed with the pink and orange colors from the setting sun, and the icicles hanging from Billy's shop glittered. I shuddered. They were much smaller, but they reminded me of the icicles hanging from the Gundy barn—and of the one that may have killed Katie.

"Humphrey, I've been expecting your call." Chief Rose's sharp voice rang in my ear.

"You have?"

"Well, sure. Officer Nottingham saw you and Troyer snooping around Uncle Billy's place well over an hour ago. How'd you finally get inside?"

Heat rushed to my face. Timothy's brow furrowed as he watched my reaction. "She knows we were inside of Billy's place," I mouthed.

Timothy ran a finger across his throat as if Chief Rose was going to cut off our heads.

I rolled my eyes. "Under the broken garage door," I said into the phone.

"A tried and true method. Find anything interesting?"

"Since you were already there, I should be really asking you that."

"More than I bargained for," she muttered.

I wanted to ask her what she meant by that, but she went on. "We need to talk face-to-face."

"About Billy?"

"Among other things. Are you available now?"

I heard a *tap, tap, tap* on the other end of the line. I imagined the Appleseed Creek police chief tapping her pen on her desk. I covered the mouthpiece and repeated what Chief Rose said to Timothy. He nodded once. "Yes," I told her. "We can meet you."

"Good. You're going to have to come to me. I need to hang around the station. Everyone goes off their rocker this time of year, and I made the mistake of giving my secretary the week off. Too much family togetherness makes some reach for the drink and others for the shotgun. I much prefer President's Day. No one hardly ever shoots anyone on President's Day." She laughed. "But I don't have to tell you about family problems, do I, Humphrey?"

My stomach dropped. Was she referring to the issues the Troyer family had or was she referring to my relationship—or lack thereof—with my own family? Having thoroughly checked my background after I moved here and my car's involvement in Becky's auto-buggy accident that killed Bishop Glick, she knew my history. That made me uncomfortable. I knew so little about her. She was a cop and had mentioned once that she grew up in Appleseed Creek. That was all I had.

She tapped her pen more rapidly. "Troyer is with you, I imagine."

"Yes, he's right here."

"Thought so. It's going to be hard to keep you two apart from each other now that you are courting." There was laughter in her voice.

I blushed.

"See you in ten minutes," the chief barked in my ear and hung up.

Timothy shifted the truck into gear. Ten minutes later he turned the truck into the small lot behind the village's municipal building right off the town square. The parking lot was empty expect for the chief's cruiser. It was after five o'clock in the evening on a day before Christmas Eve. I imagined the village staff cleared out of the building quickly to jump-start their holiday.

When Timothy, Mabel, and I walked into the department, Chief Rose was sitting with her arms folded on the receptionist's desk. Mabel trotted up to the chief's side with her tongue hanging out of her mouth.

The police chief patted Mabel's head. "What do you want, pooch?"

Timothy scraped snow off his boots on the mat at the entryway. "Fern keeps dog biscuits in her desk for Mabel when she visits."

The police chief glowered at the dog. After a moment, she opened the lowest drawer of the receptionist's desk. "These are for you?"

Mabel barked.

Chief Rose reached into the box of treats and threw two across the room into the empty waiting area, which was a grouping of uncomfortable olive-green plastic chairs. Mabel lunged after the treats and grasped them between her paws.

"Where's Nottingham?" Timothy asked. "I want to know how he saw us at Billy's when I didn't see him."

The police chief laughed. "Nottingham can't tell you that. It's a cop trick. For a kid, Nottingham's turning into a reliable officer, and if I'm not careful, he'll start gunning for my job. The village would be a lot more comfortable with him in my role since he's a man." She stood up, her tone matter-of-fact. "Let's move to the conference room to talk. The pooch will have to stay out here."

Mabel lay in the middle of the linoleum floor licking her treats, trying to make them last as long as possible.

"I don't think she will mind," I said.

The chief unlocked the door on the other side of the desk and led us into a room, bare except for one cafeteria-style table and five folding chairs. Chief Rose's conference room doubled as her interrogation and booking room. Although I'd only moved to Appleseed Creek the previous summer, I had already spent more time in this room than most of the population. Thankfully, never to be booked for a crime, though I can't say the same about interrogation.

A legal-sized manila envelope sat in the middle of table. Chief Rose held it down with a finger and dragged it toward herself.

I hung my coat over the back of my chair and took a seat across from the police chief. "What's in the envelope?"

Timothy slipped into the seat beside me.

"I'll show you in minute. We will start with Katie." She drummed her fingers on the tabletop. "We believe she was murdered."

I gasped. "Murdered? I thought it was an icicle accident."

"Yeah, I thought my death by icicle theory was a good one too." She leaned back in her chair. "However, the coroner set me straight. The icicle hit her in the head after she was already dead. The most tell-tale sign was the bruising on her neck. No way those marks were from a rogue icicle. Katie was strangled."

My hand went to my throat. An image of the pretty Amish girl being choked to death filled my mind. I closed my eyes to block the sight, but that only made it more vivid.

Timothy tapped my foot with his boot. "We didn't see any sign of that."

"I wouldn't expect you would. Her face was half-covered by her bonnet, and she was wearing a thick scarf. The coroner thinks whoever did it used the scarf to kill her and then wrapped it loosely around her neck again when it was over."

"Poor Katie," I whispered. "What a terrible way to die."

The police chief grimaced. "It wouldn't be the way I'd want to go. I'll take a gunshot straight to the brain, thanks."

Timothy blanched. No doubt my expression was much the same.

Chief Rose ran a fingernail under the lip of the envelope. "We're waiting on the full autopsy before we can say anything official. Now, here's where it becomes interesting."

Some of the color returned to Timothy's face.

"Katie Lambright being strangled wasn't interesting enough?" I asked.

She eyed me with one of her unusual peridot-colored eyes, her shimmering, forest-green eye liner smudged at the corners. "It's plenty interesting, and more than enough to keep me busy into the new year. However, then I found this." She slid the manila envelope across the table at me.

My hands hovered over the envelope, unsure if I wanted to see what was inside.

Chief Rose snorted. "It's not a snake. It won't bite you."

I flipped over the envelope and lifted the flap. Inside were a sheet of paper and a photograph of a man. The name Walter Hoover ran across the top of the page. The young man in the photo looked strangely familiar. I gasped, "Is this . . . ?"

Timothy frowned. "It's a rap sheet for Billy."

"Bingo." The police chief beamed at Timothy as if he were her prize pupil. "Troyer wins."

He settled back into his seat. "What do I win?"

"Satisfaction at being the victor." Chief Rose pointed to the second sheet. "There you will see Billy's rap sheet. I'll give you the CliffsNotes version: He went to federal prison for fifteen years. Grand theft auto. He managed a chop shop in Detroit. Eight years in, he got out for good behavior, but the moment he hits the streets he doesn't call into his probation office like he should. Instead, he disappears. He's been using the social security number of a guy who died over twenty years ago. The real Billy Thorpe didn't have a family who might have caught the illegal use of his number. I imagine Hoover bought it from some con artist."

"You can buy a social security number?" I asked.

Chief Rose darted a glance at me. "You can buy anything, sadly."

I examined the man in the photograph and racked my brain for everything that I knew about Billy. It wasn't much. He loved duct tape, was good at fixing cars—even if the ones he revived weren't the most beautiful machines on the road—and was a genuinely nice guy. Had I been wrong about the last point? I took another look at the man in the photo. He had sandy-colored hair. "He's not a natural redhead?" I asked. For some reason, this upset me. Billy always talked about how we were the only true redheads in town and now I learn that we weren't even that.

Chief Rose barked a laugh. "Of all the details to pick up on, that's the best you can come up with?"

Timothy's jaw twitched. "How long has he been in hiding?"

I watched Timothy. Billy was his friend, not mine. What did he think about this information? If I, after only having spoken to him a handful of times, was questioning if I knew the real Billy, what would Timothy be thinking right now?

"Twelve years. He was pretty good at it. We discovered his true identity when we lifted some prints from his single-wide this afternoon. Afterward, I went over to the sheriff's place and ran the prints through AFIS. The village doesn't believe it necessary that I have my own access to the database," she added bitterly. "I got zero hits for William Thorpe, but Walter Hoover popped right up."

She reached across the table and tapped the man in the photograph on the nose. "I called the Detroit Police Department to share my discovery. I can't say they were all that enthused or impressed by it." She raised her palms. "Why worry about a car thief that disappeared twelve years ago when you have gangbangers shooting each other every night on the streets? However, they said they would take him back if I found him."

"That's nice of them," I muttered. I flattened my hands on the table. "Billy," I said unable to call him Walter. "Billy was the one who introduced me to Becky's lawyer, Tyler Hart. He said that the lawyer got him out of trouble. I thought it was legal trouble."

The chief dropped the envelope onto the table. "I've cited Walter before for small violations, but nothing that would have required me to collect his fingerprints. Had I, he would be back in Detroit by now. Seems I need to have a little chat with Tyler to find out what those legal matters were."

Apparently, Chief Rose had no problem saying Billy's real name.

"He can't tell you," I said. "Anything between him and his client is confidential."

A strange look passed over her delicate features. "We'll see about that."

Timothy folded his hands on the table. "No matter what Billy may have done in his past, it doesn't mean he's responsible for Katie Lambright's murder."

Chief Rose clicked her tongue. "Troyer, you are loyal to a fault." She turned to me. "You'd better remember that about him, Humphrey. Could come in handy in the future."

"I don't think loyalty is a bad attribute," I said.

The chief ran her hand through her brown curls, and they immediately sprang back into place. "Neither do I. Troyer, you know our visit to the Lambright farm didn't go well. The Lambrights won't talk to me about their daughter. That's why I called the two of you here. I need someone," she looked directly at me. "I need someone to poke around and find out who the Amish suspects are in this case."

I pressed my palm to my chest. "You want *me* to do that?"

The chief sat back, eyeing me now. "Sure, why not? It's not like you haven't done it before. Troyer can help you out with it too." She grinned. "I know you were planning to do it anyway. Why else would you be snooping around the car shop? This way it's sanctioned by me. Unofficially, of course. My department is not liable if you break a leg or if you bust your spleen in pursuit of a suspect. Trust me, if it comes to that, I will deny this conversation ever happened."

"Thanks," I said, the sarcasm back in my voice.

As if she approved of my tone, the chief of police smiled. "That's the right attitude."

"Where do you want us to start?" Timothy asked.

"I want you to find out who was beating up Katie Lambright."

I grew still. "Beating up? I thought she was strangled."

"She was, but this wasn't the first time she had been the victim of violence. Her body was covered with bruises, and even before the autopsy, the coroner could tell that a finger on her right hand had been broken."

Timothy's brows knit together. "Growing up on a farm, a broken finger isn't that uncommon. Thomas breaks something every year."

"True, but this isn't any typical break. The coroner said it appeared to be a spiral fracture. He said the only way that could have happened was if the finger was twisted. So she either got it stuck in a vise or someone grabbed it and twisted it until it snapped."

Instinctively my fingers curled into fists to protect themselves. I thought of what Timothy said of Katie's father Jeb Lambright. Just how hot was his temper?

Chief Rose slid Billy's photograph and rap sheet back into the envelope. "What do you say, Humphrey? Are you willing to help me out again?"

Timothy gave me the slightest of nods.

I licked my lips. "Yes."

The right side of the police chief's mouth turned up. "Terrific." She made eye connect with me, then Timothy, and then back to me. "Do me a favor this time—keep me in the loop. You think of or find something important, you call me, night or day."

"Even on Christmas?" I asked.

Her brows drooped low over her eyes. "Especially on Christmas."

"Sounds fair," I said.

On the other hand, Timothy said nothing.

Chapter Eight

Christmas Eve morning, the Harshberger College campus lay still and dormant under a blanket of freshly fallen snow. The students were home with their families for the next month until the new semester began in mid-January. Only essential faculty and staff were on campus, and as the director of computer services, I was one of those people. Even on Christmas, the computer systems that kept the college moving had to be up and running, from the protective firewall to the campus e-mail.

This was my first Christmas at Harshberger, and I found the quietness of the once-bustling campus both calming and eerie. Since I was new, I opted to be the on-call person during the holiday break, hoping my staff would take their turns during future breaks. Perhaps next year I would have enough money saved to spend Christmas in Italy with my best friend Tanisha. Tee taught English as a Second Language there, and I missed her terribly. We Skyped and e-mailed often, but it wasn't the same as seeing her in person. Tanisha was more like a sister to me than a friend. Her family took me in when I was fifteen—after my mother died and my father dumped me for a new wife and new life in California.

Going to California to spend the holidays with my father, young stepbrother and stepsister, and my evil stepmother Sabrina was out of the question. Sabrina made it clear I was not welcome. Just a month ago, I had been uninvited to Thanksgiving so that the four of them could go on a cruise. At least she was upfront with her distaste for me.

My father was ambivalent, which was so much worse. The car accident that killed my mother destroyed what relationship I'd had with my father. Mom had spun off the icy road late one winter night when coming to fetch me from a sleepover party. This coming January would mark the eleventh anniversary of my mother's death.

I stepped into the server room and examined the racks of black and silver boxes. Their little green power lights blinked pleasantly at me. No red flashing lights, no alarms sounding. All was well. At least, in the server room. All was not well in Appleseed Creek. I thought of Katie. To die the way she did, it seemed too cruel. A terrible waste. What could the Amish girl have done to make someone hate her so much to hurt her like that? I found the idea that she had been physically abused deeply disturbing. If Katie had been hurt, what about Anna? Was the younger of the two Lambright sisters in danger? The Amish were particularly closed-mouthed on the topic of domestic abuse. How were Timothy and I supposed to find out what really happened to Katie?

Locking the door to the server room behind me, my thoughts turned to Billy. Should I think of him as Walter now? He had only been Billy to me—and to everyone else in Appleseed Creek. Chief Rose asked us to keep his true identity a secret, because she didn't want the information to leak in case Billy still hung around the area.

I stopped by my office to mark the log showing that I checked the servers and that all systems were normal. I wasn't in a big rush to return home. Becky was in the middle of a full-on Christmas frenzy. When we moved to the Quills' house, I told her that we could have a small Christmas party. I never expected her to jump into planning her first English Christmas party with so much enthusiasm. Our home looked like Santa's elves had an ornament fight that started in the living room and carried on into the kitchen. Becky, apparently, took her first English Christmas seriously.

Becky's favorite part about the house's kitchen was Mrs. Quills' television. When awake, she rarely left the kitchen. My cat Gigabyte was a big fan of the kitchen too, as he got the scraps from Becky's experiments. Over the last two weeks, as Becky collected recipes for the party, Food Network played 24/7 in our house. If I saw one more episode about how to make a yule log, I thought I might scream.

To Becky's delight, Young's Family Kitchen and its shops were closed both Christmas Eve and Christmas Day, so Becky was home with her best friend Paula Deen and Company while I hid in my office. Our party—really Becky's party because I had done little more for it than vacuum the carpet and clean the bathrooms—would be Christmas night. During the day Becky and I would be at her parents' home.

The only damper on the party was that the Troyers were not coming. Becky wanted her family there, but it was not the Amish way to participate in such an extravagant gathering.

As I checked my e-mail, my thoughts wandered back to Billy. Timothy said in the mobile home that it looked like he had been gone for a few days. He could be on the other side of the world by now. Did Chief Rose check flights out of Columbus for Billy's name? Was one of his automobiles missing? Did he drive out of Knox County? I made a mental note to ask the chief these questions, but it was likely she had already thought about all of this and would find my inquiries annoying. She wanted me to concentrate on the Amish, so questions about Billy's car would not be fulfilling my assignment. I turned off the computer and grabbed my coat. As much as I dreaded it, I knew I should return home and offer Becky what little help I could to prepare for the party.

Outside it was snowing again, and even though I had only been on campus for two hours, my Bug was buried under a couple inches of white powder. My only consolation? The weather was even worse back in Cleveland, as clouds full to bursting with lake effect snow blew off of Lake Erie.

I popped the trunk with my key fob and retrieved a window scraper, covering myself with snow in the process. I started in the back and began to wipe away snow, then moved around to the passenger side and ran the brush end across the window. As I did, a face stared back at me through the window.

I dropped the scraper and screamed.

The passenger door opened and Curt Fanning—the man who had harassed me since the day I arrived in Knox County and who I had hoped to never see again—stepped out of the car. I scooped my scraper off the ground and held it in front of me like a saber. I shot a look around campus in search of someone, anyone. Where was college security when you needed them?

A lazy grin spread across Curt's thin face as he leaned back against my car. "There you are, Red. I nearly froze my keister off waiting for you to show up."

"What do you want?" My hand began to ache from holding the scraper so tightly, but I didn't loosen my grip.

He ran his hand along his jawline and across his bedraggled goatee. "Is that any way to greet an old friend?"

Curt was certainly not an old friend of mine. When I first moved to Appleseed Creek he harassed both Becky and me and even threatened to kill us both "to teach us a lesson."

I waved the scraper in the air to show I meant business. "I don't have time for this, Curt. Get away from my car."

"Or what? You'll call your Amish boyfriend to come beat me up? Sorry, sweetie, the Amish won't fight for you." He smirked, and drew closer to me. "Like I would."

With my free hand, I reached into my purse for my phone.

He held up his hand. "There's no reason to call that lady cop. It's Christmas Eve, and I think both she and I would have a better holiday if we didn't cross paths."

"Then move away from my car, so I can leave."

"I will in a minute, but I'm here to help you."

"Help me?" I choked a laugh. "What could *you* do that would help me?"

He frowned. "I heard that you were looking for Billy Thorpe."

I nearly dropped the phone in the snow, but instead let it fall to the bottom of my purse. "How do you know that?"

"Little goes on in this county that I don't know about . . . legal," he paused, "or illegal."

"I believe the illegal part," I muttered. Worry bit into my gut. Did Curt have something to do with Katie's death? After the events of the summer, would I always assume Curt was involved with the crimes against the Amish? Probably. "Where's Brock?" I asked. Rarely did I see Curt without his constant companion, Brock Buckley, a huge bear of a man, bald, and with a killer temper.

Curt's face pinched. "He had things to do."

The cold began to seep into my bones. It was time to speed this up. "What do you know about Billy?"

Curt sucked on his front teeth for a second as if considering my question. "I saw him cut out of his place in a huge hurry a few days ago."

"When was this?" My voice was sharp. "Exactly."

"Let's see, today is Tuesday, so I would say it was Sunday. He was mighty upset about something. 'Course I'd be upset too if I'd just killed an Amish girl."

"He may not have done it," I snapped.

"Now, Red, why do I think that you wouldn't give me the benefit of the doubt like that?"

My face flushed because he was right. "Where was he going?"

He spiked the air with his palms "How should I know? It wasn't like he stayed to chat. The guy was in a rush."

"Did he drive away in a car?"

He nodded. "A junky brown station wagon."

I cocked my head. "What time of day did you see him?"

"It was dusk. Four thirty or thereabouts."

"What were you doing by Billy's store?"

His eyes narrowed. "That's beside the point."

I didn't think so, but I let it drop. "Did you tell Chief Rose this?"

"No, I much prefer to talk to you than to the lady cop." He winked. "She doesn't understand me like you do."

My skin prickled, like it might crawl right off my body. "Trust me. I don't get you at all."

He laughed hoarsely. "Red, it's too easy to rile you up."

I ignored his comment and moved on to my next question. "Do you remember anything else about seeing him?"

Curt thought for a moment. "He had an orange duffel bag with him. I remember because it stood out so much next to the snow."

I bet the duffel bag held Billy's toothbrush and other essentials. "Thank you for telling me."

He stepped away from my car. "Maybe things can be different," he said, his voice was low and wistful—a quality I had never heard in Curt before.

"What things?" I asked, still holding the scraper like a sword about to strike a blow.

Curt opened his mouth as if to say more, then eyed the scraper and clamped his mouth shut.

I let it fall to my side.

The smallest of smiles curved his mouth.

"Why did you help me?" I asked.

A peculiar look crossed his face, a cross between a smile and a frown. "I think you have something I want."

Even though the thought of his answer made me queasy, I heard myself ask, "And what's that?"

"I'm trying to figure it out." Then he shoved his bare hands into the pockets of his bomber jacket and loped across the snow-covered green without saying good-bye.

I stood there and watched him until he disappeared around the corner of a building. Then I brushed the snowflakes from my eyelashes and slid into my car. If Curt wanted something from me that could only mean he didn't plan to leave me alone—which was all I ever wanted from him.

Chapter Nine

I started the engine and cranked the heater to third-degree burns, then tossed the scraper in the backseat. I didn't want it in my line of vision. The first thing I should do is call Chief Rose and tell her what I learned from Curt. She would want to bring him in for questioning and would be annoyed that I didn't call her the minute I saw him. That was our deal when it came to Curt or Brock.

My fingers hovered over the chief's number on the touchscreen of my smartphone. Before I could change my mind, I pressed "call." To my relief the call went directly to voice mail. I left a brief message with the details Curt shared.

I placed the phone on the passenger seat next to me. Why had Curt been so helpful? He had helped me solve a case in November involving Amish haircutting. However, he had only done so because I had saved his best friend, Brock's, life. Could he still believe that he owed me? That didn't fit with what I knew about Curt.

Then again, why was I questioning him? Couldn't I just be grateful for the information? If it were true.

Memories of my tumultuous summer and Curt's part in it hit me. Those memories were why I couldn't trust him. My stomach clenched. Had I forgiven Curt and Brock for all their intimidation, for all their threats directed at Becky and me? I thought I had, but was it in speech only, not in my heart? Is it possible to forgive, and yet not trust?

I backed out of my spot. Now the thought of helping Becky with the Christmas party festivities sounded like the perfect way to spend the evening until it was time to leave for church. I was willing to help with whatever ridiculously complicated recipe she wanted to tackle—even a yule log.

Twenty minutes later I walked through the front door of the Quills' house. The scent of pine, cookies, and ham hit my senses. The eight-foot tree in the front window swayed, and I dropped my purse and walked over to it. About halfway up the tree two glowing blue eyes stared at me. "Gig," I said, "you know that you aren't supposed to be in there." I placed my hands on my hips. "You are in big trouble, mister."

He gave me a Siamese yowl in return.

I reached for him, and he wiggled deeper among the boughs. The tree began to sway more, and I grabbed it around the trunk to keep it from toppling over. The last thing I wanted was for the tree to land on the Quills' mini-grand piano. "Gig, you get out of there this very minute!"

"*Yowl.*" The tree stopped swaying.

I let it go. "You're going to be grounded, which for you means no more of Becky's sweet eats."

His paw batted at me from two feet above my head. This was another one of those times when I wished I were six inches taller.

"We'll talk about this later," I threatened. I could have sworn I heard him laughing when I stomped away.

I stepped into the kitchen. "Gigabyte is inside the tree. I can't get him out."

Becky had the television cranked to the sound barrier, and—surprise, surprise—it was turned to a cooking show. She was at the stove, melting chocolate in a double boiler. A gingerbread house stood in the middle of the granite-covered island, and a piping bag with red icing dripping from its tip lay on the island next to the house. Powdered sugar dusted the floor as if a donut had exploded in the room. A buffet table stood against the wall opposite the sink, and that's where Becky's finished creations waited for tomorrow's party. I was pleased—and relieved—to see that the yule log was already complete. At least I wouldn't have to hear about that any longer.

A streak of green icing marred Becky's right cheek. "Chloe, you're home. Wonderful. Can you help me?"

I grabbed an apron from a peg on the back of the pantry door. "What do you want me to do?"

"Can you finish piping the roof of the gingerbread house?"

I examined the intricate crisscross pattern she had applied to the roof. "Um, Becky, you're the artist. If I touch that with a piping bag, you will have one huge blob on the roof."

She laughed. "Okay, come over here and stir the chocolate. All you have to do is stop it from burning."

Easier said than done. I didn't tell her that, though, because it was a much simpler task than the roof piping.

Becky picked up the piping bag and began making slate rectangles on the roof with red icing. She worked quickly and with zero mistakes. Becky excelled at every form of art she tried. She had the dexterity and the eye to make a simple piece spectacular. She blew a lock of her white-blonde hair out of her eyes as she worked. "I think I might have made too much for tomorrow's party."

I pointed a thumb at the buffet. "You think?"

She chuckled. "We can take some to the Christmas program at the schoolhouse. I'm so happy that we are able to go. It was always my favorite day when I was in school." She frowned. "I miss it sometimes." She drew in a deep breath and forced a smile. "That's silly. I've been out of school for years."

"But you're going back," I reminded her.

Her clear brow creased. "If I pass the GRE."

I stirred the chocolate. "You will pass. You've passed every practice test I've given you."

"That's different. I know those tests don't really count, so I'm not nervous."

"Then pretend the test is practice. That will help."

She set the piping bag down and started placing candy pearls strategically around the roof. "But it's not true."

Chocolate dripped from my spoon. Should I tell Becky about my run-in with Curt? "That's the most blinged-out gingerbread house I've ever seen."

"You think so?"

"Trust me—everyone will think so."

She grinned. "Timothy is bringing Aaron to the party," she said cheerfully. Her voice was light and bright now that the conversation had moved away from school and onto a subject that she enjoyed—Aaron.

I frowned. Aaron Sutter took a risk by coming to our home for the party, even if he was Timothy's best friend. He was Amish, baptized and everything, and the son of Deacon Sutter. The deacon barely tolerated Becky and Timothy visiting the Troyer family and would have put a stop to that all together had Bishop Hooley not stepped in and allowed it.

Recently, Aaron started working at Young's Family Kitchen as a host. I suspected the close proximity to Becky everyday was the main reason Aaron took the job. He was smitten with his best friend's little sister. Becky cared about him, but I wondered if her affection for him ran as deeply as his did for her.

"Did I tell you that he was coming?" Becky asked.

I laughed. "Only fifteen times." The chocolate was becoming more difficult to stir. I made a face. Some must have burnt on the bottom. Maybe Becky wouldn't notice.

Her forehead creased. "Do you think he will be in trouble for coming?"

I shrugged and pretended to concentrate on the chocolate. "He knows how his father would feel about it. How is he going to leave his family on Christmas Day? Isn't that a time his family will get together?"

She worried her lip. "He said his sisters are coming to his farm in the morning, and then in the afternoon the family is going to his oldest sister's farm. She lives in Holmes County. Aaron is going to beg off, saying he's too tired for the long drive."

Aaron was paralyzed from the waist down as the result of a construction accident during his *rumspringa* when he was about Becky's age. An accident that Timothy felt partly responsible for, so much that it was the catalyst that caused him to leave the Amish district.

"So, he's going to lie to the deacon?" The chocolate began to smoke, and I stirred faster. Double boiling was no joke.

"No," she said aghast. "He really will be too tired. That's a long day for him. He can come here and head back long before his parents arrive home from his sister's house. That will be a much shorter day for him." She set the container of candy pearls on the island. "Okay, maybe he's not telling the deacon the whole truth, but there's no other way for him to come. You know what the deacon would do if he found out. He would forbid Aaron to speak to me, or worse, have him shunned from the church." She picked the piping bag back up again and held it listlessly in her hands. "He's taking a risk because of me." Red icing spurt on the countertop. "But . . ."

I stuck the spoon in chocolate. It stuck straight up like a peg in a board. "But what?"

"I can't go back to being Amish now that I know what the *Englisch* world has to offer. I care about him, but I can't be what he needs me to be. I can't be Amish."

"Did Aaron ask you to be Amish again?" I tried to keep my voice casual.

"No." She blinked tears from her eyes. "He would never do that."

"Have you told Aaron how you feel about being Amish?" I poked the spoon with my index finger. It didn't even budge. "It may be best if you told him now before he becomes too attached."

She scooped up another handful of candied pearls. "I'm sure he knows."

I gave up on the chocolate. "He needs to hear it from you. You may think that he knows, but you need to be sure. It's only fair." I swallowed. "If he leaves the church for you, he'll be shunned. It won't be like how it's been for you and Timothy."

"*You* don't have to tell me how the Amish world works, Chloe. I'm the one from there. You're not."

Her words were like a slap across my face. The sting lingered in the air between us for a few seconds. "You're right." I pointed at the stove. "By the way, I ruined your chocolate. Sorry."

There was a solid ten seconds of tense silence followed by the front door opening and slamming shut.

"Hello!" Timothy called from the living room. He carried a huge basket into the kitchen.

"What's that?" I asked.

He removed his stocking cap. "I was at Young's this morning just to check if the guys closed up the jobsite right for the next couple of days. Ellie was there and forced this on me. It's stuffed with cookies and treats from the bakery." He smiled at his sister. "I told her Becky was making enough food to feed the entire district, but she insisted."

"How is Ellie?" I asked. One of Ellie's thirty-year-old twin sons died just before Thanksgiving. The first Christmas without a loved one was the hardest. I wished I could tell her it got better, but it took many years for things to improve after the loss of my mother.

"She seemed cheerful, but I imagine she doesn't feel that way when she is alone. She is professional, always on the job." He sniffed the air. "Is something burning?"

"The chocolate," Becky yelped.

I stepped out of the way while she charged the stove. "I told you I don't know what I'm doing."

Becky lifted the boiler off the stovetop and moved it to a cool burner.

Timothy chuckled. "Where should I put this?" Every flat surface in the room was covered with food in varying stages of preparation.

I pulled out one of the chairs sitting around the kitchen table. "Right here will work."

Timothy set the basket on the chair, then looked over at his sister. "How many people are you expecting?"

Becky was back to piping. "Thirty or so. I invited a lot of people from church and work." She frowned. "I wish that our family would be here."

Timothy shook his head. "It's better this way. *Daed* would not be comfortable at an *Englischer* party. We will see them today at the Christmas program and then again tomorrow."

Becky sighed and cleaned the tip of her piping bag. "At least the party isn't until tomorrow. I might need to go back to the market later today for more chocolate."

The smell of burnt chocolate hung in the air. "I can buy it. I'm the one that burned it," I said.

"No, it's okay." She walked across the room and gave me a hug. "I'm sorry about what I said earlier. It was mean." She lowered her voice. "I got mad because I know you're right, and I don't want you to be."

I hugged her back. "No worries, Becky. Sisters fight."

She smiled and went back to her piping.

Timothy gave me a quizzical look, but I just shook my head.

He shrugged. "I have some more stuff in my truck." He turned toward the kitchen door.

"I'll help you," I said as he was stepping out the door. I was better at carrying stuff than at cooking. When I caught up with Timothy outside, Mabel was in the Quills' front yard eating snow.

Timothy removed a basket of fresh-baked rolls from the truck.

"How much stuff did Ellie give you?"

"You know Ellie," he said with a laugh. "Why give someone one pie when you can give them three?"

I cleared my throat. "I need to tell you something."

He frowned. "Does this have anything to do with what you and Becky were just talking about?"

I waved that idea away. "No. That was just girl stuff."

He waited.

I took a deep breath. "I saw Curt Fanning today."

Timothy dropped the basket and the rolls bounced into the snow. Mabel loped over and ate one whole.

Chapter Ten

Timothy's breath caught. "What happened? Are you okay? Did he try to hurt you?" His questions came at me rapidly, his voice sharp.

I squatted to pick up the rolls. "Do you think Mabel will become sick from eating these? I think she ate seven of them."

Timothy held out a hand to help me up. He gripped my fingers tightly. "Chloe, did he hurt you?"

"No. He wanted to tell me he saw Billy leave the auto shop in a hurry late Sunday afternoon in a brown station wagon. He knew about Billy's connection to Katie Lambright's death." I didn't add that Curt had broken into my car. It would only distract Timothy.

He let go of my hand. "How could he know that? Greta told us not to tell anyone."

I shook my head. "I didn't tell anyone. I didn't even tell Becky."

"Neither did I."

"He could have heard it from someone else that was at the scene."

Timothy touched his chin. "Maybe. Or he could be making it up to cover his own tracks. I can't think of a better suspect for Katie's murder than Curt Fanning."

Mabel finished off the remainder of the rolls and rolled back and forth in the snow.

"I don't think he did it," I said.

Timothy's brow shot up. "Why's that? Did he say something to make you think that? Does he have an alibi?"

I frowned. "I didn't ask him about an alibi."

"I'm sure you will have another chance since he seems dead set on seeking you out all of the time," he said bitterly. "Was Brock with him?"

"No. Curt was alone."

"That's new. I thought Tweedledee always needed Tweedledumb."

I laughed. "What do you know about Tweedledee and Tweedledumb? You can't tell me you read *Alice in Wonderland* as an Amish kid."

He gave me a small smile, but it didn't quite make it to his eyes. "I saw the movie after I left." He paused. "With Hannah."

"Oh." I knelt to pet Mabel, who was on a carbohydrate high. I scratched her belly. Hannah was Timothy's Mennonite ex-girlfriend. They broke up long before I moved to Appleseed Creek, but it was still painful to know he might have any good memories of their time together. Hannah was less than pleased when I came to town and Timothy showed interest in me. As far as she was concerned, she and Timothy were meant to be together. I was only a temporary nuisance.

I straightened up. "Whatever Curt's motive may have been to tell me, he gave us a valuable clue. If we knew when Katie died, maybe we could have a sequence of events."

"Chief Rose would know the timing of Katie's death. If she doesn't know yet, she should soon."

As if on cue, my cell phone rang, the readout declaring, *Chief Rose.*

"Humphrey," the police chief barked in my ear. "Where do you get off leaving me a voice mail that Fanning told you something about the Lambright case?"

"I thought that you would want to know."

"Yes, I want to know, but you could have called me back or left a text telling me it was important." She took a deep breath. "Never mind. It's good info to have. It fits in with my timetable."

"Your timetable?"

"Yep. I forgot to mention to you and Troyer that the coroner said Katie died twenty-four to forty-eight hours before you stumbled upon her. She was still in fairly good shape because she was packed in snow."

I tried not to gag. "Did the Lambrights mention when you visited them that Katie was missing?" I asked, raising my brows at Timothy.

He shook his head.

In my ear, the police chief continued, "No. They hardly spoke to us at all. That's why I asked for your help, remember? Now, get out there and talk to some Amish." She ended the call.

I slipped the cell phone back into my pocket.

Timothy wrapped his arm around my shoulder. "I'm sorry that I got upset. I don't want anything to happen to you."

"Nothing will," I promised.

"That's what you said last time."

He had a point. I removed his arm from my shoulder and held his hand. "Come with me. I want to give you your Christmas gift."

He pulled back on my hand. "I thought we were going to exchange gifts in front of my family tomorrow."

"You already broke that rule, remember?" I said as I touched the chain around my neck.

He grinned. "Oh, all right. But is this a bribe to forget about Curt and Brock?"

"Um."

His blue eyes sparkled. "Because I'm not saying that I won't be bribed."

I rolled my eyes. "Come on." Still holding his hand, I led him to the garage, while Mabel galloped behind us.

"My gift is in the garage?" His voice teased.

I entered the code into the keypad and the automatic door went up. The gift was wrapped in silver paper and sitting on Mr. Quills' workbench. I led Timothy by the hand to the bench. "Open it."

"Are you sure you want me to open it now?"

"Yes." I clenched my hands. *Would he like it?*

He sat on the stool and began removing the paper. As he realized what it was, he ripped at the paper more quickly, then he rested a hand on the box and didn't say anything.

I was right. It was an unromantic gift. "I can return it and find something else," I said quickly. "I know it's a strange first Christmas gift."

He turned around and faced me and held out his hands. I grasped them.

"Chloe," he whispered. "I love it. It's the perfect gift."

The worry circling like a storm cloud around my heart evaporated. "It is?"

"How did you know I wanted a ratchet set just like this?" He stood with a wide grin on his face. "It has ninety-four pieces and more sockets than I know what to do with."

My shoulders relaxed. "Last time we were at Billy's . . . before," I paused, "before he disappeared, you were admiring his set and wishing for your own."

Timothy flinched at the mention of his friend—a friend who was missing—an escaped convict who was potentially wrapped up with the murder of an innocent Amish girl.

I cleared my throat. "Later, I went back and he told me where to buy one just like it. He was excited to help because he cares about you."

Timothy ignored my commentary on Billy's feelings about the gift. "I didn't even know you were paying attention to what we were saying."

"I'm always paying attention to you," I whispered.

He pulled me close and whispered. "And I'm always paying attention to you."

THE AMISH DISTRICT'S ONE-ROOM schoolhouse was thirty minutes by foot from the Troyer farm, ten minutes by buggy, and two minutes by car. Timothy, Becky, and I arrived at the schoolhouse before the rest of their family.

As Timothy parked his truck a little way from the line of Amish buggies tethered to the hitching post, I was instantly charmed. The schoolhouse looked like it had been dropped right out of a giant postcard. A white-washed rail fence surrounded the schoolhouse, swing set, teeter-totter, and outbuildings, all covered with a thin layer of snow. Child-sized boot prints ran every which way across the schoolyard. Mothers in heavy winter caps and bonnets stood next to their husbands in their thick wool coats and black stocking caps. The children's coats were more colorful—blue to purple to maroon. They were dots of color in a sea of black and white. A boy chased a classmate with a snowball, and his father reached out and grabbed him by the collar. The child squealed and then melted into laughter until his father released him.

I wished I could take a photograph of the scene, but I stopped myself from reaching inside my purse for my cell phone to snap a picture. Any photography would insult the Old Order district.

"This is where you went to school?" I asked Becky and Timothy.

"Yep," Becky said and hopped out of the truck.

"It's so darling," I told Timothy.

Timothy laughed and squeezed my hand across the seat. "Trust me, I didn't think that when I was a student here. All I wanted to do was finish school so that I could go to work as a carpenter."

The Amish only attend school through the eighth grade. With two master's degrees behind me, this was difficult for me to fathom. School had been my escape. "You didn't want to go on to high school or even college?"

He shook his head. "School's not for me. I did pass the GRE because it would be easier from a business standpoint. I took a couple of business classes at the community college too, but never earned a degree. I couldn't stand to sit there and listen to an instructor talk about how to do something. I'd rather do it and learn for myself."

I twisted my mouth. I had loved school. I cried when I graduated from my last program and even considered applying for my doctorate so I could stay another four years at the university. The fact that my student loans hung over my head like the sword of Damocles stopped me. After I paid them down, it was likely I would go back to school. What would Timothy think about that decision? Would he believe it a waste of time?

Sparky clomped onto the schoolyard pulling the Troyer's largest buggy behind him as Timothy and I slipped out of the pickup. Grandfather Zook and Mr. Troyer sat in the front seat, and most likely, Timothy's mother and the three younger Troyer children were in the back of the buggy.

Grandfather Zook parked Sparky next to Timothy's truck. Timothy tethered the horse to a tree and rubbed the white star in the middle of his forehead. Thomas leaped out of the buggy wearing a striped nightshirt and a cloth over his clothing and a band on his head. The seven-year-old spun in place, so that we could appreciate the full effect of his outfit.

The rest of the family piled out of the buggy. Ruth was the last to slip out, and from the scowl on her face it was clear she didn't want to be there.

Thomas kept spinning and almost toppled over. His father caught him and reprimanded him in Pennsylvania Dutch.

Mrs. Troyer shook her head. "He insisted on wearing his shepherd's outfit all day long."

He lifted his chin. "I'm playing a shepherd in the Christmas pageant. I have a line too," he said proudly.

"What's that?" I asked.

"Do you hear the angels singing?" he recited just below a shout.

Ruth winced.

Naomi giggled and clutched her faceless doll by the leg.

I squeezed her hand. "It won't be long before you are in the Christmas show too. Maybe next year?"

She grinned and nodded.

"Maybe you will be a sheep to Thomas's shepherd."

Thomas shook his head. "A person can't be a sheep. We have *real* sheep for our play."

As if on cue, Bishop Hooley and his eldest daughter, Sadie, who was Becky's age, walked around the corner of the farthest outbuilding led by three lambs on a rope.

"Those are mine," Thomas said proudly.

"They aren't yours," Ruth corrected. "The bishop is only letting you borrow them for the pageant."

Thomas wasn't listening. He was already halfway across the schoolyard to the Hooleys. As usual, Naomi ran after him.

A thin, young woman stood at the door, holding a large brass bell in her hand. She smiled broadly as she rang the bell. "Time for school," Timothy whispered in my ear.

He moved away and walked with

his father and grandfather toward the schoolhouse. He was trying to keep a low profile among the Amish; however, my attending the Christmas program as the Troyer family's guest spoke volumes. Timothy and I could have danced around the schoolyard holding hands, and it would have made no difference. The community knew Timothy was courting me. What the majority of them thought about it remained to be seen.

Becky fell into step beside me. She sighed. "I need to get used to being stared at when I come back into the community."

The Amish were not subtle in their examination of us in our English clothes. "Just pretend they are staring at me," I said.

She grinned. "They probably are."

"Thanks a lot." We stepped into the schoolhouse and scraped the snow off of our boots on the mat.

Thomas and the other children in the pageant stood in the back corner of the room receiving last-minute instructions from their teacher. While the children made final preparations, parents and families were allowed to roam around the room and view their children's projects.

The classroom held thirty metal and wooden desks, which weren't that different from the ones I had in grade school. Each desk had a flip-open lid, so that students could store their pencils, paper, chalk, and slate. In the front of the room sat the teacher's wide wooden desk, and behind that was a green chalkboard running the entire length of the wall. The alphabet in print and cursive letters hung above the chalkboard. The Amish still taught their children to write in cursive. I took handwriting in school too, but Tanisha's eleven-year-old brother never had. The public schools in Cleveland now taught keyboarding. That would never be a curriculum concern for the Amish school.

Welcome messages were written side-by-side in Pennsylvania Dutch and English on the chalkboard. Colorful paintings hung from every open wall space in the room and chain links of red and green construction paper hung from the rafters.

A painting of a horse hung on the back wall. It looked like it could gallop right out of the painting. I recognized it immediately as one of Becky's pieces, and she saw it too. "I thought my teacher would have taken this down when I left the community."

I patted her shoulder and smiled. "It's too pretty to take down."

I scanned the room for the Lambright family. Anna was the youngest and the only one still in school. She wasn't there, and neither were her parents. I hadn't really expected to see them. They were in the middle of the Amish tradition of three days of mourning a death in a family.

The younger of the two teachers, a pretty brunette not much older than Becky, rang the school bell again. She spoke in their language, and everyone found a seat. Out of habit the children went to their assigned desks, and the parents and family sat in the three rows of metal folding chairs set up in the back of the classroom.

After each of the seventh and eighth graders, including Ruth, read poems they wrote about the holidays, the Christmas pageant began.

Mary and Joseph spoke about their trip to Bethlehem, how the innkeeper turned them away with a claim of no vacancy, and they traveled on to the manger. The expressions on Mary and Joseph's faces were so exaggerated that I stifled a laugh. The tiniest of smiles crept onto on Mr. Troyer's usually stern face. Conversely, his father-in-law beamed from ear to ear.

A small choir of girls sang, "Hark! The Herald Angels Sing" in English, and then it was Thomas's big moment. He stepped onto center stage, in front of Mary and Joseph, gripping the leashes to the three lambs in his hand and tilting his head back as if mesmerized by some celestial being from above.

Had acting been an option for an Amish child, Thomas might have considered it for a career.

"Do you hear the angels singing?" he shouted in top voice, startling the lambs. The animals *baaed* and ran in opposite directions from Thomas, pulling their leashes from his hand.

Children jumped out of their desks and began chasing the lambs around the room. This only made the animals more terrified. A latecomer opened the schoolhouse door, and the Amish man was nearly run over by a lamb making her great escape. The children cornered the other two by the teacher's desk.

Parents' mouths hung open, and Mrs. Troyer covered her face with one hand. Mr. Troyer just shook his head before he and Timothy went outside to track down the bishop's lost lamb. Grandfather Zook doubled in mirth. I had to look away from him or I would start laughing too.

Thomas's eyes were enormous as laughter erupted in the room. The two teachers tried to restore order by lining up the three wise men for their cue. Then Bishop Hooley quietly walked two of his captured lambs outside.

Thomas regained his composure. "I think the lambs heard the angels." He bowed and stepped aside, so that the magi could take center stage from the east.

I could not contain my laughter any longer. I covered my mouth with my winter hat to stifle the fit of giggles that overtook me. When I could breathe again, I glanced across the room to find Deacon Sutter glaring at me.

The sight sobered me up like nothing else could.

Chapter Eleven

After the pageant ended, the teachers laid out cookies and punch for the children and coffee for the parents. Thomas popped up at my side still in his shepherd's outfit. "How did I do, Chloe?"

I kept a straight face. "You were memorable."

He nodded, his lower lip protruding. "Too bad about the sheep. I'm glad that Timothy was able to catch the third one. I would have felt bad if I lost one of the bishop's sheep."

"It was a good thing," I agreed.

He ran away to talk with one of the wise men. It was nice to know that shepherds and wise men got along.

The line for punch and cookies snaked around the room, and I could feel the curious stares of the Amish coming from it. During the program, their focus had been on the children. Now that the program was over, their curious looks focused on me. I stepped out of the schoolhouse into the snow.

Ruth disappeared around the corner of the outhouse. In the Appleseed Creek district the Amish had indoor plumbing, but apparently that nod to technology didn't extend to the schoolhouse.

Thinking she might be upset or embarrassed by her brother's antics, I followed her. The snow muffled my footsteps. As I got closer, I heard Ruth speaking to someone in her native language. I hesitated. The last thing I wanted to do was make Ruth more upset by making her think I was spying on her.

She turned and waved toward me. This was a first. Ruth never asked me to come and talk to her. Of the Troyers, she was the least comfortable with me being involved with the family. If she had her way, I think she would happily see me return to Cleveland.

I stepped around the side of the outhouse "Ruth, is everything okay?" I pulled up short. I had expected her to be talking to a classmate, and she was. I had not expected for that classmate to be Anna Lambright.

Anna was pretty. Not quite as beautiful as Katie had been, but it was clear within the next couple of years that she would be. She had sandy-blonde hair, almost the color of caramel, and wide-set brown eyes that made her look even more innocent than the typical Amish girl. Tears ran from those eyes.

"Anna, are you all right?" I asked.

Tears fell faster, and I mentally kicked myself for the stupid question. Of course she wasn't all right.

She licked her chapped lips. "I need your help."

"Mine?"

She nodded. "Ruth said that you can find the man who hurt my sister."

My mouth fell open. "I . . . I . . ." I couldn't find the words to say.

Ruth tucked her arms under her cloak. "You solved those two other murders."

"Well . . ." Again, the words wouldn't come, because she was right. Did I tell her that Chief Rose basically gave me the same assignment? I thought not. Most Amish had distrust for the English police.

"You found out what happed to the bishop and Ezekiel Young," Ruth pressed.

I shifted. "Maybe I can help." The chief *had* just told Timothy and me today that Katie's death was a homicide. "How do you know she was murdered?"

Anna shivered. "The lady police officer came back to the farm today. I heard her tell *Daed.* He was so angry that I thought he was going to throw her off the farm."

"Why? It's not Chief Rose's fault about what happened to Katie."

She lowered her gaze. "*Daed* knows that, but that's my father. He's angry." Her voice sounded monotone.

The memory of Chief Rose describing how Katie's finger had likely been broken came to mind. How did I ask Anna about that and not lose her trust? I exhaled slowly. "I will try to help. When was the last time you saw your sister?"

Anna looked away, her expression closed.

"Anna, if you want me to help you, I need to know this."

She twisted the end of her cape, her eyes staring off into the distance. "Saturday morning."

I tilted my head. "Timothy and I didn't find her until Monday morning. Was she missing for two days?"

"*Nee.* At least I didn't think she was missing like she was in trouble."

"What kind of missing could she be?"

"I thought she'd run off. That's what *Daed* said happened." Tears rolled down her cheeks. "I thought that she ran off and left me. I was so angry at her that I decided I would never forgive her for leaving me there, and now, she's dead." She ran her hands up and down her arms. "I was hating her and she was already dead."

Ruth wrapped her thin arms around her friend, and together the girls cried. The pair reminded me so much of Tanisha and me after my mother's death that it took my breath away.

I let the pair comfort each other for a few minutes before moving on to my next question.

"Did Katie want to leave the church?" I asked. "Did she ever mention it?

She pulled away from Ruth, sniffing and gnawing on her lip. "Maybe. She talked about what it must be like to be *Englisch* and what it would be like if she could live without rules. I never thought she was serious. We've all said that before." She looked to Ruth for confirmation.

Ruth nodded and took her hand.

"But she knew *Daed* would never forgive her if she left the church, whether she was baptized or not. The bishop said that it was all right for the Troyers to see Becky and Timothy even though they left the Amish way, but my father said many times that he would never allow that. He thought Simon Troyer was weak and that his weakness led his children to leave the way."

Ruth stiffened.

"Can you tell me who Katie spent the most time with?"

Her forehead wrinkled as if she hadn't expected that question. "My sister was popular with the young men in the district." She swallowed a sob. "Because she was so pretty. I think that made lots of the girls in the district jealous. She didn't have any girlfriends. Other than family, she spent the most time with Nathan Garner. They were courting."

Garner? That name sounded familiar.

"His family owns a large Amish furniture warehouse between here and Fredericktown. Lots of *Englischers* shop there. Some Amish too."

That was it—the furniture store that Grandfather sold his small wooden kitchen accessories to. I pressed on. "Did she spend time with anyone else?"

"There were other young Amish men too. I told you that they all wanted to court my sister."

"But she only had eyes for Nathan?"

She gnawed on her lip. "Just lately. Until a few months ago, Caleb King was courting her."

"Caleb is here," Ruth said. "I saw him earlier. Two of his younger brothers were in the Christmas pageant."

"I'd like to talk to him," I said.

Ruth's mouth fell open. "You can't talk to him here. Someone will see you."

Anna blinked her brown doe eyes at me. "You don't want to talk to Caleb. He will get angry. He is much like my father in that way."

"He will be mad over a few questions?"

"Katie said he was angry over everything. That's why she asked him to stop courting her. Nathan was better. He was kind to her."

Again the broken finger came to mind. "Did he hurt her?"

Anna frowned. "She never said so. She only said he was angry one time to me, and that was right before they stopped courting."

"When was this?" If I had an approximate time, maybe the coroner could estimate when her finger was broken and if the two were related.

"Summertime. Close to the same time she started working at the warehouse Nathan's family owns."

My body tensed. "What did she do there?"

"I don't know exactly, something in the office." She twisted the end of her cloak with her hands. "My sister was so smart. She should have been a teacher and maybe this would have never happened."

I peeked around the corner and the schoolhouse was emptying out.

"I need to go home before my *daed* knows that I'm gone," Anna said. "He was out checking the ponies in the far pasture, and he should be home by now." She reached for my hand. "Chloe, my sister didn't deserve this." With tears in her eyes, she added. "*I* didn't deserve this. Please help."

I squeezed her hand. Even through my glove, her fingers felt cold. It was like holding a Popsicle. "I'll try."

She nodded, adjusted her bonnet, and gave Ruth a crushing hug, whispering something to her in their language. Then she ran in the opposite direction of the schoolhouse.

Ruth drew in a shaky breath.

"What did she say to you?" I asked.

Her voice was barely above a whisper, and I had to lean in to hear her. "She can't be my friend anymore. Her father won't allow it."

Katie's father rose higher up on my suspect list, and I wrapped an arm around her shoulder. "Let's go back."

She nodded.

I spied Timothy by the door leading into the schoolhouse, scanning the yard. I knew he was searching for me. Of all the attendees, I was the easiest to identify in my purple coat and black wool trousers. A navy blue ski hat covered my bright red hair.

Timothy's blue eyes lit up when they met mine, and something inside my chest fluttered.

Ruth yanked on my arm. "Chloe, Caleb King is by the swing set."

I turned in that direction and saw two Amish boys in their late teens or early twenties laughing and jabbing at each other.

Timothy followed my line of sight and frowned. He gave the slightest head shake. *No.*

I pretended I didn't see him and started in that direction. Ruth didn't follow me.

The boys' laughter was low as they spoke to each other in a mixture of Pennsylvania Dutch and English.

"Caleb?" I asked.

Both boys examined me.

"*Ya*?" the taller of the two said. His sharp cheekbones were a stark contrast to his friend's round face.

"We met at the Troyers' farm. I'm Chloe."

"*Ya*. Everyone in the district knows who you are. You made Timothy Troyer turn *Englisch*."

Timothy left the Amish long before I ever showed up in Appleseed Creek, but I didn't bother to correct him.

Caleb's friend laughed.

"I'd like to talk to you about Katie Lambright." The sentence popped out of my mouth before I could think of a better opening. If it hadn't been for Katie's death, I would have had no reason to speak to the Amish man.

Caleb paled. "What do you know about Katie?"

My eyes slid to the friend again. "Can we talk alone about this?"

His friend opened his mouth, but Caleb cut him off in their language. After a minute of arguing, the friend sauntered away.

Caleb scowled at me.

I cleared my throat. "I'm sorry about Katie."

He folded his arms. "It is a shame to lose anyone from the church, but I don't know why you think Katie was of a special interest to me."

"You courted her for a long time."

Caleb cracked his knuckles. "Who told you this? Timothy Troyer? What would he know? He left the district when I was still a child in the Christmas program."

I took a small step backward. "I didn't hear it from Timothy."

"It is no matter."

"Why did you stop courting Katie?"

"Unless you have something important to say to me, I have nothing to say to you." He started to move away.

"What about Nathan Garner? Should I speak to him about Katie? Isn't he a friend of yours?" I asked my questions quickly. Even though my voice was low, I became aware of the adults exiting the schoolhouse watching us. I should have heeded Timothy's headshake. The schoolyard was not the right place to question Caleb.

Caleb froze in place and spun on his heels to face me. A black cloud passed over his face. "Nathan Garner is not my friend."

"Because of Katie?"

He clenched and unclenched his gloved hand, glaring at me. Then he turned and stalked away, uttering in Pennsylvania Dutch.

"Chloe Humphrey, you are one gutsy woman," Timothy said from behind me. "What were you doing talking to Caleb King like that? He's three times your size."

I gave him a wry smile. "So you think this wasn't the best time?"

He buttoned the top button on his coat. "No, it wasn't. What did he tell you?"

I told him, then I conveyed my conversation with Anna and Ruth behind the outhouse.

From across the schoolyard, Deacon Sutter glared at us.

Timothy shook his head. "Well, I watched the two of you the whole time to make sure he didn't try anything."

"What would he try?"

Timothy pursed his lips. "Who knows? He's unpredictable. You on the other hand are brave to march right up to him like that."

"Me? Brave?" I never thought of myself that way. My best friend Tanisha had always been the brave one. *She* was the one living halfway across the world in a foreign country. I was barely three hours from the town I'd lived in my entire life.

"I can tell you don't believe me."

"I don't."

He squeezed my hand. "And that just makes the quality even more attractive."

Chapter Twelve

All the lights were on in the simple, white-steepled church in the middle of Appleseed Creek. The lamppost in the yard wore a Christmas evergreen spray and a big red bow. The front doors, which led from the greeting hall into the sanctuary, had green wreaths with matching bows.

The Mennonite congregation of Appleseed Creek was not conservative. The women wore everything to services, from long, almost Amish-looking skirts to jeans. Becky and Timothy were members of the choir, but there was also a praise band with an electric bass player. What had Timothy and Becky thought the first time they stepped into this church? Although the service wasn't much different from those I once attended with the Green family in Shaker Heights, they must be a world apart from the all-German services Becky and Timothy grew up with in which men and women sat on different sides of the living room of an Amish family's home.

The organ music began, and the choir marched down the center aisle singing "O Little Town of Bethlehem." As Timothy walked by in his royal blue choir robe, he winked at me. The shimmery fabric was a far cry from the plain style he'd worn most of his life. Becky looked angelic. If she sprouted wings and started strumming a harp, I wouldn't be the least bit surprised. If Aaron had been there, he would have fainted dead away. As a baptized Amish man, Aaron spent Christmas Eve with his family within the Amish district.

The choir members took their places in the loft, and the pastor began his greeting. My pew was half full. At the far end was a young family with a baby gumming a teething ring. Between the family and me sat a middle-aged couple, the woman wearing a long skirt and her hair pulled back into a bun, much like the Amish.

Someone stopped at my pew. "Is this seat taken?"

The voice sent a chill down my body. I couldn't look at him. "No."

Curt slipped into the pew and stood next to me. "I'm glad, because I was hoping that we could sit together, Red."

Reflexively, I slid over in the pew and knocked into the heavyset woman on my other side. She shot me a dirty look. *So much for the Christmas spirit.*

Becky watched from the choir, her mouth dropping open.

Timothy's eyes bored into me and looked ready to lunge off the stage.

I bit my lip. Should I move? Should I stay?

The pastor finished making announcements, and the first hymn began. The congregation rose as one. Curt, not knowing the cue, jumped up at the last minute. I opened my hymnal to the correct page and handed it to Curt. He held it in his hands as if it had teeth and might snap closed like an alligator's jaw.

I pulled a second hymnal from the back of the pew and found my page as the organist began the first notes of "Angels We Have Heard on High."

The woman next to me belted out the carol as if she was

performing in center stage at Severance Hall. I used her volume to my advantage and slid a glance at Curt. "What are you doing here?" I hissed.

The corner of his mouth curved up. "What, Red? You don't think I am worthy enough for your religion?"

Heat rushed to my face, and I turned my eyes down to the music in my hands. Mercifully, the song finally ended and the congregation sat.

I shifted uncomfortably in my seat through the Scripture reading and congregational prayer. Curt stared straight ahead, never once glancing in my direction. Was he paying attention? Was he interested in what he heard? The organ started up again for yet another carol, "O Come, All Ye Faithful."

Curt popped up to standing, but this was the hymn in which the congregation was asked to remain seated. People in other pews stared at Curt. His forehead bunched and his face turned red. In the many times Curt and I had come face-to-face, I'd seen almost every emotion cross his face, but I had never seen him self-conscious. He didn't sit down. His knees locked into place.

I stood and handed him the hymnal, and he gave me the first real smile I'd ever seen from him. It wasn't a smirk or a leer, but a tiny and genuine grin. By the second verse the entire congregation was standing, even the irritated woman next to me.

The song ended, and Curt sank into his seat.

My gaze shifted toward the front where Hannah Hilty wrinkled her nose as she examined my companion and me. She tossed her head and her silky brown hair hit the woman behind her in the mouth.

I bowed my head to cover laughter bubbling up from within me. Who knew that I would spend my first Christmas Eve in Appleseed Creek with two of the people in the world who disliked me so much? All I needed was my evil stepmother to finish off the glaring trifecta.

When I brought my face up again, I found Timothy watching me. His expression moved from anger to concern as his hardened eyes softened. He raised his eyebrows as if to ask whether I was okay. I gave the smallest of nods, *yes*.

I sat the rest of the service, hyper aware of Curt's proximity to me. I scooted closer to the woman to my right. She set her purse, which could have passed for a saddlebag, between us to stop my encroachment on her space. Curt didn't seem to notice. He watched the front of the church with studied attention.

Finally, the pastor gave the benediction and filed out, followed by the choir. Timothy paused beside Curt.

"Nice dress, Buggy Boy," Curt said just loud enough for both Timothy and me to hear.

The choir member behind Timothy tapped him on the back with his bulletin, urging him to start moving again.

Curt leaned against the back of the pew. "Guess Buggy Boy's not too happy about us being together."

"We aren't together," I shot back.

Curt sucked on his front teeth. "That hurts. It really does."

I almost apologized, but I stopped myself. The pew emptied out into the side aisle, and I stood. "What are you doing here? Really?"

"Can't a man celebrate the birth of Baby Jesus?"

"Yes. I—I didn't mean—"

He stood and was inches from my face. I smelled the chew tobacco on his breath. "Merry Christmas, Red." Then he melted into the line of parishioners leaving the church. I fell back onto the pew bench stunned. What just happened? Had I just spent my first Christmas Eve service in Appleseed Creek sitting next to Curt Fanning, my arch enemy?

I whispered a prayer. "Dear Lord, what is going on?"

Five minutes later Timothy slid into the pew next to me, his brow furrowed. "What was that?"

I shrugged. "I wish I knew."

"What did he say to you?"

"Not much. A few snide comments, but I've heard much worse from him."

Timothy's fingers intertwined with mine on the pew's smooth wooden seat.

"I think he was just here to go to church."

Timothy snorted. "I don't believe that for a second. If that's true, why'd he seek you out? He wanted to scare you, like before."

I didn't feel scared, only confused by Curt's action. "When I saw him earlier, he was alone just like tonight. This is the second time I've seen him without Brock."

"Maybe they had a falling out."

"Maybe . . ." my voice trailed off.

Timothy clenched his jaw. "There is something more to this. He wants to torment you. That's all he's ever wanted since the day you met him."

I frowned, remembering how Curt was so embarrassed about standing up at the wrong time and so grateful I stood beside him. I shook my head. Maybe I imagined his grateful attitude. Maybe Timothy was right. Curt was trying a new way to torment me. He'd tried everything else. Why not bother me in church too?

I sighed and glanced around the sanctuary. Ladies from the church were up front watering the poinsettias on either side of the altar. "Where's Becky?"

Timothy stood and pulled me up beside him. "Handing out invitations to her Christmas party tomorrow."

I cocked an eyebrow. "I thought she already sent invitations."

"She has. Twice. This is the third set she's passing out. She's also begging for RSVPs. I've never seen her so excited about something like she is about this party."

Hannah walked up the aisle with a companion and stopped at our pew. "Timothy, I'd like you to meet someone." Her too-sweet voice set my teeth on edge.

Hannah and a dark-haired young man stepped in front of us. The guy was *tall.* Timothy was six foot one and the guy with Hannah had five inches on him.

Timothy and I slipped out of the pew.

Hannah looped her arm through her companion's. "This is Justin. He's my boyfriend."

Boyfriend? The last time I checked, Hannah had been determined to give Timothy that title. By the way both of his eyebrows rose, Timothy appeared surprised too.

Hannah gazed up into Justin's face. "He's home from college for Christmas. He plays basketball for the University of Kentucky."

The basketball I could understand, considering his height.

Timothy held out his hand to shake Justin's. "Nice to meet you. Are you from Knox County?"

"Mount Vernon," Justin said, his voice deep and rumbling, but his eyes wide in a semi-stunned expression.

Hannah flipped her silky brunette hair. "Justin's mother and mine are old friends. We've known each other since we were children." She leaned her head against Justin's shoulder.

I tried not to gag. "That's so nice for you both."

"It is." Hannah removed her arm from Justin's. "Go get my coat."

The basketball player leaped into action and hurried out of the sanctuary.

Hannah stared at Timothy. "He's everything I ever hoped for and could never find in anyone else."

Timothy just smiled at Hannah's dig. "He seems to be very attentive."

"He is," she said smugly, half-turning toward me. "Merry Christmas to you both," she said, and then left the sanctuary.

Timothy's eyes twinkled. "Hannah finally found the perfect boyfriend."

"I hope so. It would be the best Christmas present that I could ever receive."

Timothy led me down the church's center aisle. "Even better than the necklace that I gave you?"

I winked at him. "A close second, at least." Together we collected Becky in the greeting hall as she passed out party invitations by the fistful.

I grimaced. The Quills had been gracious and told us we could throw a small holiday party in their home. I suspected that our landlords' interpretation of small varied greatly from Becky's.

"Okay, okay," Timothy said as he approached his sister. "Everyone here has heard about the party. Stop pestering people."

She narrowed her bright blue eyes at her brother. "People need to know about it. I put a lot of time and energy into planning this."

Timothy stacked the remaining invitations in his hand and gave them to me. "Trust me, we know." Before she could argue, he added, "And the party will be great. Full of special surprises."

Becky's scowl evaporated, and her face broke into a grin.

I dropped the invitations to the bottom of my purse. "Special surprises? Like what?"

Becky started to laugh and then hurried to the cloakroom to collect our coats.

A mischievous twinkle lighted Timothy's eyes in a way I hadn't seen before. I gaped at him.

"What?" he said.

Becky came back with our things, and Timothy helped me into my winter coat.

I wrapped my scarf around my throat. "You're not going to tell me?"

Becky bounced up and down, and Timothy reached over and covered her mouth as if afraid she'd burst out and share the secret.

"I'll figure it out for myself," I huffed. "I am a detective of sorts. Ask Chief Rose."

That only made Timothy and Becky chuckle.

We stepped out into the cold, snowy Christmas Eve night, and I was left hoping for a good surprise—and no more bad surprises like the one we found behind the Gundy barn just the day before.

Chapter Thirteen

On Christmas morning my eyes opened automatically at six a.m., as if my alarm clock had rung, and I still had no idea what the big surprise was. Laying in the bedroom of one of the Quills' grown daughters, I had to remind myself where I was and that today was Christmas morning. Back in Shaker Heights there would have been little doubt. Tanisha's younger brother Tyson always ran around the house at five thirty a.m., trying to convince the adults to wake up because it was time to open presents. Usually, Tanisha and I took little coaxing. I thought of my friend in Italy realizing her Christmas was half over by the time I had opened my eyes.

Gigabyte circled my head and yowled. As long as I was awake, he saw no reason why he shouldn't be entitled to breakfast. I ran my hand along the coarse hair of his tawny-colored back. From the bookshelves, dozens of pairs of eyes watched me. Growing up, the Quills' daughter had been a collector of porcelain dolls. Since she left them here when she moved out, I could only assume she was over her doll phase. That or her husband refused to let them in their home. If that's how he felt, I agreed with him. Fifty or so dolls sat on specially made shelves directly across from the bed. It had taken me a few weeks to be able to sleep in the same room with all those staring eyes.

I slid my feet into my blue fuzzy slippers. "Is Becky awake?" I asked the cat.

He gave me a haughty look, as if to say, "If she were awake, do you think I would be talking to you?"

Becky spoiled my cat with bacon and sausage in the morning, and tuna and hamburger in the evening. The best I could offer was a can of cat food. I poked his belly with my index finger. "You're getting a little round around the middle. If you're not careful, the vet's going to make me put you on a diet."

He swiped at my hand with claws out.

I retracted my finger. "Okay, okay." I guessed no one appreciated criticism about their waistline—even a cat.

I grabbed my hoodie off the carved, pink provincial desk chair and slipped it on.

In the kitchen, I stared out the back window that faced east and opened into a view of lush farmland. No partition divided the Quills' property and the farm more than a mile away. The sky had that gray quality that promised dawn and perhaps more snow. It was a beautiful Christmas morning. Perhaps the most naturally beautiful I had ever seen.

There weren't sunrises like this in Cleveland, yet still, I felt hollow. Happy as I was to be in Appleseed Creek with the Troyers, for the first time, I wondered if I should have gone home for the holidays and spent Christmas with the Greens. The Greens were my home. Tanisha's mom invited me several times, but I'd insisted that I wanted to stay in Appleseed Creek. *Was that a mistake?* As much as the Troyers included me, here I was still separated by language, by tradition, and by the past.

Thoughts of Christmas traditions made me think about my parents, about Christmas before my mother died, before my father turned cold. I remembered my mother, who loved Christmas as much as a kindergartner, and how she would wake us up at five on Christmas morning to open gifts. I remembered the homemade French toast my father made for breakfast while Mom and I cleaned up the wrapping paper scattered around the living room floor.

Did my father, Sabrina, and the children like the Christmas gift cards I sent them? Gift cards seemed so generic, but I learned from painful experience that it was better to do that than to pick something out myself that Sabrina would complain about having to return to the store.

I glanced at the stack of Christmas cards on the kitchen counter. A card was all I received from my father's family this year. My stepmother had signed the card simply, "The Humphrey Family." The signature came off as a pointed insult, a marked exclusion. The urge to rip the card in half was almost overpowering when I read it. Instead, I buried it in the stack of more sincere holiday greetings.

I touched my cell phone in the pocket of my hoodie. Should I call Dad and Sabrina and wish them a Merry Christmas? Isn't that what a good daughter would do? The clock on the microwave read six thirty a.m. It would only be three thirty in California—far too early to call. Relief and guilt mingled in my stomach. I filled a glass with tap water and drank it down.

Gigabyte gave my ankle a small nip to remind me of the business at hand.

"Ouch!" I lifted my foot up in the air.

He sniffed at the other exposed ankle.

I knew I should have remembered to put on socks before coming downstairs. "I think we should buy you one of those automatic feeders. It might save me some bloodshed."

He eyed me as if my joke wasn't the least bit amusing. I reached into the overhead cupboard and removed a can of cat foot. "Yum, tuna and liver." I opened it and gagged at the smell. Too early for cat food. With a spoon, I dished half a can into his dish that said *Man of the House* on the side. Wasn't that the truth?

He sniffed the cat food with disdain.

"Don't worry. You will have a second breakfast when Becky wakes up, you little hobbit."

He took a small bite and hunkered down with his face buried in the dish.

Becky walked into the kitchen rubbing her eyes. "Merry Christmas," she said with a yawn. She had been up past midnight cleaning and preparing for our party that evening. I begged off at twelve.

I rummaged through the cupboard for coffee mugs. "Merry Christmas. How late did you stay up?"

She squinted at me with bloodshot eyes. "Two. Do we have any *kaffi*?" she asked, using the Pennsylvania Dutch word for coffee. That told me she was especially tired. Becky always made a conscious effort to use only English words.

I opened the refrigerator and pulled out the coffee and half and half. "I was about to make some."

Gig wrapped himself around her legs and pleaded in his high-pitched Siamese voice.

"Oh, Gig, did she give you that muck for breakfast? You poor thing."

That muck was mostly gone.

I poured water from the carafe into the coffeemaker and hit the power button.

He yowled, pleading his case. Becky picked him up and scratched behind his ear. "Don't worry. I'll make you a real breakfast. What do you want—bacon or sausage patties?"

Gigabyte gave me a triumphant Siamese smile over her shoulder.

"Showboat," I muttered as I headed back upstairs to shower.

By the time I got back downstairs, Gigabyte had polished off his luxury breakfast, and Timothy and his housemate, Danny, sat at the kitchen table, eating scrambled eggs, bacon—apparently that had been Gig's choice—and pancakes. A smile broke across my face and my melancholy from the morning faded away. "Merry Christmas!"

"Merry Christmas, Chloe," Danny said. He was a lanky guy close to my age. Like Becky and Timothy, he grew up Amish and left during his *rumspringa*, but he was from a stricter district in New York State. His family refused to see him, even though he'd never been baptized.

Timothy smiled. "*Frehlicher Grischtdaag*! We need you to practice saying Merry Christmas in Pennsylvania Dutch. *Grossdaddi* will be impressed."

Becky handed me a plate of pancakes. I took it and said. "Frelick Grisdaag."

Becky, Danny, and Timothy started to laugh.

I put my hands on my hips. "Okay, my pronunciation isn't that great. Eat your breakfast, so we can go to church and then the farm. Grandfather Zook will appreciate my effort."

Danny forked a bite of pancake and changed the direction of the conversation. "Tim told me about you two finding that girl. I was sorry to hear that."

"Did you know Katie?" I asked.

He shook his head. "Not really, but I gathered that a kid at one of my stops knew her pretty well. When he found out that I used to be Amish, he asked me if I knew her. I was sorry to disappoint him."

For one of his many jobs, Danny drove a truck delivering produce from the farm to local restaurants and grocers in the area.

Timothy's glass of orange juice stopped halfway to his mouth. "You didn't tell me that."

"I just remembered when Chloe said Katie's name."

"What's the kid's name?" Timothy asked.

"Jason. I don't know his last name. I only know his first because that was what his name tag said. He works at that Appleseed Marketplace right here in town."

"Jason?" I poured myself a mug of coffee. "That doesn't sound like an Amish name to me."

"The kid is definitely an *Englischer.*"

Becky flipped another pancake on the stove. I didn't know who she thought was going to eat it because Timothy and Danny both had stacks in front of them that were eight pancakes high. She waved her spatula. "Why would Katie Lambright be friends with an *Englischer*?"

I took one pancake from the serving dish and sat at the table. "It strikes me as odd too, especially since Jason is a guy."

Danny snorted. "He's not much of a guy. A real skinny kid, who looks like he spends most of the time playing video games."

"I bet Chief Rose doesn't know about Jason." I stirred half and half into my coffee. "I want to talk to him before I tell her."

Timothy broke a strip of bacon in five small pieces. "I don't think Greta's going to like that. She'll want you to tell her right away."

I cut my pancake. "She'll scare him off."

Danny laughed. "Let Chloe talk to him first. She's not the least bit scary."

I swallowed my bite of pancake and rolled my eyes. "Gee, thanks, Danny."

"Anytime," he said with a smirk.

Chapter Fourteen

Later that morning the church bells rang joyfully overhead as Timothy and I walked down the church's front steps after the Christmas morning service.

Danny clapped Timothy's shoulder. "Hey, let's go. I want to get to the farm. I can hear your mom's bread pudding calling my name. Do you think she made the date-flavored one?"

Timothy smirked. "Probably since she knows that you're coming."

Danny rubbed his chapped, bare hands together. "Excellent. Let's hit the road. Where's your sister?"

Timothy shook his head. "Inside. Reminding people about the party."

I suppressed a sigh. If everyone that she invited showed up, we would be in violation of the fire code.

A few seconds later Becky appeared in the doorway. As she skipped down the steps her long, white-blonde braid bounced on her shoulder underneath her stocking cap.

Hannah and her new boyfriend Justin were a few steps behind. Hannah stood a good foot away from Justin, but when her eyes fell on Timothy, she hooked her arms through a crook in the tall boy's arm and looked up at him, adoringly.

I suppressed a gag. Little did she know that her pointed display of affection was completely missed by Timothy as he and Danny talked about the horses that would be up for sale at the next Amish auction.

"Everyone's here," I said, ushering our group to the parking lot. The sooner I moved Timothy away from Hannah, the better.

Timothy gave me a quizzical look.

I smiled brightly. "Danny made your mom's bread pudding sound so good that I think I'm eager to try some too."

Timothy's eyes narrowed as he scanned the churchyard. When he spotted Hannah and Justin, a grin tugged at the corners of his mouth. "Yes, it's time to go," he said, giving me a knowing smile.

A blush crept up my neck. Maybe Timothy knew me too well.

Outside of the Troyers' barn, the fields were a blanket of sparkling white. Mercifully, the snow had started and stopped that morning.

Becky fingered her long blonde braid. "I hope we don't stay long."

"You don't want to upset your parents by running off the first chance you get, do you?"

She dropped the braid. "I guess not. It would be a whole lot easier if they would just come to our Christmas party and we could see them there." She held up a mittened hand. "Before you say anything, I know why they can't come . . ."

I winked at her. "I wasn't going to say anything."

Thomas flew out of the barn, his arms and legs pumping as he ran. He catapulted his body into his big brother's arms, and Timothy stumbled back, trying to regain his balance. "How do you think I did yesterday at the Christmas program?" Thomas asked excitedly.

"Do you want to know what we thought before or after the bishop's lamb got loose?" Becky asked.

Thomas frowned. "That wasn't my fault. The lambs got scared. Teacher told me that they must have had a case of stage fright."

Danny snorted. "Sheep with stage fright."

"It is no matter," Thomas said. "Teacher said that I did a *gut* job and everyone would remember my performance."

"She's right about that." I ruffled his blond bowl-cut hair. "You did an excellent job, Thomas. I can tell you can keep a cool head under pressure just like your big brother here." I let my hand fall to my side. "Where's your hat? It's freezing out here."

He wiggled out of Timothy's arms, rolling his eyes. "You sound like *Mamm*."

Danny removed a huge basket from the back of his SUV. "Becky, what did you put in here? Cinder blocks?"

"Stop complaining, Danny, you're the one who asked for my monkey bread."

His eyes lit up. "Monkey bread? Really?" He lifted the corner of the basket's lid and peeked inside.

Becky slapped his hand away. "Consider it your Christmas present."

He licked his lips. "I will."

Even though she had spent days making food for the Christmas party we'd be hosting at the Quills' house, she still made five or six—I lost count—dishes to bring to her mother's table for dinner.

We all helped Becky carry her creations and our gifts inside. As I removed my gifts from Timothy's truck, I wondered if the family would like them. I bought simple gifts and wrapped them in plain brown paper. I tucked the gifts under my arm and picked up one of Becky's casserole dishes. If her dream of being an art teacher didn't pan out, she could always be a chef. She had so many talents that the possibilities for Becky's future were limitless. What *was* difficult was making her realize she had those talents, and that she was smart enough to pass the GRE with flying colors and be accepted into any higher education program.

Mrs. Troyer pursed her lips into a thin line. "Becky, do you think I will not feed you when you come home? I said you didn't need to bring anything today."

"I know, but I've tried out some new recipes. You will like them, I promise. I brought jambalaya."

"That sounds like a horse's name," Mrs. Troyer said.

Becky removed her pink stocking cap. "No. It's food, and it is wonderful. It has just enough of a spicy kick."

"Hm," Grandfather Zook said from his seat at the head of the kitchen table. "I didn't like those burritos you made a few weeks ago."

"It's a different kind of spice," she told him.

Timothy opened the door and Mabel slipped inside.

Mrs. Troyer pointed at the dog. "Timothy, you know what I think about animals in the house."

Thomas pulled on his mother's apron. "But *Mamm,* it's Christmas. Weren't animals there the day Jesus was born. I bet there was a dog. What stable doesn't have a dog?"

I hid a smile. Thomas turned into quite a little actor when he wanted to.

Mrs. Troyer folded her arms. "Because it is Christmas, she can stay, but not in my kitchen. Take her to the living room. If she doesn't behave herself, she's out." She shook her finger at her youngest son. "This won't happen again."

"Until next Christmas," Thomas said.

His mother frowned.

"*Danki, Mamm.*" Thomas and Mabel shared a grin and the two slunk off to the living room.

As Grandfather Zook and Becky compared the merits of

Mexican and Cajun cuisines, I carried the gifts into the living room. Naomi followed me.

Mabel lay in front of the fireplace as if she'd been there every day of her life.

Naomi pulled on my sleeve. "What are those?"

"What do they look like?" I teased.

Her eyes sparkled. "Gifts. Are any for me?"

I shrugged. "Maybe."

With one finger Thomas pulled on the edge of my brown paper sack to peer inside. "Should we open them now?"

Mr. Troyer walked to the base of the stairs, which led to the second floor. "We will open gifts in a few minutes, Thomas. Do not pester Chloe."

"I'm not pestering her." He turned his soulful blue eyes up at me. "Am I?"

I tweaked his ear. "Maybe a little."

Mr. Troyer sat in his easy chair. "The sooner everyone comes into the living room, the sooner you will be able to open your gift."

Thomas flew into the kitchen. "*Daed* says that we need to open gifts now."

Mr. Troyer shook his head at his youngest son.

Becky guided Grandfather Zook into his rocking chair by the fireplace. One by one the rest of the Troyer family and Danny found places to sit in the living room. Ruth sat on the first step of the stairway, which was as far away as she could be from the rest of the family without leaving the room.

"Ruth, come sit by me," Grandfather Zook said.

The thirteen-year-old frowned.

"You won't sit by your *grossdaddi* on Christmas?"

Mr. Troyer's eyes narrowed. Ruth noticed her father's expression too and stood up and moved across the room to sit at her grandfather's feet.

I knew that Ruth was preoccupied by Katie and Anna. Murder was a heavy subject to occupy such a young girl's thoughts.

I stood in the middle of the room, unsure where I could place my gifts. As if Becky understood my dilemma, she took the gifts from my arms and set them on the oak chest that the Troyers used as a coffee table.

"I'm the oldest, so I will start," Grandfather Zook said and pointed at a rectangular-shaped package sitting beside Mabel near the fireplace. "Ruth, give that one to Chloe, and I see a few packages there, too, for your brothers and sisters, and maybe even Danny." His eyes twinkled.

Danny chuckled. "You got me a gift too, Grandfather Zook?"

"Just this once," the older man said with a laugh.

Ruth set the gift in my lap, as Grandfather Zook spoke, "Chloe, that is from not just me, but the whole family."

I adjusted the package on my lap. "It's so heavy. I have no idea what it can be."

Grandfather Zook pulled on his beard with a twinkle in his eyes. "Open it and find out." He glanced about the room. "All you *kinner* open your gifts."

The sound of tearing paper floated into the air. Naomi held up a small wooden chair that was the perfect size for her favorite doll, and Thomas laughed with delight at his wooden train.

Becky ran her hand over the rosette carved into the wooden handle of the hairbrush she received. She looked up. "Chloe, you haven't opened your gift yet."

Carefully, I removed the brown paper to find a jewelry box the size of a breadbox in my lap. An intricate Amish farm scene complete with horse and buggy was carved into the jewelry box's lid. "Thank you," I said. My hands trembled as I lifted the lid and touched the cranberry velvet-lined compartments.

Grandfather Zook pulled on the end of his white beard. "I

think that will work for any jewelry you might have received this Christmas."

Mr. Troyer's head whipped in his father-in-law's direction at this comment.

Did Grandfather Zook know about Timothy's gift to me? "I love it," I said. "It's perfect. Did you make it, Grandfather Zook?"

He smiled. "*Ya.* It makes me happy that you like it."

"I do." I knew the perfect place to put it on the dresser in my bedroom. I might have to move a few of the Quills' daughter's dolls to make the space. "I have gifts for each of you too."

Mrs. Troyer frowned. "Chloe, you needn't give any gifts to the adults."

I blushed. "I know, but you've all been so kind to me, that I wanted to." Typically, the Amish only gave gifts to the children for Christmas, but since it was my first holiday with the family, I wanted to give something small to everyone, even the adults. I bit my lip, hoping that I wouldn't offend Timothy's father. I picked up my brown sack and began handing out packages. When I finished, I said, "Go ahead and open them."

More ripping sounds echoed through the Troyers' living room.

I watched each person open his or her gift: a metal trivet for Mrs. Troyer, a new pair of pliers for Mr. Troyer, and for Grandfather Zook, a beard comb.

The oldest member of the family examined the comb. "Oh my, I will have the best whiskers in the county now. That's for certain." He ran it through his cotton-white beard, which hung two inches below his chin. It had been much longer until a few weeks ago when Grandfather Zook was attacked. The attacker had cut off his beard, which was a deep insult to an Amish man.

Naomi squealed with glee when she found the purple dress for her beloved doll, and Thomas hugged the baseball to his chest like it was a teddy bear. Ruth folded the embroidered handkerchief I'd given her and tucked it into her apron pocket.

Thomas practiced holding the baseball like a pitcher would. "Where is Timothy's gift, Chloe?"

Timothy laughed. "Chloe already gave it to me. It was too heavy to bring here today."

Thomas's brow knit together. "Too heavy? What was it?"

"A ratchet set," Timothy said.

Mr. Troyer shot his wife a worried look. "That is an expensive gift."

It was expensive, but Timothy's reaction had been worth every penny.

"Christmas is not about how much money you spend." Mr. Troyer's voice was firm.

"*Daed*," Timothy said, letting the name hang in the air.

Time to change the subject. I handed Grandfather Zook a second gift.

His brow shot up. "What could possibly be better than that comb?"

I smiled, tickled that he liked the comb so much. It had taken me days to decide what to buy him. "This one is for Sparky."

He opened the brown paper sack, peeked inside, and removed one of the extra large carrots from the bag. "Sparky will love them. We should give him one."

Ruth popped up from her place on the floor. "I'll do it."

Her parents shared a glance.

Ruth saw their look, too. "I can check on Gertie and her new calf, too. The calf had a cough earlier today."

"*Ya*," Mr. Troyer said, "She did. Gertie's calf was a surprise to come this time of year. We must do our best to keep her healthy and warm. Gertie, too. She's one of my best milkers."

Ruth removed her bonnet and cloak from the peg on the wall. "I will return quickly."

Naomi brought her doll to me and held out the new dress.

"She wants to wear her new outfit?" I asked.

The four-year-old nodded.

I helped Naomi change the doll's clothes while all the time watching the door leading into the kitchen. That was the way Ruth had gone. I slid Naomi from my lap and stood. "I think I want to tell Sparky Merry Christmas myself." Timothy watched me as I slipped into the kitchen. To my relief, he didn't follow me.

I grabbed my coat from the mudroom and slipped into my snow boots. Through the glass door, I saw the breeze kick up snow in a swirling wave. Large snowdrifts gathered around the outbuildings and towering trees throughout the farm.

The path to the Troyers' barn, however, was hard packed with uneven snow. Despite the sensible boots that Becky insisted I buy for my first winter in the country, I had to be careful. The barn's side door was open a crack. I stepped inside and let my eyes adjust to the dim light. There were no electric fixtures in the Troyers' barn, and Ruth hadn't lit one of the gas lamps. The only light came from the sun's rays streaming in from the high windows. The angles of the light created bright spots and shadows throughout the hollow building.

Ruth stood in front of Sparky's stall. Each of the Troyers' horses had a stall to themselves near Grandfather Zook's workshop. The family's livelihood, the dairy cows, huddled at the far end of the barn about a half-basketball court away in one large pen. They mooed and exhaled heat from their nostrils into the frigid air. The large back entrance of the barn was open, allowing the cows to move in and out to the pasture as they wished. However, it looked like most of them decided to stay inside. A stall next to Sparky held a mother cow, Gertie, and her new calf. Gertie rolled a brown, round eye at me as I passed, and I took it as a warning to leave her calf alone.

Sparky folded the last of the carrot into his mouth and nuzzled Ruth's palm.

I rubbed his forehead. "Merry Christmas, Sparky."

The horse's ears flicked in my direction. I liked to think that he recognized my voice.

Ruth crossed the floor and perched on a hay bale across from Sparky's stall. "I expected you to come out here. You want to talk to me, don't you?"

"Naw, I wanted to wish Sparky a Merry Christmas."

She flushed. "Oh."

I laughed and sat next to her on the hay bale. "I'm only teasing you, Ruth. I do want to wish Sparky Merry Christmas, but I want to talk you about Anna. It was brave of her to come to the Christmas program yesterday."

She pushed her black bonnet back, revealing the white prayer cap underneath. "You think so?"

I nodded. "Is she afraid of her father?"

She played with the black ribbon of her bonnet. "Afraid? Her father is stern, but she never said she was afraid of him."

"Maybe she didn't say she was, but did she ever seem to be? How did she act when she talked about her father?"

"Sad," was all Ruth would say.

I dropped my questions about Anna's father for the time being and pulled my gloves farther up on my wrists. "Did Anna ever mention Katie having an English friend named Jason?"

Her head snapped in my direction. "How did you know about him?"

"Danny knows Jason from his delivery job."

Ruth blushed. She had a terrible crush on Danny. It didn't

matter that he was ten years older and had left the Amish. "Is he Danny's *freiden*?"

I shook my head. "Only an acquaintance, but Jason has spoken to him about Katie. Was Jason a boyfriend of Katie's?"

Ruth wrinkled her nose. "*Nee*. He's an *Englischer*, and Nathan Garner courted Katie. Anna and Katie's *daed* would be furious."

We were back to the dad again. "Why?"

She shivered. "Anna's *daed* has a temper, and he doesn't like *Englischers*. He thinks they are lazy."

"Do you know why Caleb stopped courting Katie?"

She shook her head *no*. Abruptly, she stood. "Christmas dinner will be soon. I should go inside and help *Mamm*." She left the barn without waiting for me to walk back with her.

I let Ruth go, knowing she wanted to be alone. All of the changes in her life—Becky leaving, Katie's death, my arrival in Appleseed Creek—couldn't be easy for the Amish teenager. She had always been told what to believe, and her brother and sister, whom she respected and loved, decided that they wanted to believe something else and have a different, non-Amish kind of life. Ruth told me once that she would never consider leaving the Amish, but her siblings choosing another path had to give her pause. My relationship with Timothy must make it that much more difficult.

I had only been a year older than Ruth when my mother died. I knew how a girl in her early teens wasn't equipped for dramatic upheaval. Ruth was upset, and her friend, Anna, was mourning.

My cell phone was heavy in my coat pocket. It was after eleven in the morning in California. I could no longer argue with myself that it was too early to call.

I gritted my teeth and called my father.

"Yes?" Sabrina's brisk voice snapped in my ear.

"Merry Christmas, Sabrina. This is Chloe."

"I know it is you, Chloe. Your number came up on up on your father's phone."

I laughed hollowly. "Can I speak to Dad?"

"What about?" Her voice was sharp.

"I—I just want to wish him a Merry Christmas."

"Your father's not available right now. He's with his children. He works so hard. I insisted that he spend the day with his children. No interruptions."

And what was I? An interruption? A stab of jealousy hit me in the gut. "Oh."

"Did you receive the Christmas card I sent?" she asked.

"Yes, thank you," I murmured.

"Good. I hoped you weren't upset that we didn't send you a check this year, but I told your father since you're finally working—even if it is out in the middle of nowhere with a bunch of cows and pioneer people—that you didn't need the money."

Did she consider Amish "pioneer people" or just anyone living sixty miles away from the closest shopping mall? I placed a finger over my left eye to hold back the twitch forming there.

She continued. "You should be able to take care of yourself from now on and are no longer our responsibility."

Heat filled my face. *Their responsibility?* I hadn't been *their* responsibility since they dropped me at the Greens' doorstep on the way to California almost ten years ago.

"Chloe, about our gifts," my stepmother went on, as if completely unaware of how hurtful her words were to me. "The gift cards were fine, but four different stores? Honestly, Chloe, it would be much easier for me if you got them all from the same place. I don't have time to spend running all over the city, spending gift cards." She gave a suffering sigh. "I suppose it's too late to change anything for this Christmas, but do keep my convenience in mind for the future."

"I will."

"Good. Was that all?"

"Can you tell Dad that I called and said Merry Christmas?"

"I'll do that," she said and hung up.

I closed my eyes for a moment, vowing not to waste another tear on my father. Again. I stood and scratched Sparky along the bridge of his nose. He backed up and ran his big horsy lips along the palm of my hand. I held my hand flat with my fingers out of the way of his square teeth just as Grandfather Zook had taught me, then laughed to myself. I'd come a long way for a city girl.

Slam. The door to the barn closed. I yelped, and Sparky whinnied and backed into the corner of his stall. The four other horses stamped the ground. A cacophony of moos came from the dairy cattle. "It's okay. It's okay," I said to myself as much as I said to the animals.

Slowly, Sparky returned to the gate. He rolled one large brown eye toward the swinging door.

"It's okay, Sparky. It's just the wind."

Thwack, thwack. The door slammed against its frame. Ruth must have forgotten to latch it when she left the barn. Sparky retreated to the corner of his stall again.

"I'll bring you another nice big carrot before I go home today," I told the retired racehorse before I left.

Outside the barn, I firmly latched the door, then watched my feet while I walked the icy path, trying not to trip over them. To my left, boot tracks headed away from the barn and across the snow-covered field. They weren't Ruth's. The track was too long, too wide, and the tread more closely matched the size of a man's work boot. Had they been there when I walked to the barn to talk to Ruth? Maybe I had been too preoccupied on my way to the barn to notice them.

I shivered. Had the door slamming been from the wind or from someone peeking into the barn and watching me?

I pulled my cell phone from my pocket and took several close shots of the tracks. After e-mailing them to myself, I ran the rest of the way back to the farmhouse.

Chapter Fifteen

When we returned to the Quills' home, Becky ran into the kitchen, muttering about a cheese ball she needed to finish before the party. Mabel trotted into the house. Gigabyte, lounging on the back of the couch, hissed at the affable dog before fleeing upstairs. It was for the best. Gig didn't like crowds, and at last count, Becky's party had grown to forty. I started to regret telling her it was a good idea to host a Christmas party.

I picked up my iPad from the coffee table and opened my e-mail, staring at the images of the boot prints on the screen.

Timothy walked up behind me. "What are you looking at so hard?"

I turned the iPad around so he could see.

His forehead wrinkled. "Footprints?"

"Boot prints actually. I found them outside the barn after Ruth and I went out to see Sparky."

He handed the iPad back to me. "*Daed*'s boots?"

I shook my head. "I don't think so. They were directed away from the house, across the field." I swallowed. "I think they were fresh. And could have been made while Ruth and I were inside the barn."

Timothy closed his eyes for a few seconds as if he didn't like the thoughts flying through his head. He opened his eyes. "You think someone watched the two of you?"

"I—I don't know. Maybe it was someone making a short cut through the farm who wanted to step out of the cold. When he heard our voices he decided to keep going."

He cocked his head. "It's ten degrees? You think someone was just out for a walk?"

"Maybe not," I admitted. Was someone watching or listening to us? Curt immediately came to mind. Could he be watching me again? Was his claim that he was interested in church even true?

He scratched his head. "Why didn't you tell me while we were still on the farm?"

"I didn't want to ruin Christmas for your family." I tapped the iPad screen. "In any case, I e-mailed the photographs to Chief Rose. We will have to see what she says."

"You might hear today. Becky invited her to the Christmas party."

My brow shot up. "Becky didn't tell me that. Is the chief coming?"

He shrugged.

"Who else did she invite that I don't know about?"

"Her probation officer and her lawyer."

I snorted a laugh. "This will be the first Christmas I celebrate with a probation officer. What about you?"

Timothy grabbed both of my hands. "It's the best Christmas ever."

I tried to smile, but the memory of Ruth's sad face stopped me.

"Would someone please help me?" Becky called from the kitchen. "The turkey is stuck in the oven."

"That's because you bought a bird big enough to feed a marching band," Timothy muttered as he headed into the kitchen.

An hour later, Timothy left to take Mabel home before the party, and I stepped into Becky's room, which was much smaller than mine but had the benefit of being free of dolls. As soon as we moved into the house, Becky offered to take the smaller room. At the time, I thought it was out of the kindness of her heart, but now, I wondered if she had an ulterior motive—like staying away from those dozens of unseeing doll eyes.

Becky sat on the bed brushing her white-blonde hair. It was so long that when she wrapped it around the front of her, it resembled a horse's tail. "I still want to cut it," she said between strokes. Becky mentioned more than a month ago that she wished to cut her hair.

The first time she brought it up, I had been hesitant because this would be the final sign that she had no plans to the return to the Amish way of life. "Did you pray about it?"

"Yes, and I still want to do it." She braided her hair. "I've been thinking a lot."

"About something other than this party?" I teased.

She groaned. "Yes, well, sort of. I've had so much fun preparing for the party that I think this is what I want to do. I want to take the GRE, then go to culinary school, have my own bake shop, and maybe my own television show, just like Paula Deen."

My brow shot up. This was new. "I thought you wanted to be an art teacher."

"I did, but this is like art in a way. I can still use my creative side."

I thought of the gingerbread mansion sitting downstairs. "That's true."

"Can you hand me a hair band from the dresser?"

As I chose a red one from the small dish, I wondered how Aaron fit into this plan. "Your parents won't be happy."

"I know that." She sighed. "Chloe, you are always so concerned about what my parents will think, but what about your own? What do they think?"

I sat next to her on the bed and smoothed my skirt. "What do they think about what?"

"About your life? About you living here?"

I laughed off her questions. "We were talking about *your* family."

"We always talk about my family, Chloe. What about yours?"

The doorbell rang. Saved by the bell.

I secured the end of her braid with a rubber band. "Time to start the party."

She started to stand up, and I held her by the shoulder. "You're the only one who can decide about your hair, Becky. Do whatever is best for you, okay?"

"Will you go with me to have it cut?"

"Of course. We can make a day of it." I tugged on her braid. "You have more than enough to donate to charity."

"To charity?"

"To donate to children who lost their hair to disease."

Her face lit up. "I want to do that!" The doorbell rang again.

"You'd better get down there or your party will be over before it even starts."

She turned her neck and smiled at me. "Thank you, Chloe." She hopped off of the bed and ran down the stairs.

A half hour later Christmas carols rang through the Quills' house as I moved around the room carrying a tray of miniature Amish whoopie pies that Becky had made. The tray was half full, and I think that I ate more than I handed out. Everyone gains weight during the holidays, right?

Timothy stood next to Aaron's wheelchair by the grand piano tucked in the corner of the room. I popped another whoopie pie into my mouth. Hopefully, Aaron would not be in too much trouble with his father for attending the party.

I wove through the crowd to the pair.

"Merry Christmas, Aaron."

His face broke into a grin. "Merry Christmas, Chloe. This is quite a party. I've never seen anything like it."

"It's all Becky. I only helped a little when she would let me."

His eyes lit up. "I'm happy she invited me." Aaron reached up from his wheelchair and grabbed one of the chocolate pies. "Why does everything taste better when it's bite size?"

Timothy laughed. "Because you can pop it into your month before thinking about how bad it may be for you."

Aaron swallowed his second pie, then poked the air with his forefinger. "That must be it."

"You look very Christmas-y, Chloe."

I looked down at my green-and-white snowflake sweater and corduroy skirt. "This is nothing. You should see my friend Tanisha. She takes Christmas clothing to a whole other level." I chuckled remembering Tee's red sweater with the grinning reindeer face in the middle of it. Did she take it to Italy with her?

"I'm sorry you and Timothy were the ones to find Katie." His voice turned solemn. "She was a sweet girl. Everyone liked her. She was popular in the district."

I set the tray on an end table. "How was she popular? Did she have a lot of friends?"

"*Ya*, but she was more popular with the young men. Many wanted to court her."

"Like who?"

He thought for a moment. "Oh, all of them."

Timothy tapped the wheel of Aaron's chair with his toe. "Even you?"

"Nope. Not me." His eyes scanned the room and fell on Becky again.

"Do you think she may have upset one of the would-be suitors?" I asked, causing Aaron to tear his eyes away from Becky.

Aaron tilted his chin upward. "Enough for them to kill her?" He shook his head. "I don't know. Caleb King is angry, I'm sure. He was courting her for a long while. The next thing I knew Nathan Garner was driving Katie around the county in his buggy and taking her to singings. I saw the two of them on a buggy ride about a week ago. That's always a tell-tale sign that someone is courting."

Timothy's brow rose. "I thought Caleb and Nathan were friends."

Aaron cleaned his fingers on a paper napkin. "They were. Speaking of friends, I hear Billy from the auto repair shop took off."

"How do you know that?" Timothy asked.

"Everyone knows."

Becky's musical laughter floated across the room. She chatted with two young men from the Mennonite church.

Aaron frowned and released the brake on his wheelchair. "If you will excuse me." He rolled in their direction.

Becky turned, and her eyes sparkled when she saw that it was Aaron. The two Mennonites scowled at each other.

Timothy sighed. "At first, I thought their liking of each other was cute, but now I think it may be trouble."

"Because Aaron is baptized."

"Yes."

My conversation with Becky about Aaron came to mind. Should I tell Timothy about it, so that he could warn his best friend about the coming disappointment? I bit my lip. No. Becky needed to tell Aaron herself. I cleared my throat. "I wonder why Katie broke it off with Caleb. Don't Amish girls usually commit to one boy?"

"Most of the time, but she was still very young. There is another possibility too. Maybe he was the one who broke it off."

I remembered how angry Caleb was when I asked him about Katie at Thomas's school program. "I want to talk to him again."

He laughed. "I figured."

"Tomorrow. Where can I find him?"

"Nathan's family owns a furniture warehouse just outside of Appleseed Creek."

"That's the one Grandfather Zook sells his napkin holders to."

Timothy nodded. "Right. Caleb works there too."

I grimaced. "That must be uncomfortable for both of them. Let's go there tomorrow."

"We can't. The warehouse will be closed tomorrow. Amish businesses are closed on Christmas Eve, Christmas, and Second Christmas."

"Second Christmas?"

"That's what we call the day after Christmas. What do you call it?"

I laughed. "The day after Christmas. They call it Boxing Day in England, though."

"Boxing? Like punching?"

I laughed. "No, not that kind of boxing, like boxing up gifts." I frowned. "I don't like the idea of having to wait another day to talk to Caleb or Nathan, for that matter."

Timothy nodded. "Lots of folks are out and about on Second Christmas even if all the shops are closed. It's a big day to visit extended family. I'll see if I can find out where Caleb might be."

I suppressed a sigh. It was the best plan that I had. "At least we should be able to track down Jason since he's English."

Timothy's cell phone rang.

My eyebrows shot up. Usually the only calls he received were from the job site at Young's, but that was shut down for the holiday.

He took the call and moved away from me. "Hello?" Did he think that I would try to overhear? I admit I was curious about the call, but not *that* curious. I watched him talk on his phone on the other side of the room. Becky appeared at my side and her body reverberated with excitement as she clasped her hands in front of her chest. Something was definitely up. Of the two, I was most likely to crack Becky. I sidled up to her. "What's going on?" I asked.

She jumped. "Nothing. Nothing's going on."

"Becky, you are the worst liar in the world, even for an Amish girl." I made a "gimmee" gesture with my hands. "Spill."

Her brow knit together. "You want me to spill something? Won't that ruin the Quills' carpet?"

I chuckled. "It's just an English expression. It means tell me what you know."

"Oh." She pursed her lips together. "I can't. I promised."

"Who did you promise?"

Becky seemed to consider whether or not she could answer that question. Her eyes moved to Timothy, who was watching us while still on the phone. He shook his head at his younger sister.

"I can't tell you," Becky said finally. "I can't."

"Why not?"

"Because it will ruin everything."

"Just tell me if it is good or bad."

She rolled her eyes. She was becoming a bit of an expert eye roller. "Just wait and see. Let's eat some gingerbread house. It will make you feel better."

"Becky, you spent three days making that house, and you want to eat it?" I pointed to the intricately decorated house. Becky had even made a tiny Siamese cat representing Gigabyte out of modeling chocolate. It was a work of art. Several partygoers walked around it, including Becky's lawyer Tyler Hart. I hadn't seen him come inside.

"That's what it's for," she said, practically.

"Well, don't expect me to take a bite out of it."

Becky placed a finger to her cheek. "I think I need a bigger knife to cut into the roof." She went to the kitchen.

I joined Tyler at the gingerbread house.

He nodded to me. "It was nice of you girls to have this party. Everyone seems to be having a good time. Myself included."

"We're glad that you could come."

He smiled. "It's my pleasure."

"Can I ask you about Billy?"

He adjusted his glasses. "I was wondering when you'd bring him up. I had a nice chat with Greta just yesterday about my client."

"What did you tell her?"

"Chloe, I can't tell you exactly what legal matters I helped Billy with, but I can assure you I didn't know about his past. Had I known, I would have never agreed to have taken him on as a client."

"So if we find him, you won't help him now?"

He examined the tiny chocolate replica of Gigabyte. "I didn't say that."

"Do you have an idea where he could be?"

"I'm afraid not. I spoke with Billy when he needed my assistance but didn't know him well enough to know where he might have gone under these circumstances." He glanced around the room. "Is Greta here? She said that she might drop in."

"Becky invited her, but I haven't seen her."

He frowned slightly. "Are there any more whoopie pies?"

"I think there might be in the kitchen."

He nodded to me and headed in that direction.

Across the room, Timothy's cell phone rang again and he answered. A minute later he walked across the room to me. "I have a Christmas gift for you."

I touched the necklace around my neck. "You already gave me a gift."

"I know." His face broke into a grin. "This one is better."

The doorbell rang.

"Are you going to answer that?" Timothy asked.

Becky skipped across the room and stood next to her brother.

I looked back from one to the other. "I don't know what's going on here, but okay, I will play along."

The doorbell rang again. Whoever was on the other side was decidedly impatient.

"I'm coming," I muttered.

I opened the door and stumbled back as the person on the other side catapulted herself into my arms.

I found my voice. "Tee!"

Chapter Sixteen

"Are you surprised?" my best friend asked. She bounced up and down and her wild ebony curls flew in all directions.

I wiped away a tear. "Yes, I'm surprised." I turned to Timothy and Becky. "You two knew about this?"

Tanisha showed off her dazzling white smile. "Of course they did. How else would I know where you lived? Let me tell you, my GPS was no help at all. I would have been here earlier, but my Garmin took me way off course. I had to call Timothy and describe where I was. His directions were to take the right fork at the intersection where the old barn burned down. Who says that? This county really should invest in some road signage." She spoke a mile a minute just like always. I had to wonder how she taught her Italian students English. It would be an intense class with Tanisha at the helm.

"Let's sit down," I said.

Timothy touched my arm. "I'm going to take Aaron home. I'll be back in a few minutes."

I noticed guests were beginning to leave. It was nearing ten in the evening. I hadn't realized that the party had gone so late.

Becky turned toward the kitchen. "Let me grab my coat. I want to go with you." A second later she reappeared in her winter coat. "I'm ready. Chloe, is it okay if I go? Tanisha, I'm sorry to run out on you like this so fast."

Tanisha laughed. "I'm sure we will have plenty of time to visit. I'll be here for a couple of days."

"You will?" I beamed.

After Becky, Timothy, and Aaron left, followed by the rest of our departing guests, I fell next to Tanisha on the Quills' flowered couch. She glanced around the room and picked up a porcelain figurine of a ballerina. "Um. Since when have you been into ballet?"

I laughed. "I told you this house came furnished. The elderly couple who lives here is in Florida for the winter. They will be back in April, and then we will have to find a new place to live. Honestly, I hope we do sooner than that. This is too far from town."

"No kidding. And hello? Did anyone ever hear of streetlights out here?" She removed her magenta-colored coat, revealing her ugly reindeer sweater underneath.

I burst out laughing. "You wore it!"

She tweaked Rudolph on the nose. "I had to wear it. It's Christmas."

"Did you already see your parents?"

"Oh yeah." Tee rolled her eyes. "I would have left earlier, but Mom wouldn't let me out of her sight. I'm surprised I didn't lose an arm while leaving the house, she was yanking on it so hard."

"I don't want to keep you from your parents."

"Please." She whispered out of the side of her mouth. "I had to check out Timmy." She fanned herself.

I covered my mouth. "I don't think anyone calls him 'Timmy.'"

"Good. That can be our thing, then. Timmy and I need a special relationship. I mean I *will* be the maid of honor at the wedding."

"Whoa there," I said, sounding like Grandfather Zook talking to Sparky. "You're getting a little ahead of yourself."

"Not that far," she insisted. "Let me see the necklace."

I pulled the necklace from its place under my sweater. I had e-mailed her about the gift from Timothy, but I left out the part about finding the dead body by the barn.

The hammer and computer mouse charm reflected the yellow light from the pewter lamp on the end table. "That's the sweetest gift I have ever seen. How romantic! How did he even think of it? Maybe I need to find me an Amish boy while I'm here. It's much nicer than anything Cole ever gave me."

I tucked the necklace back under my sweater. Cole was Tanisha's former fiancé. He lived in Florida and broke up with her in an e-mail while she was in Italy. "Have you heard from Cole?"

She shook her head. "Not even a Christmas e-card. He wasn't too happy when I told him I threw his ring into Lake Como. I hope the fish that ate it enjoyed it because I never want to see that ring again." She bumped my shoulder. "Cole never looked at me like Timmy looks at you. I've only been here a few minutes, but I can tell he is completely besotted."

"Really?" My voice squeaked.

She laughed and stood. "Got any food around here. I'm starved."

I stood too. "You have a full gourmet spread."

"What? You moved to the country and learned how to cook? If you tell me you started knitting, I'm going to faint dead away."

"No way. Becky's the chef. I'm clean up."

She grinned. "Sounds like my kind of arrangement."

Gigabyte was in the kitchen eating a piece of ham in his dish that Becky must have given to him. Tanisha dropped to all fours. "Gig! I missed you."

The Siamese cat arched his back and hissed. He then slunk under the kitchen table, the ham clenched between his front teeth.

Tanisha jumped to her feet. "At least some things in your life haven't changed. Gig is as friendly as ever. He only likes you."

"He likes Becky." I lowered my voice. "I think he likes Becky even more than me now. She gives him bacon for breakfast every morning."

"If someone made me bacon for breakfast every morning, I'd love her too." She loaded her plate with leftovers from the Christmas party. "So what are we going to do tomorrow? Will I meet Timmy's family?"

I picked up a baby carrot from the buffet. "Yes, I think so. You will love his grandfather. As for what else we are doing, maybe you can help me with a project."

She bit into a croissant and closed her eyes for a minute to relish the taste of it. "If it's something with computers, count me out."

"No computers," I promised. "We're looking for a murderer."

The croissant dropped from her hand.

Chapter Seventeen

The sun rose just above the stand of evergreen trees that hid the Gundy barn from sight. Tanisha's leg sank halfway up to her calf in a snowdrift, and she struggled to pull her leg out. "Ugh! Tell me again why you brought me out into the wild."

I gave her my arm to steady her, and she pulled her leg and foot free. "This was your idea, remember? You were the one that bounced into my room at five thirty in the morning wanting to do something."

She carefully edged around the next snowdrift. "I can't help it. I'm still on Italy time. It's the afternoon over there. All I said was I wanted to see the sights."

I pointed to the barn. "This is one of them. Besides, you walk everywhere in Italy."

"Might I add that walking around Milan is different? I'm not walking through four feet of snow around the *duomo*." She brushed snow off her pant leg. "At least Becky and I have the same size feet. Thank goodness she let me borrow her boots." She held up her foot to show off the sturdy black boot.

"The ones you brought with you are impractical for the country. There's no *duomo* or cathedrals around here."

"Are my boots impractical? Yes. Worth a month of a teacher's salary? Absolutely." She sighed when she stepped into another snow drift. "I didn't see Becky this morning. Where was she?"

"She works at Young's Family Kitchen, the local Amish restaurant. It's about two miles from our place. She was filling in at the bakery this morning so she had to leave early to bake pies."

"I don't think I've ever met a single person who can bake a pie."

"That's an exaggeration."

"You're right, but you don't see Mom trying to bake a pie, do you?"

"That would be a disaster." Tanisha's mother was as gifted in the kitchen as Tee and I were. Her lack of cooking prowess led to us not being able to boil water either. But we could dial a phone really well for takeout.

"We'll swing by Young's later. Timothy will be there too. He's the contractor on a job there." I walked on. "You will love it, and Ellie—she's the owner—will kill me if I let you leave Knox County without trying a piece of her pie."

Tanisha caught up with me. "Speaking of killing people, tell me why we are tramping cross-country like a couple of fur traders. Seriously, I feel like it is 1800. If Davy Crockett came out of the woods wearing his coonskin cap, I wouldn't be a bit surprised."

"Davy Crockett was never in Knox County, but you might have seen Johnny Appleseed planting trees around here back then."

"You said that this had something to do with the murder."

"It does. We are walking to the barn where Timothy and I found Katie."

"Katie is the dead girl?"

"Yes." I looked at the unspoiled snow-covered ground. We

passed through the stand of pine trees and found pastel-colored sunlight washing over the weathered barn.

Tanisha whistled. “What did they keep in there? Dinosaurs?”

“Horses, I think. The Gundy family that lived here moved to Colorado years ago. Timothy said they still own the land though.”

Tanisha stuck her hands deep into her coat pocket. “Why don’t they sell it? They could make a fortune.”

I shrugged.

Tanisha picked up her pace. Although we could see the barn, it was still a half mile away. She glanced over her shoulder. “What’s taking you so long? Giddyup!”

“I think you’ve been watching too many Westerns in Italy.”

“Hey, I’m starved for English-speaking TV over there. If you’re up late at night they show American Westerns or *Seinfeld*. I’ve told my students to watch them because listening to English is the best way to learn. But I have noticed that lots of them are getting a Western twang. You should hear it with an Italian accent. It’s hilarious.”

“I hope you like cooking shows because if not, you and Becky will be spending tonight fighting over the remote.”

“As long as they are in English, I’m good.”

The closer we came to the barn, the more nervous I became. Had someone been watching Ruth and me at the Troyer farm yesterday? Was it related to Katie’s death? Would that person come here? I glanced at Tanisha. Maybe I shouldn’t have brought her here. What if something happened? “Tee, maybe we should go back.”

She stopped shaking snow from her boot. “Back? Why?”

“I didn’t think this through . . .”

“Chloe, don’t be such a worrywart. Where did you find her?” Tanisha asked. Her voice had a hushed quality and lost its joking tone.

“On the other side.” We walked around the outside of the barn. I stopped and stared down at the place Timothy and I found Katie.

With the freshly fallen snow, our tracks and the impression Katie made in the snow had vanished. It was like she had never even been there.

"Are you okay?" Tee asked.

"I think so. It seems so strange there's no sign that she was ever here."

"What was she doing here?" Tee asked the logical question that I had asked myself dozens of times in the last three days.

"I don't know. I think if we learn the answer to that question, we will learn what really happened. One thing we know for certain was she wasn't here alone. Someone else was here and strangled her."

Tanisha's hand flew to her throat. "How gruesome."

"I hoped that I would find some kind of clue as to what happened to Katie, but the whole scene is covered by snow."

"What's inside of the barn?"

"That's where it becomes really strange." As we walked around the side of the barn I filled her in on Billy—who he was and how he was involved in the case.

She stopped and held up a hand. "So you are telling me that this guy who fixes everything with duct tape—and I mean *everything*—is an escaped convict and has been hiding in Amish country for nearly twelve years."

"That's what I'm telling you."

She raised both palms toward the sky. "See, Mom doesn't want me to go back to Milan because she's afraid it's not safe for a girl on her own, and look at you—exactly how many people have been killed since you moved here?"

"Please don't tell your parents. The last thing I want them to do is to come down here and get me."

Tanisha played with the zipper on the parka she borrowed from Beck. "Does your dad know any of this?"

I narrowed my eyes. "Why would he?"

She held up her hands in surrender. "I know the 'dad' talk is off-limits."

"That's another thing that hasn't changed in my life."

Tanisha opened her mouth as if she was about to say something else, but then she snapped her mouth closed again. Fine with me. If it was about my father, I didn't want to hear it.

We slipped through the broken barn door, and a scraping sound like a piece of metal moving across stone filled the air. Tanisha tugged on my sleeve and opened her mouth. I held a finger to my lips and moved farther into the barn.

The scraping came from the far end of the barn close to where Billy had stashed his extra car parts and became more pronounced as we crept in that direction. A large pen stood between us and the auto graveyard. We stopped. Inside the stall, a thin man bent over and then straightened. Then he did it again. I craned my neck and could just make out the handle of a shovel in his hands.

"He's digging something," Tanisha whispered in my ear.

I held my forefinger to my lips again, urging her to stay quiet. Then I felt for my cell phone in the pocket of my winter coat but didn't remove it. It would take Chief Rose the better part of an hour to reach the Gundy barn, more than that if she was outside of Appleseed Creek. I couldn't turn and leave. The man in the stall could be the killer. Chief Rose would never forgive me it I let him escape without catching a glimpse of his face.

I cupped my hand over Tanisha's ear and whispered, "Go wait outside the door and stop him if runs out."

"What if he tries to hurt you?" she hissed.

"I'll scream and you come running."

Her eyes grew wide, her voice hoarse. "I don't think this a good idea."

"I have to see who it is."

She grimaced, but nodded and carefully walked back to the door. When I saw that she had stepped outside, I tiptoed closer to the man with the shovel, stopping to pick up a tire iron from the stack of Billy's car parts, its heft reassuring in my hand.

Through the six-inch wide slats that surrounded the stall, I had a clear view of the man. Puffs of his breath were visible as he threw shovelfuls of near-frozen earth into a wheelbarrow. I shivered in my thick coat. The hole he dug was at least two feet deep. I saw the sheen of metal as his exertion revealed the top of whatever had been hidden in that spot. He ran the back of the shovel across the top of the metal object, making that scraping sound again that Tanisha and I first heard when we stepped inside the barn.

He straightened up suddenly, as if sensing my presence. "Who are you? What are you doing here?" he demanded.

I held the tire iron in front of me. "I think you're the one who should answer that."

"I'm not the one sneaking up on people."

"I'm not the one digging a hole in a barn I don't own."

He paused, eyeing me. "How do you know this isn't my barn?"

"Because it belongs to the Gundy's, and they're Amish. You're not."

He didn't have a response for that. He stepped into the light for a better look at me. In turn, I was able to get a good look at him. He was a gawky teen, maybe eighteen or nineteen years old with glasses and braces. He wore his sandy-brown hair long and it flopped into his eyes and curled around his ears.

His eyes glowed with recognition when he saw me, but I didn't recognize him. Could he have seen me in town and remembered me even when I hadn't noticed him? There weren't too many redheads in Appleseed Creek, so I tended to stick out in most places around town.

He focused on the tire iron and then looked down at his shovel. "Who are you?"

"My name is Chloe. Now, it's your turn."

"Forget it. I'm not telling you anything." He turned the shovel around in his hand so that the blade end pointed to the sky.

My fingers began to cramp from holding the tire iron so tightly. "You won't tell me what you're doing here, or what it has to do with Katie Lambright's death?"

He gripped the handle of the shovel like a sword. "I didn't have anything to do with Katie's death," he shouted. "I would never hurt anyone, especially her."

I stepped back. "If that's true, why don't you drop the shovel?"

He looked at the shovel as if seeing it for the first time, his eyes suddenly wide. He lowered it and drove the spade into the dirt ground of the stall until it stuck there.

"What are you digging?"

"It's none of your business, and you'd better leave. Now."

I shrugged as if what he said didn't bother me, but inside my entire body trembled. Thankfully, about thirty feet and the wall of the stall stood between us. I could run out the door before he reached me. I removed my cell phone from my pocket. "Maybe you would like to tell Chief Rose and the police, then?"

His chin jerked upward, then he ran out through the back of the stall. The kid must have been a track and field sprinter because he was on the other side of the barn before I found my footing. I dropped the tire iron and gave chase, but no way would I be able to catch him.

But Tanisha could. She dove at the teen's feet like she was back on her college volleyball team and he was the ball. Instead of bumping him over the other side of the net, however, she grabbed him around the ankles. He went down like a felled tree. On landing, he pinned his own arms under himself.

Before he could roll over, Tanisha sat on the boy's back. "My old volleyball coach would be proud of me if he had seen that dig. I jumped three feet."

"It was impressive," I said, bending down to examine the kid's face. "Did you hurt him?"

"How could I have hurt him? He landed on snow."

I stepped around the prostrate teenager. He was trying to hold his face up out of the snow, but with little success. "What's your name?"

"It doesn't matter."

Tanisha bounced on his back. "Come on, kid. Spit it out."

The boy winced and groaned. "Will you tell her to climb off of me?"

I crossed my arms. "No, not until you tell us your name."

"So you can tell the police?"

"That is the idea."

He squirmed back and forth. "Then forget it."

Tanisha dug her knee into his back and reached into the pocket of the kid's jeans and removed his wallet. She waved it at me. "I say we check his ID."

He kicked at her with his long legs, bending them back and trying to smack her with his heels.

She slapped at one of his boots. "That's not very nice. You cut that out."

I took the wallet from Tanisha's hand and opened it. The picture ID inside read *Jason Catcher.*

Jason. I knew that name. Was he the English boy Katie had called a friend?

Jason began to thrash back and forth. "I can report you both for assault."

Tanisha snorted. "What are you going to tell the police—that a girl sat on you? Please."

I rifled through his wallet some more. Behind the driver's license was a Harshberger College ID. That's why he recognized me. I held it up for him to see. "You go to Harshberger, then."

"So what if I do."

I shrugged. "I just find it interesting since I work there." I peered at the card. "It says you're a freshman."

"So. Is that a crime?"

I tucked his IDs back into the wallet. "No, but vandalizing property is."

He twisted his neck. "Vandalizing what? I didn't do that."

"What do you call the great big hole you were digging in the barn?"

"That's not vandalism. No one cares about that barn anyway."

"That's something you will have to talk to the chief about. She may not agree."

Tanisha smacked at his foot as he tried to kick her again. "Now, why were you digging a hole in the barn?"

"Get her off of me. I can't breathe. She's crushing me." His squirming became more violent.

Tanisha's brow shot way up. "Did he just call me *fat*? Because I think he just called me fat." She bounced on his back.

Jason gave up the fight. "Ooph."

Tanisha was far from fat, but as a tall, muscular athlete she wasn't a lightweight either. I held out a hand to my friend. "Climb off of him. He's no good to us if he can't breathe."

"I'm freezing, too, lying on the snow like this."

"Poor baby," Tanisha muttered.

"Tee."

She took my hand, allowing me to hoist her up. "Fine."

Jason grunted as he struggled to his feet. "Give me my wallet."

Tanisha turned to me. "I think you should hold onto it," she said.

The kid scowled. "If I'm pulled over while driving home, and I don't have my license, I will be in deep trouble."

Tanisha brushed off the snow Jason had kicked onto her. "That sounds great to me."

I gripped the wallet. "I'll give it back to you when you tell me why you were digging in the barn."

"Because I was told to." He held out his hand. "Can I have it back now?"

"*Who* told you to?"

He dug a fist into his side. "That wasn't a condition. You keep cheating."

Tanisha snorted. "This kid has a lot of nerve." She scanned him up and down. "That will work for you in prison, buddy."

Jason paled. "Who said anything about going to prison?"

"Whoever killed Katie is going to jail," I said.

"I told you already—it wasn't me."

I crossed my arms and cocked my head. "Tell us about your relationship with Katie Lambright."

"This has nothing to do with Katie!" he bellowed.

Tanisha put a hand over one ear. "Geez, kid, there's no reason to break the sound barrier."

"Katie was your friend, wasn't she?" I asked.

He glanced away, and tears sprang to his eyes. "She was my best friend."

Tanisha stuck a hand on her hip. "Your best friend was an Amish girl?"

A tear slid down Jason's nearly frostbitten cheek. "Please give me my wallet, so I can go home. I knew I shouldn't have come here."

I held out the wallet to Jason and he ripped it from my hand. Without a backward glance he took off and ran across the field.

"Why did you give it to him?" Tanisha asked.

"Because it was his, but I didn't give it all back." I waved Jason's student ID at Tanisha before slipping it into my pocket. "The chief will be able track him down with this. I've seen her in action. It's impressive. We did have an important victory here."

Tanisha jumped from foot to foot. "What is that?"

"He left whatever he was digging up in the barn."

Tanisha let out an excited gasp and ran for the barn door. "Let's go see what it is."

Inside, we stared into the two-feet-deep hole in the barn's dirt floor. "It's some kind of safe-deposit box," I said. "Help me pull it out."

We dropped to our knees on either side of the box, reached inside the hole, and tugged.

"This thing weighs a ton," Tanisha complained.

I agreed, but focused on the task before us. "On the count of three. One, two, three!" We yanked the box from the frozen earth, wrestling it out of its hole, and set it on the ground.

Tanisha blew out a long breath. "Is this how the Amish bank? By burying their wealth, underground?"

"I'm not sure this belongs to an Amish person." With my glove, I wiped dirt away from the box's latch and lifted it. It stuck at first, but then gave way.

"I guess whoever buried it didn't think that it needed a lock underground," Tanisha said.

I lifted the heavy lid and peered inside. A folded cotton sheet covered the contents. I found a windshield wiper in one of the milk crates and used it to move a piece of the cloth back to reveal a framed photograph and a wad of money held together with a rubber band.

"Are those hundred-dollar bills?" Tanisha asked.

I nodded.

She reached for the money with her bare hand.

I grabbed her wrist. "Don't touch it."

Tanisha pulled back. "I would guess that's at least a thousand dollars."

"If they are all hundred-dollar bills, it's a whole lot more than that." I knelt for a closer look at the photograph without picking it up. It was a picture of a middle-aged woman and man. In between then was a younger, thinner version of a man I recognized. "That's Billy," I said. "The guy I told you the police were looking for."

"Why would he bury all this?"

"I guess he wasn't really ready to give up his old life, the one he had before he went to prison." I sighed. "I wish there was some clue in here about where he may have gone. He might lead us to Katie's killer."

"He might *be* Katie's killer," Tanisha said. "This time capsule, or whatever it is, is giving me the creeps."

"Why didn't he come here first to collect this before he fled?" I wondered aloud. My fingers had gone numb from the cold. Slowly, I stood up. "We've got to take this box with us."

"Isn't that tampering with evidence? You know they show old *CSI* episodes on television in Italy too."

"If we don't, Jason might come back and take it, and Chief Rose needs this for the case." I removed my cell phone from my pocket, and speed-dialed the chief's number. Again, I got voice mail. We couldn't sit around all day until she decided to check her phone, and I didn't believe this merited a 911 call. "She's not answering. We have to take it with us."

Tanisha shook her head. "We can carry it a few feet, Chloe, but not a mile. It will take forever."

I spotted a piece of metal—sheeting from a car door. All the innards of the door had been removed. I tapped it with my boot and it moved easily. "Let's put the box on this piece of metal." Tanisha helped me hoist the box onto the old car door.

Inside one of the milk crates, I found several large bungee cords.

"What are you going to do with those?" she asked.

"Watch." I secured the box to the sled with one set of bungee cords. Then used two more bungees to make pulls on either side of the car door.

"What is it?" Tanisha asked.

I handed her one of the pulls. "A sled."

"Wow," Tanisha said. "You've really gone country. That or you've been watching a lot of *MacGyver* reruns. We get those in Milan too. If I needed to, I could make a small bomb with a paper-clip and gum."

I pulled the makeshift sled toward the door. "Let's hope that particular skill does not become necessary."

Chapter Eighteen

We stepped into the Appleseed Creek Police Department and set the box on the floor. Tanisha glanced around the sparse room. "They could use a decorator in here," she whispered.

The door that led into the interrogation room opened and Chief Rose stepped out. "Sorry I missed your call. I was in the middle of a traffic stop." She pointed at the box. "What do you have for me, Humphrey?"

"Something Billy left behind."

She narrowed her eyes, which were outlined in bright blue. "You mean Walter."

"It's simpler to call him Billy. That's who he is to us."

She shrugged and glanced at Tanisha. "Who is this?"

"This is my friend, Tanisha. She's visiting from Italy."

The chief raised an eyebrow. "You're Italian?"

Tanisha shook her head. "I'm teaching over there. Love your eyeliner, by the way."

"Thanks," the chief drawled. "Did Walter leave this gift for me?"

I shook my head and told her how Tanisha and I found the box. Then I handed her Jason's college ID.

She arched an eyebrow. "He gave this to you?"

Tanisha suppressed a smile. "We borrowed it for you."

Chief Rose snorted and knelt by the box. She pulled a pair of latex gloves from her pocket, and as she slipped them on said, "I would have preferred you leave the box there and hang around until I had showed up. This evidence has now been compromised."

I flushed. "We thought that he would come back and take it."

The chief scowled and picked up the wad of money with a whistle. "Looks like this was Walter's getaway stash. He must have buried it in the Gundy barn when he first moved to Appleseed Creek."

"Why didn't he take it with him before he disappeared?" I asked.

Chief Rose stood and leaned against the side of the desk. "There are a couple of possibilities. Either he didn't leave of his own free will or he was too spooked by finding or killing Katie Lambright."

"Do you really think he did it?"

The police chief sat at her receptionist's desk and flipped Jason's ID on the desktop. It spun until it came to rest in the middle of the flat surface. "I think he could have and that's enough for me."

"How does Jason know Billy?" I asked.

"I don't know," the chief said, "but I'll be sure to ask him."

"Are you going to arrest him?" Tanisha asked.

Chief Rose leaned back in her chair. "For digging a hole?"

"For trespassing."

"Then I would have to arrest everyone who goes out to that old barn." She eyed me. "Including Troyer, Humphrey . . . and you." She stood up and removed her gloves. "I need to take this over to the sheriff's department. Maybe one of the techs can pull a fingerprint off the box." She examined us. "Did either of you touch any of this?"

"We wore gloves," Tanisha said.

She nodded. "Smart girls. What else do you have for me?"

I swallowed. "Katie was courted by a couple of Amish guys—Caleb King and Nathan Garner. Caleb was upset when she started dating Nathan."

"I know that. Humphrey, I gave you this assignment to find out stuff I didn't know."

I frowned.

She sighed. "I'm not saying that you did a bad job. Thanks for the box. Next time you find something, wait for me. I will come to you."

Tanisha and I walked out of the police department. "Is she always like that?"

I laughed. "Yep."

"Where to now? Food? Crime fighting makes me hungry."

"I know just the place to take you."

Twenty minutes later, Tanisha burst out laughing when we turned into the parking lot at Young's. "What's so funny?" I asked.

"This restaurant is *enormous.* Are you sure it doesn't have its own zip code? My friends in Italy always say how huge things are in America and I guess they're right. I notice it more now." She rolled down the window, allowing the cold winter air to circulate inside the Bug. "Look at all those buggies. Aren't they charming? I have to take some photos. My friends in Italy will love them."

"Be careful not to take pictures of the Amish themselves. They don't like it. Or if you take a photograph, don't let them see you."

She nodded.

I drove around to the back of the building. "Where are you going?" she asked. "Wasn't the entrance in the front?"

"It is, but Ellie, the owner, lets the Troyer family park by the kitchen in the back."

She smirked. "She lets the Troyer family, and you are counted in that number. You still think you and Timothy aren't serious?"

I ignored her question and parked my Bug a few feet away from Sparky standing in front of Grandfather Zook's buggy. "Hey, Spark," I said as we passed him.

Tanisha threw a glance over her shoulder. "You're friends with the horses too?"

I laughed.

Instead of walking through the kitchen, I led Tanisha to the side door by the office entrance. I knew that would be closest to the hostess stand where we would most likely find Ellie.

We walked down the short hallway past the offices and restrooms. A group of English tourists who waited for their table played checkers on a white wooden table between matching rockers. Others read Amish Country brochures in front of the burning fireplace. Although an Amish home would not have a Christmas tree, a simply decorated one stood in a corner next to the fireplace. The only ornaments were handmade bows and silver glass balls. Naomi and Thomas stood in front of the Christmas tree examining each ornament with studied attention.

Grandfather Zook sat on a rocker closest to the hostess station. He stacked his metal braces against the wall behind him. "Chloe, we have been waiting for you," he said. "Becky told us that you had a friend visiting."

"Grandfather Zook, this is Tanisha."

Tanisha held out her hand to the older Amish man, and he clasped it between his two wrinkled ones. "It is *gut* to meet you. Chloe has spoken about you and your family many times."

Tanisha smiled her dazzling, white smile. "Every time she e-mails me she writes about your family."

"E-mail? Yes, I know this is some computer mail. I prefer a letter, which you can keep and save."

"When I arrive back to Italy, I will send you a letter then."

"Oh, make it a postcard. I would love to see a picture of where you live." Grandfather Zook winked at me. "I bring in the mail every day, which is a *gut* thing. Who knows what my son-in-law would think about me getting mail from Italy." He let go of her hand. "You say Chloe writes about us, but she must mention Timothy the most?"

A blush worked its way up my neck. Between Tanisha and Grandfather Zook I would have no rest from the teasing.

Tanisha leaned toward Grandfather Zook. "She talks about him all the time."

I placed my hand on the back of Grandfather Zook's rocker. "Okay, okay, you two. I'm standing right here."

The hostess stand was only a few feet away. Ellie returned from seating an English couple and dropped a stack of menus into a holder on the side of the podium. The line to be seated was nearly to the front door. "Your table should be ready in one minute," she said to the next couple. "They are bussing it now."

The couple thanked her, and Ellie caught sight of Tanisha and me standing by Grandfather Zook. "Chloe, I have been holding Joseph's table for twenty minutes. What took you so long?"

Tanisha raised her brow at me. With so many tourists and Amish in close eavesdropping range, I couldn't really say anything about Jason, the box, or our conversation with Chief Rose. "We got held up. I'm sorry."

Ellie sniffed and placed her hands on either side of her hips. "Held up. This is an *Englisch* problem, I see." She had on the same blue dress worn by all of the women on her staff—even the English ones—and a black apron with "Young's Family Kitchen" embroidered on the hip pocket. Her steel gray hair was parted in the middle and tied back at the nape of her neck in the Amish style. "Who is this?" She nodded toward Tanisha.

"Ellie, I'd like you to meet my good friend, Tanisha."

Ellie inspected Tanisha from head to toe.

Tanisha shot me a nervous glance. I smiled back. Ellie could be pushy, but she was harmless.

Ellie nodded as if she had decided something. "If you are a friend of Chloe's, you are a friend of mine. You look a bit thin. I hope you came here to eat."

"I did. I'm starving. Chloe said that this was the only place to go."

Ellie nodded with satisfaction. "That is the truth." Then it was my turn to be scrutinized. She watched me, curiously. "I heard you've made another unpleasant discovery. How are you holding up?"

The last person I found in Katie's condition was Ellie's thirty-year-old son, Elijah. His death was only a month ago and I knew the pain was still raw for Ellie, as well as Uriah, Elijah's identical twin. "I'm okay. How are you?"

"It comes and goes. *Gott* gave me much work to do, which is a blessing. My mind wanders when my hands are still."

Thomas led Naomi by the hand. "Chloe, you came. We have been waiting."

"I know. Ellie just told me. I'm sorry to make you wait so long."

The seven-year-old shrugged. "Did you see the Christmas tree? It is so pretty."

Naomi clutched her doll in its new purple dress in her arms. "It sparkles."

"I wish *Daed* would let us have one."

Grandfather Zook shook his finger at his young grandson in mock scolding. "Oh no. You don't go asking your *daed* that. I'll be the one who is blamed for putting the idea in your head."

Thomas and Naomi giggled.

I smiled at them. "I'd like you to meet my friend, Tanisha."

The two Troyer children smiled shyly at Tee. "You live in Italy," Thomas said. "I showed my teacher where you lived on a map. It looks like a boot."

"That's right," Tanisha said.

Movement over Tanisha's shoulder caught my eye. Curt was watching us. My body clenched, and I turned my back to him. Do I tell the family about Curt's presence here? Ellie knew his history with the Troyers and would certainly kick him out of Young's if she recognized him. I took a deep breath, steeled myself, and spun back around.

He was gone.

Had I been hallucinating? Or should I go look for him to make sure he was really gone?

Tanisha laughed at something that Grandfather Zook said and gave Naomi a hug.

No. I would not let Curt ruin another moment for this family.

"I'm starved," I said. "Let's go to the table."

"That's what I've be trying to convince you to do for the last five minutes," Ellie said. "Now, scoot with you." She handed me a stack of menus. Tanisha helped Grandfather Zook up, and Thomas handed his grandfather his arm braces.

I led the way into the dining room. The aroma of roast beef, yeasty bread, and cinnamon permeated the air. My stomach growled. I had been so caught up in finding Jason in the barn I had not realized that I was hungry until that very moment. Naomi and Thomas walked right behind me, followed by Tanisha and Grandfather Zook. Tourists stared at us as we made our way to the table Ellie always reserved for Grandfather Zook. I'm sure we were an unexpected sight—an elderly Amish man on metal braces, two Amish children, a red-headed English woman, and Tanisha with her wild curls and dark skin.

Like an experienced waitress, I placed the menus on the table by the large window overlooking the snow-covered cornfield to the property's west. When everyone was seated and studying their menus, I asked, "Where's Ruth?"

Grandfather Zook shook his head. "She didn't want to come today. She wanted to stay back and help her *mamm*."

Ruth complained about chores constantly, so I found Grandfather Zook's excuse hard to believe.

Thomas pulled on my arm. "She's sad because she can't see Anna anymore."

I frowned. "I know." More likely, that was the real reason Ruth hadn't joined us. "Did Mr. and Mrs. Troyer stay back at the house because Ruth didn't want to come?"

Grandfather Zook rubbed a paper napkin back and forth across his mouth, mussing his beard. "*Nee*, my son-in-law wanted to visit his mother in Holmes County today. She hasn't been well."

"I'm sorry to hear that."

A waitress in a Young's uniform approached us. Tanisha let Grandfather Zook order for her, and he selected the meat trio. Tanisha rubbed her hands together. "It's nice to have a break from pizza and pasta."

Thomas's mouth fell open. "Tired of pizza? Becky made us a pizza a week ago and it was the best thing I've ever eaten. I could eat a whole one all by myself."

Grandfather Zook shook his teaspoon at Thomas. "Don't let your *mamm* hear you say that. What about her roast turkey? You like that?"

Thomas nodded, seriously considering Grandfather Zook's alternative for the best food ever. "But the pizza has cheese on it."

"Mushrooms," Naomi piped up.

Grandfather Zook shook his head. "Of all the *Englisch* words, she knows *mushrooms*."

The little girl squeezed her doll tightly to her chest. From Tanisha's expression, I guessed she wanted to stick Naomi in her pocket and take her home. Most people felt the same way about the little girl.

Conscious of all the calories I'd taken in over the holidays, I opted for salad. While the family continued to discuss the merits of Becky's pizza, I wove across the room to the salad bar. I pulled a plate from the stack inside the chilled case, and Becky sidled up to me with a square, two-tiered metal cart with salad refills.

I piled shredded iceberg lettuce onto my plate. "You're on salad bar duty today."

"Yes," she said with a sigh. "No tips, but we all have to take our turn at it." She switched out the coleslaw containers. "If you want to see Nathan Garner, he's right over there." She nodded toward a long table near the back wall. I counted heads—nearly twenty people sat there, all of them Amish. I recognized Nathan Garner from seeing him briefly at the Troyer barn the day Timothy and I found Katie. His dark, wavy hair was barely contained by the Amish bowl haircut, and a dimple just like his father's appeared in his right cheek. On looks alone, I could see why Katie Lambright would agree to let him court her over Caleb. The young Amish man laughed at something the person next to him said and his dimple caught the light. His father, Levi Garner, sat at the head of the table laughing and joking with his guests.

Becky placed the empty pickled beet tray on her metal cart and replaced it with a fresh one. "Nathan's one of the most handsome boys in the district."

"Even more handsome than Aaron?"

Becky blushed and ducked her head.

I added broccoli to my salad. "Do they come here a lot?"

"The Garners bring their family and those that work for them here every year on Second Christmas."

"It's like a Christmas party?" I whispered back.

As if he sensed my gaze, Nathan glanced in my direction. We made eye contact for a few seconds. He didn't look particularly upset over Katie's death. What did he think about the *Englisch* girl holding a spoonful of black olives over her plate at the salad bar? I might never know because the Amish were experts at hiding their emotions. That trait had taken some getting used to for me after living with Tanisha and the demonstrative Green family since I was fifteen. This aspect of the Amish reminded me of my father. Dad always hid how he really felt—except for his disappointment in me.

Becky gripped the handles of the cart. "I'd better head back to the kitchen. We are out of diced ham and eggs. They are always favorite toppings."

"Stop by our table if you have a minute. Tanisha is here with us."

She promised she would. I moved further down the salad bar and contemplated my dressing options. The most popular in this area was the Amish-made sweet and sour, but I opted for ranch. Just like Tanisha needed a break from pizza, I needed a break from Amish food.

Nathan stood up from the table and headed for the front of the restaurant. I set my salad on the bar and went after him. An English man stopped me and said, "You forgot your salad."

"I'll grab it later," I said.

"She must really have to use the john," he said to his companion.

I reached the front of the restaurant in time to see Nathan walk down the long hallway toward the restrooms. Ellie led a couple to their table and muttered, "Where's the fire?" as I passed her.

The checker players were no longer in front of the Christmas tree as I hurried past. I caught up with Nathan at the door to the men's room. "Nathan Garner?"

He spun around. "*Ya?*"

"I'm Chloe Humphrey. I was wondering if I could talk to you for a few minutes."

He pointed his thumb at the men's room. "Now?"

Heat rushed to my cheeks. "Whenever it is a good time for you."

"Now is not a *gut* time."

My face burned. "I'm so sorry."

He pushed on the door and half-turned his body. "What is it you wanted to ask me? Is it about furniture, if so you'd be better off asking my *daed.*"

"It's about Katie Lambright."

His hand slid from the door. "Are you the police?"

"No."

"Then, I don't have to talk to you." Nathan's skin went pale, as if he might be sick. "I can't talk about Katie."

"I know this must be difficult, but it's important I talk to you. I'm not the police but I'm working with Chief Rose to find out how Katie died."

The dimple receded into his cheek. "I already know how she died."

"How?"

He pushed the door opened wide. The sound of the paper towel dispenser going on and off echoed into the hallway. "I don't owe you an explanation. Leave me alone, *Englischer.*"

"Should I ask Caleb my questions? Would he know what happened to her?"

His eyes flashed. "*Ya,* he would know," he paused. "Because he killed her."

The door to the men's room slammed in my face. A heavyset English man cleared his throat behind me.

"I'm sorry," I murmured and stepped out of the way.

Thomas ran down the hallway. "Chloe, there you are.

Grandfather Zook sent me after you. He thought something was wrong when you didn't come back to the table."

I ruffled his silky blond hair that felt like a baby-fine version of Timothy's. "I'm fine. I need to go to the salad bar and pick up my plate."

"You haven't gotten your salad yet?"

I shook my head.

He took my hand. "I will have to help you then because this is taking too long."

I let Thomas lead me back into the restaurant and to the salad bar but not before shooting a backward glance at the men's room door.

Chapter Nineteen

The first salad I made, which had disappeared from the bar by time that I had gotten back there, was much healthier than the one Thomas helped me create. I believe he dumped the entire container of croutons onto my plate when I wasn't looking. We reached the table just as the waitress placed the rest of the group's meals in front of them.

Tanisha was gap-mouthed when she saw the pieces of chicken, roast beef, and ham along with the green beans and mashed potatoes on her plate. She pulled her camera out of her bag. "I need a picture of this to show my friends in Italy."

Thomas pointed at his drum leg. "Take a photograph of mine. They will want to see it too."

Naomi, too, pointed at her plate.

In the end, Tanisha took photographs of everyone's plate for her friends back in Milan to enjoy. "They will love seeing real Amish home cooking. Most of them have never heard of the Amish before."

Thomas's fork stopped halfway to his month. "They don't know the Amish?"

Tanisha cut into her roast beef. "There aren't any Amish living in Europe."

Thomas seemed to consider this. "But most of the people I know are Amish."

Tanisha laughed. "That's because you live here."

Grandfather Zook chuckled. "Let's bow our heads and thank *Gott* for this, His beautiful meal."

Thomas sat between Tanisha and Grandfather Zook. He folded one hand into Tanisha's slim brown one and the other into his grandfather's white wrinkled one. I took Tanisha and Naomi's hands and bowed my head too.

Grandfather Zook said the prayer in English. "*Gott*, please bless this food we are about to receive to our bodies, and let us remember Your birthday every day, not just during Christmas. We pray for continued comfort for Katie Lambright's family and friends. Amen." He picked up a knife and fork and began cutting Naomi's ham slice into tiny pieces. Thomas advised him where to make the cuts.

Tanisha leaned toward me. "What took you so long over there? Couldn't you decide between the crumbled blue cheese and the shredded cheddar?" She examined my plate. "I see you went for both."

"I saw one of the boys who courted Katie Lambright," I whispered. "I wanted to talk to him."

Her eyes widened. "What did he say?"

I placed my napkin on my lap. "He knows who killed her."

Tanisha jumped up in her seat, her hip hitting the underside of the table. I saved her water glass before it tipped over. Grandfather Zook and Naomi stared at Tanisha, while Thomas held the drumstick in his teeth, about to bite down.

"Oops," Tee said with a laugh.

Thomas lowered the drumstick. "Did you get stung by a bee? I jumped like that when I was stung." He leaned across the table. "It stung me in the behind when I was going down the slide."

Grandfather Zook chuckled. "There are no bees this time of year. Maybe it was a spider." He lowered his voice. "Don't tell Ellie I said that. She'd chase me with a wooden spoon if she thought I told folks there were pests in her place."

"No bees or spiders. I'm fine." Tanisha insisted.

Thomas squinted at her as if he wasn't quite buying her story.

Tanisha gave me a desperate glance.

Thankfully, Becky approached the table. "Is everyone having a good meal?"

Thomas nodded. "Tanisha got bitten by a spider."

Becky took a step back from the table. "Did you kill it?"

"There wasn't a spider," I said.

Thomas shook his head and mouthed "spider" at his older sister. Then he held out his hands as if to say the spider was roughly the size of a Chihuahua.

Becky backed farther away from the table. "I'll just return to the kitchen, then. I'll see you later tonight, Tanisha."

Grandfather Zook pointed his fork at his grandson. "Thomas, you know your sister does not like spiders."

"She doesn't?" Thomas asked in an innocent voice.

Naomi pulled on my sleeve, and I bent my head toward her. "What is it?"

"He stares," she whispered.

I straightened up and noticed Curt two tables away, watching us. A chicken dinner sat in front of him, but it didn't look like he had taken a single bite.

I dropped my gaze. I hadn't been imagining Curt's presence. He was here. Did Becky know? How could I convince him to leave without making a scene in Ellie's restaurant?

A waitress, thankfully not Becky, stopped at Curt's table. He said something to her and she nodded. Their exchange seemed pleasant enough. Maybe he didn't plan to make trouble, but his presence made trouble for me, no matter his intention.

The waitress returned a minute later with a to-go box and his check. Curt packed up his uneaten meal, placed a stack of bills on the table, and left.

Tanisha pulled on my sleeve. "Tell me again what this guy said."

Guy? Curt? I blinked at her. No. She referred to Nathan. "Later," I whispered.

Tanisha nodded and turned her attention back to Grandfather Zook and the children.

When we finished eating, I looked across the room, but the Garner table stood empty. Two young Amish women removed the dirty glasses and dishes from its surface. When had they left?

"Now, can you tell me?" Tanisha whispered as we followed Grandfather Zook, Thomas, and Naomi across the dining room.

I leaned toward her, my voice low. "He said his rival for Katie murdered her, but considering the source, it could just be his jealousy talking."

Tanisha's eyes sparkled. "Let's go talk to him." She was really getting into this sleuthing thing. "We can decide whether or not he's lying. You ask the questions, and I will put on my liar glare."

"You have a liar glare?"

"I'm a schoolteacher. It's an occupational requirement."

"It's too late. He's already gone."

She glanced around. "Well, then, let's find out where he lives and stake out his house."

"Tee . . ."

As we stepped into the restaurant lobby, Grandfather Zook turned. "Tanisha, have you ever been on a buggy ride before?"

Tanisha seemed to forget about Nathan Garner and the stakeout. "No."

"I think the *kinner* and I are going to take a short one around town before we head back to the farm. Do you want to ride with us?"

My best friend stopped just short of jumping up and down. "Yes!"

Grandfather Zook pulled on his beard. "*Gut*. Chloe, do you want to come too?"

I shook my head. "I think I'll go find Timothy."

A knowing grin spread across the old man's face.

Thomas took one of Tanisha's hands and Naomi took the other. "*Grossdaddi*'s horse is named Sparky," Thomas said.

"Really?" Tanisha followed Thomas and Naomi out the side door near the offices.

Grandfather Zook cocked his head. "You be careful around Nathan Garner."

"I—"

"You're surprised I overheard you, aren't you?" He yanked on his right ear. "My legs might not work right, but my hearing is just fine. The Garner family has a lot of money and influence in the district. Even Deacon Sutter doesn't pester them."

"Why? I thought they owned a furniture store."

He removed his black felt hat from the peg by the hostess stand and placed it on his head. "They do, and it's one of the most successful businesses in the county." I helped him in to his coat. "Just be careful. I don't want my grandson's heart broken because something happened to you." He squeezed my hand. "I don't want my heart broken either."

"I'll be careful." I held the door as Grandfather Zook maneuvered outside with his braces. I was anxious about him navigating the icy ground, but thankfully, Sparky and the buggy were only a few steps away. Thomas ran over and held onto his grandfather's elbow the rest of the way to the buggy.

Tanisha waved at me from the backseat. She had her camera out, ready to snap photographs. I hoped that if she caught any of the children in the shots, Mr. Troyer wouldn't care.

When the buggy pulled away, I let the side door close and headed toward the offices in search of Timothy. I had to tell him everything that I learned since I saw him last. Thankfully, my search was short-lived because he walked toward me.

"What's wrong?" he asked as soon as he saw my expression.

"Is there somewhere we can talk?"

He put his arm around my shoulders and led me to the office in the back. It once belonged to the late Elijah Young, and his twin Uriah let Timothy use it as a home base for the pavilion project. The split-paned window looked out onto the jobsite. When the project was completed, I wondered if I could enter the pavilion again without remembering the sight of Elijah dead on the dusty floor with shears stuck in his back and his beard cut. His murderer was at Knox County jail awaiting trial.

Mabel lay under the desk. I arched my brow. "Does Ellie know she is in here?"

He grinned. "No, and I hope to keep it that way. It's too cold to leave her in the pavilion."

Mabel rolled on her back exposing her belly to us. I gave it a good scratch, and she wiggled back and forth with a happy dog expression on her face. If only Gigabyte were as easy to please.

There were no computers. Just paper ledgers and metal filing cabinets that held receipts. The only signs of English technology were the electric lights, which the bishop allowed for businesses, and a battery-operated calculator.

I sat on the armchair in front of Uri's desk and told Timothy everything that had happened today, from finding the box, to

Tanisha slide tackling Jason Catcher to the ground outside of the Gundy barn.

"I wished I had been there to see that."

"I'm sure she will reenact it if you ask her to."

He laughed.

I straightened the stack of papers on the desktop. "The only thing that would finish this day off would be an appearance by Deacon Sutter. I haven't seen him since the Christmas pageant at the schoolhouse, but he does have a knack for popping up when you least expect him."

"Don't wish for that," Timothy said. "What are you going to do next?"

"I'll call Chief Rose and give her a heads-up, and then we need to find Billy. He is the missing piece that holds all of this together."

"Good." He pressed his lip into a thin line. "Because I think I know where Billy is."

I dropped the stack of papers onto the desk. "Where?"

"I'll tell you on the way."

"Shouldn't we call Chief Rose? She will want to be there when we find Billy."

Timothy slipped into his winter coat. "We'll call her if he's there."

I bit my lip. I knew Chief Rose would not be happy with that. Why wouldn't Timothy call her?

As Timothy, Mabel, and I walked out the side door to his truck, I called Tanisha's cell phone. "Can you ask Grandfather Zook to drop you at my house? I have to run an errand."

"I'm glad you called. He just asked me if I wanted to see the family farm. I really do, so do you care if we go over there now? You can pick me up later."

"That's perfect."

"Great! Chloe, I'm having the best time." And then she hung up.

I couldn't help but smile. Tanisha was someone who always had the best time. I could use a little of her enthusiasm.

"Ready to go?" Timothy asked.

I nodded. "You really think Billy is wherever we're going?"

Timothy's jaw twitched. "If he's not, he left Knox County for good."

That's exactly what I feared.

Chapter Twenty

Timothy tapped his fingers on his truck's steering wheel. "I hope I'm not wrong about this."

Mabel leaned her head over the backseat, so that I could pat her head. I slid a glance at Timothy. "Now you are having doubts?"

He shrugged. "It's the only place I can think of where Billy could hide in the county and feel at home."

"Where is it?"

"It's twenty minutes away. There's an old auto parts factory off Route 13 close to Fredericktown. It closed down ten years ago. I'm wondering if Billy didn't gather most of the parts he stashed in the Gundy barn from this factory. The company went under big time and everything was sold piecemeal at rock-bottom prices. I got three parts for the truck I owned back then for twenty dollars. Anywhere else it would have cost me hundreds."

"What did the factory make?"

"Rearview mirrors, headlights, and other small parts."

Timothy passed the exit for Fredericktown but turned left off 13 before we reached Mount Vernon, the county seat. The drive was smooth and quiet. "Wow. This route is better paved than most around here," I said.

"The auto parts company had it repaved so that their workers could make it into work even during the worst Ohio winter. Unfortunately, that didn't save the company."

A large red brick building came into view a half-mile down the road. Timothy drove the pickup through a gate with ice-covered hinges. The galvanized chain, its lock broken, hung listlessly from the fence. He brought the truck to a stop in front of the building, or at least what I thought was the front. It was hard to tell. Snow blew in through the broken windows. Dead ivy caked in ice snaked up the four corners of the building while overgrown evergreen bushes grew over the windows on the first floor.

Timothy sighed. "Signs of the rust belt," he said.

"I'm from Cleveland, remember, and there are parts of the city that have four or five burned-out factories like this. Lots are being reclaimed for fancy apartment buildings and small business suites though."

Timothy removed his key from the ignition. "That kind of transformation isn't going to happen in Knox County. There aren't enough people to live in those fancy apartments or shop at those upscale businesses. The building will sit empty until the elements eventually knock it to the ground."

"Looks like the elements are halfway there. Do you really think Billy could be staying inside? How could he survive? With all those broken windows he must be half-frozen by now."

Timothy placed his hand on the door handle. "I can't think of anywhere else he might be. He's a big guy and a loner. There aren't many places he can hide this deep into Amish Country without someone noticing. The Amish would never hide him, knowing his connection to Katie's death."

I pulled my pink hat farther down over my ears. "Let's go, then."

"I want Mabel to wait in the truck." He pointed at the busted windows. "There's going to be a lot of broken glass in there, and I don't want her paws cut."

My heart melted a little at Timothy's concern for his dog. Mabel seemed to understand what he said because she settled onto her haunches in the backseat. She didn't look particularly disappointed about staying behind. "Doesn't look like she's going to argue with you," I said.

Timothy laughed. "I didn't expect her too." He opened his door and got out. I followed.

Our boots crunched across the frozen earth. Tall bushes blocked the entrance, and I didn't see how we were going to get inside. "Where's the door?"

"There." He pointed to a cluster of overgrown bushes. Stacks of snow six inches high sat precariously on the branches. They didn't look like they had been disturbed in the last millennium.

"He can't be in there. You'd need a machete to break through those branches. It's clear no one has entered the building through that door in the last decade."

"He must have gotten inside another way," Timothy said, not giving up on his idea that this was Billy's hideout. Who was I to question him? He knew Billy better than I did.

"If you really think he's in there, maybe we should call Chief Rose, and she and her officers can search the building."

He placed a hand on my cheek. "Chloe, he's my friend. I owe it to him to ask him myself before I hand him over to Greta."

"Okay."

"Let's walk around the building and find another way inside. It should be pretty obvious. Billy's built like a garbage truck."

The bushes thinned out as we rounded the back side of the building. A metal door stood open a crack. Timothy's face brightened.

I touched his shoulder. "But there aren't any footprints."

"It has been snowing pretty hard. If he came through this way, they would be covered by now."

Timothy placed his gloved hand onto the metal door. It didn't move. He pushed a little harder. It didn't budge. "Back up," he said.

I took a big step backward.

Timothy rammed his shoulder into the door, and it opened just wide enough for him to squeeze inside. His hand appeared in the door opening, so I took hold of it and stepped through.

I stood beside Timothy for a moment, letting my eyes adjust to the darkness. It was a shock after being outside with the sun glaring off the snow.

Timothy's laughter echoed throughout the hollow space.

"What?"

"It would help if you removed your sunglasses."

I touched my face. "Oh, right." I tucked them in the inside pocket of my ski jacket, then grinned at him. "Much better."

He squeezed my hand.

"Should we keep our voices down? He might hear us." My voice reverberated off of the walls just like Timothy's laughter had.

"I'm not sure it matters. The quietest whisper seems to cause an echo in here."

Shards of glass the size of my leg and jagged pieces of metal covered the dusty concrete floor. Chains that used to transport heavy pieces of equipment hung from the ceiling, resembling instruments of torture. I wrapped my arms around myself. "This place could double for the set of a horror movie."

"I've never seen a horror movie."

I shivered. "Trust me, after coming here, you don't need to."

I stepped over a rusted bar. "Where could Billy be? I certainly wouldn't want to spend more than five minutes in this place. It gives me the creeps."

"He has to be in here somewhere," Timothy said.

"Why do you think that? Did he talk about this place? Did he come here a lot after it closed?"

Timothy set his jaw. "I know Billy, and he's most at home around cars. There's no other place like this in the county."

"Chief Rose thinks he left the area and found a new place to hide."

"That would have been the smart thing to do, but I'm betting he didn't do the smart thing. I know this, though—Billy didn't kill Katie Lambright. My guess is that he will hang around until Chief Rose arrests someone else."

I wasn't so sure. Billy ran before, why wouldn't he run again? I lowered my voice. "You think he's looking for the killer?" The image of Billy, three hundred pounds with bright red hair, sneaking around and spying on Amish farms didn't seem to work for me. I was self-conscious in the Amish community because of my hair color and my clothing, but at least I was small.

"No. But I think he's hanging around until his name is cleared from this crime."

I wrinkled my brow. "He didn't hang around Detroit."

Timothy shook his head. "That's because he knew he was guilty."

Rather than argue, I said, "Let's look for him. I'm freezing."

Timothy nodded and we moved deeper into the factory. Every step revealed another hazard set on skewering us—from sharp metal rods to exposed nails. The windows on either side of the office door were busted. With so many broken windows in the factory, I wondered if some teenagers had broken in and used the place for target practice.

In the middle of the factory, a metal staircase rose up to the second level. "What about up there?"

Timothy tilted his head up. "The foreman's office. It does look like the most likely place for Billy to hide. You stay down here, and I'll go up."

The rusted stairs looked like they would give under my cat's weight. "Are you sure the staircase will hold you?"

"I'll be fine." Timothy placed a foot on the step and the rusted metal gave way beneath him.

I rushed over. "Are you okay? Did you cut yourself?"

"I'm okay," Timothy said, breathing hard. "Good thing it's winter, and I'm wearing a lot of layers. The metal didn't even touch me." He glanced down at his torn pant leg. "I can't say the same for my jeans."

I grabbed Timothy by both of his arms to help him balance and he pulled his leg free of the metal. He brushed off his leg. "We need to be more careful."

"You're not going to be able to go up there. You're too heavy. I'll go up."

He shook his head. "No way. If the stairs can't hold me, there is no way they held Billy."

"We can't come all the way here and not check."

Timothy pursed his lips.

I squeezed his arm. "I'll be up and down before you know it."

Timothy started breathing hard. "No."

"Timothy, what . . ." And then I realized what was bothering him. I wrapped my arms around his waist. "Nothing like Aaron's accident is going to happen to me."

His eyes widened. "How did you know that I was thinking of Aaron?"

I cinched him closer. "Because I know you."

He kissed the top of my head. "I know you too." He tilted my chin up. "You're going up there, aren't you?"

I nodded.

"Okay. Be careful." He removed the flashlight clipped to his belt and handed it to me.

"I'm always careful."

He rolled his eyes, reminding me of Becky.

I skipped over the demolished first step and moved to the second one. It gave a fraction of an inch, but it held my weight. I moved to the next step. The higher up I went, the more stable the stairs became. I hopped onto the landing and waved to Timothy a floor below.

"Hurry up," he said, the expression on his face strained.

I moved along the landing to the office door, which was open halfway, and I pushed it in the rest of the way with my boot. The room was dank and smelled of sour milk. I felt the wall for the light switch and flicked it on. Nothing happened. I should have remembered that electricity to the building had been cut off years before.

I shone the flashlight around the room. There was no sign anyone had been inside the office for decades. Beyond the first room was a second door that led into an inner office. I picked my way across the room and tried the doorknob. It turned easily.

It wasn't an office but a large closet. Three wire hangers hung from a wooden pole, and empty cardboard boxes lay on their sides. I sighed. Timothy would be disappointed I took the unnecessary risk of checking the second floor to find nothing. I was beginning to believe that Billy wasn't inside the factory and never had been there. Chief Rose was right. He was halfway to Mexico by now.

I closed the closet door and left the room. I stood on the landing and waved to Timothy.

"Did you find anything?" he called.

"No." I moved along the landing to the next door. It opened into another office suite. This one was laid out identically to the first. Thankfully, it didn't smell as badly, but it was in the same disarray as its matching office. I opened the closet door and shone the flashlight into the tiny space. The light bounced off a large orange duffel bag. I looked closer. Curt had said that Billy took an orange duffel bag when he left. There was also a small stockpile of canned food and dozens of empty beer bottles. A shiver overtook me. Timothy was been right—Billy had been camping out in the factory.

Still, I couldn't understand how he got up to the landing. How had the stairs held his weight when they couldn't hold Timothy's?

I backed out of the office to the landing.

"Find anything?" Timothy asked.

"Yes. Billy's not here, but I found his stuff." I paused. "He's living here."

"Great. You should come down now."

I pointed to the last door. "There's one more."

Timothy blew air out of his mouth. "Okay, but be quick."

As I moved to the last door, the landing narrowed slightly. I realized it was because a large piece of it had broken off and fallen to the floor below. Carefully, I tried the handle of the third door. It wouldn't budge. "It's locked," I called down to Timothy.

"Okay, we've been here long enough. Come down."

Tentatively, I made my way back across the landing and to the staircase. I placed my foot on the first step and a bolt gave way. I gasped. The staircase crashed to the floor. I gripped the hand rail and pulled myself back onto the landing, my heart inside of my throat. Dust from the factory floor billowed into my face. I scrambled to my feet. "Timothy!"

He coughed as the dust settled. "Are you okay?" His voice was sharp with concern.

I took a deep breath. "Yes. I'm fine."

I stood twenty feet above him. Jumping down on the shard-covered concrete floor was not an option. "There must be another staircase down."

"Was there an exit through the offices? Maybe there is back way out."

I gripped the railing. "No for the first two, and the third one is locked."

"We need to call for help then," Timothy said.

"I think it's time to call the chief."

Timothy grimaced. "Let me try Danny first. He can bring the extension ladder from our house."

Why was Timothy so reluctant to call the Appleseed Creek police chief? Should I call her myself? I was about to ask him both of those questions when Timothy removed his cell phone from his pocket. "There's no reception in here. We're too deep into the factory. I'm going to have to go outside."

I removed my cell from my pocket and found the same thing.

Timothy's forehead creased. "I don't like the idea of leaving you up there."

"I'll be fine. You'll only be gone for a few minutes. No one is here, including Billy."

He grimaced. "Don't move."

I lowered my chin. "Where would I go?"

He shook his head and walked back toward the entrance to the factory. I sat in front of the third office door, leaning my back against it, and hoped it wouldn't be a long wait for Danny to bring the ladder. I wished I had told Timothy to call Tee while he was outside. I didn't want her to worry when we did not return back at the expected time.

I heard a sound behind me, and strained to identify it. Just then, the door flew open in toward the office and I fell on my back. Hands grabbed me by both of my wrists and dragged me into the dark office.

Chapter Twenty-One

The hands let me go. The flashlight that had been sitting on my lap was nowhere to be found, but enough light shone through the broken windows of the office that I could make out the enormous shape of a man blocking my only way out of the office. Slivers of the sun's rays backlit his red hair, but his face remained in the shadows. Could he see me clearly?

I scrambled to my feet, my hands touching something wet on the floor. I shivered to think what that might be. "Billy, what are you doing?"

"Why are you here?" His words slurred and his breath reeked of alcohol.

I wiped my hand on my jeans. How many empty beer bottles had I counted in the second office? Fifteen? Twenty?

He swayed. "No one was supposed to find me here. Everyone was supposed to leave me alone. Why are you here?" He bellowed the question again.

I took a huge step back and my heel connected with the corner of a cot. I spun around and squinted in the gloomy space, able to make out an army cot and two plastic rolling crates. One crate overflowed with enough rolls of duct tape to wrap me into a human cocoon. I faced Billy again. Even in the dim light, he didn't look so good. Definitely drunk. Sober Billy had been affable and endearing. I had no idea what drunk Billy was like and had no desire to find out. "I'm here with your friend, Timothy."

He ran his hands down the length of his face. "He won't be my friend when he knows what I've done."

I shivered. "What have you done, Billy? Do you mean Katie Lambright?"

"No," he bellowed. "I had nothing to do with that Amish girl."

"Do you mean—"

"Chloe!" Timothy voice sounded muffled and far away. "Danny's on his way."

Billy launched at me and pressed his meaty hand across my mouth. His other arm wrapped around me, pinning my arms to my side.

"Chloe?" Timothy's voice pitched up an octave.

I struggled against Billy's grasp, smelling the alcohol on his clothing and his breath. I bit the inside of his bare hand. It tasted like salt and dirt. I gagged as Billy yowled and yanked his hand away. He bent over, nursing his injured hand, and I pushed him aside. He barely moved an inch, but it was enough for me to squeeze by him and throw open the office door. I half stumbled, half fell on to the narrow landing.

Timothy stared up at me. "Chloe, what's going on?"

I gasped for breath. "Billy. In. Office."

Timothy ran to the spot just below me. "I thought you said no one was up there."

"I guess I was wrong."

Behind me, Billy cried in anger. I dashed out of the way of the doorframe. With nowhere else to go, I ran to the end of the railing as Billy stumbled onto the landing. The mesh metal surface groaned under his added weight. Could it hold the both of us?

In the light, I saw Billy's bloodshot eyes. His clothes were caked with dirt and dust from living inside the warehouse, and the sleeve of his coat was torn. He gripped a roll of duct tape in his hand as if it were a life preserver. Billy had some of the most creative uses for duct tape, and I hoped he didn't have me in mind for any of them.

Billy took another step onto the landing. The metal screeched in protest. I moved to the far end of the platform, below a twenty-foot drop to the unforgiving floor.

Timothy's voice was tight. "Billy, stop. The landing can't hold both of you. Go back into the office."

Billy's eyes flicked away from my face and down to Timothy. "What are you doing here? You don't belong here. You're going to tell the police where to find me."

Timothy held out his hands. "Billy, please, what do you plan to do? Chloe's done nothing to you."

"She's here. You're both here, and now my one safe place is no longer safe. You are forcing me to leave."

"No one is forcing you to do anything. Chloe is your friend." Timothy's voice was confident, commanding, yet I could see the fear in his eyes. "You don't want to see her hurt, do you? If you keep walking on that platform, it's going to give and you both will be seriously hurt—or worse."

I leaned up against the railing with my back, and it gave a fraction of an inch. It was in as good of shape as the stairwell—which lay in pieces on the floor. Could I escape to the first office to hide? Did the door lock work? I couldn't remember if I saw a lock when I searched the room earlier, and the last thing I wanted was to be trapped in another office with Billy. I darted a glance toward that office. I had to try. Timothy was right—the landing couldn't hold the both of us much longer. I inched toward the first office door, roughly ten feet away from me.

Halfway along the landing, Billy's eyes seemed to focus on me, so I stood still, trying to steady the rise and fall of my chest. "Billy, you said that you had nothing to do with the death of the Amish girl. If something happens to me, no one will believe you. You will be charged with both crimes."

"Billy, she's right." Timothy's voice was tight.

I began inching to the first door again.

"I didn't hurt that girl." He closed his eyes for a moment as if reliving the discovery of Katie's body behind the Gundy barn. "She was already dead, long dead before I found her."

"Why didn't you tell the police?" Timothy asked. "Why did you run?"

I held out my hand. It was one arm's length from the doorknob.

He rounded on me, and I froze, still too far from the office door. His eyes clouded over. "Because I knew what would happen. *This* is actually what would happen. They would find out about my past and believe I did it. But I tell you I didn't." His voice rose. "I promise you I didn't. You know I've been to prison, don't you?"

"I . . . well . . ." I stumbled over my words.

"Billy, whatever you did years ago doesn't matter. What you do today does." Timothy voice was growing hoarse.

Billy's eyes grew sober. "You're wrong. The past *does* matter. I know the police chief believes I did it. She took one look at that barn and knew I was the one using it for storage. I have been for years. No one knew or cared what I did in the barn. There are no animals, and the Gundys have been gone for a long while now. I would never hurt anyone."

"Prove it by not hurting Chloe." Timothy's voice wavered ever so slightly.

Billy's eyes flashed and his brows lowered, but just as quickly the anger in them faded away. He slid to a seated position on the landing in front of the second office door. "How are we going to get down?" Billy moaned. "You've destroyed my sanctuary. This was my escape from all the bad in the world."

"You climbed the stairs to the landing?" Timothy asked.

Billy nodded. "Yes. I knew they were weakening and tried to only go up and down once per day."

My hand closed around the doorknob and I threw the first door open, only to discover my worst fear—a broken lock. My safe haven had disappeared. Billy may have seemed harmless sitting defeated on the landing, but his mood was unpredictable. And he still had the duct tape.

I shuffled back to my place at the end of the landing. I pressed a hand to my chest and felt the rapid beat of my heart. Danny was on the way, but would he arrive before the landing gave away completely?

Timothy held his useless cell phone in his hand. I knew what he was thinking. Was I safe enough for him to run outside and call Chief Rose? Like me, I was sure that he regretted not calling her from the very beginning. I cringed to think of the chief's reaction to our stupidity.

Billy pointed a sausage-like finger at his friend. "Don't call the police. I will throw her off this landing if you do, and you'd better hope you are a good catcher."

My stomach roiled. How could Billy say that to his friend? Timothy's lips stretched into a thin line as he tucked the phone back into his pocket. "What happened to you?" The sound of betrayal was thick in Timothy's voice.

Billy dropped his hands to his lap and refused to look at Timothy. Instead, he turned his gaze on me. I shivered in light of his wild expression.

"Should I call you Walter, then?" Timothy asked, making a grab for Billy's attention.

The larger man's head snapped around. Timothy's ploy had worked. "I don't go by that name any more. That was my past. I've changed."

"Have you changed, Billy? If you are willing to put Chloe in harm's way like this, I don't think you've changed at all. It looks like you are still living a life of crime. I don't know you at all. You really are Walter. Billy is gone."

Billy shook his head like a stubborn child, his chin lowered toward the floor. "No. No. I'm not like that at all. I'm not that man anymore. I made mistakes, and I paid for them."

Timothy tilted his head back farther. "If you paid for them, why is there still a warrant out for your arrest twelve years later?"

Billy struggled to his feet, his movement too much for the already taxed platform. The landing underneath my feet groaned, followed by an awful snap as the support gave way. Billy clawed the air for something to hold onto—and found nothing.

I squeezed my eyes shut and gripped the rickety railing, willing it to hold me. I whispered a prayer. Billy and his portion of the platform crashed to the floor, dust billowing into the air.

"Chloe!" Timothy screeched.

I waved the dust from my face, and coughed. "I'm okay. I'm still on the landing." I coughed again. "Where's Billy?"

Billy let out a deep, torturous groan. At least that told us he was alive.

Through the haze the dust created, Timothy knelt beside his friend. "Billy?"

Billy whimpered.

At this point, the platform was too unstable for me to take one step away from my little corner. The cloud of dust in the air was too thick for me to see how badly Billy was hurt.

Billy said something in a choked sob, but I couldn't understand what. The sound of screeching metal and his crash landing played over in my head.

Timothy coughed. "I think his leg is broken. It's at a weird angle, and he has a gash on his head that's bleeding pretty badly."

The dust began to settle enough for me to see their faces. Timothy ripped off his black wool winter coat and wrapped it over the wound on Billy's head. "This is not going to stop the bleeding without some pressure," he said.

I knew he was right. "Go call for help, then. But return as fast as you can, so you can hold that to his head."

"Right." Timothy jumped up and sprinted from the factory.

"Billy? Billy, it's going to be okay." My teeth chattered.

He moaned softly. I took any noise he made as a good sign. Billy's face was turned away from me, and I couldn't see his expression. I felt helpless trapped twenty feet above while Billy could be bleeding to death.

Timothy ran back into the factory. He fell to his knees beside Billy and held his coat down on the man's wound. "Paramedics and the police are on the way."

"Did you speak to Chief Rose directly?"

"No, I got Officer Nottingham. I'd still be on the phone if I had spoken to her. She's going to chew me out. That's for sure." Timothy glanced down. His tan sweater was soaked with blood. "Head wounds bleed a lot," he said. "It doesn't mean it's life threatening."

I didn't know if Timothy said that more for my benefit or for his.

Danny walked into the room carrying a ladder. He set it on the ground. "Whoa. Looks like I missed all the fun."

"Emergency is on its way," Timothy barked.

"Um, Tim when you called and said that you needed me to bring a ladder to get Chloe down you didn't say anything about

Billy bleeding from the head, and man, his leg don't look so good either."

"It just happened," Timothy said through gritted teeth. "Can you help Chloe down, please?"

"Oh, right." Danny picked up the ladder and placed it against the open end of what was left of the platform. "How'd you get up there?"

"Stairs."

He arched an eyebrow.

"There *used* to be stairs."

"If you say so." He raised the extension, and locked it at the proper height. "All you have to do is climb down."

Easier said than done. "How do I do that?"

"Swing your left leg around the side and then the right."

I gripped my railing, reluctant to let go of it. "Will it hold me?"

"This ladder holds good old boys four times your size for hours on end. Of course, it will hold you. Now, move it because I can't say the same for that platform."

The sound of sirens broke the air. I wanted to be down on the ground before Chief Rose showed up. She would not be a happy camper.

I swung my left leg onto the ladder. It didn't budge, but I wasn't as confident about moving my right leg. The platform under it wobbled. Before I could change my mind, I swung that leg onto the ladder too. A toaster-sized piece of the landing crashed to the floor.

Timothy watched me, gap-mouthed.

I waved at him from the security of the ladder.

Voices shouted back and forth to each other, and the sound of running footsteps echoed through the cavernous building. The cavalry had arrived. Carefully, I progressed down the ladder. Out of the corner of my eye, I saw three EMTs push Timothy away and start working on Billy.

"Will he be okay?" Timothy asked.

Three rungs from the floor, I heard, "Humphrey, you better have a good reason for this mess."

I hopped off the last rung to face Chief Rose, her face redder than I had ever seen it. If smoke began to pour out of her ears, I wouldn't be a bit surprised.

Timothy wrapped his arms around me, whispering in my ear, "Thank the Lord you weren't hurt." Dirt and dust caked his white-blond hair, giving it a grayish cast. He turned to the chief. "This wasn't Chloe's idea. She wanted to call you. I didn't. I was stubborn."

She narrowed her eyes at me. "I find that hard to believe. Typically, it's Humphrey getting you into trouble, not the reverse."

Timothy shook some of the dust from his hair. "It was my idea to come here and look for Billy. I knew this was the only place he could hide in the county. Anywhere else someone would have seen him in an instant."

Behind Timothy, an EMT gave Billy a shot in the leg. The mechanic cried out in pain.

Chief Rose's face was impassive. "I'd say you found him. I won't bother telling you both how stupid it was for you come into this deathtrap looking for him or that he may have been armed or that you are lucky that he's the one they are loading on the stretcher and not you." Her yellow-green eyes bored into Timothy. "Troyer, I thought you had grown up over the last few years. I'm disappointed to see that I was mistaken, sorely mistaken. I can't even look at either of you. Nottingham will take your statements and then you can go." She stomped away.

"I don't think I've ever seen her that angry," I said.

"She has every right to be. Everything she said was true. I let my pride get the best of me. I thought I could find Billy and talk him into turning himself in." His entire body shook, his voice uneven. "When I think what may have happened to you . . ."

I wrapped my arms around him. "Timothy, I'm fine, I'm safe. It was my idea to go up to the landing, remember? I can be just as stubborn as you can."

He pulled my arms away from him. "I'm sorry. I can't. I need to be alone."

"Alone?" My eyes traveled around the room. How did he expect to be alone? The place was crawling with police and emergency workers. In addition to Chief Rose and her crew, county deputies had arrived since technically they were outside of Appleseed Creek's village limits and the chief's jurisdiction.

Timothy's lips were pale. "I did it again."

Hoping that he wouldn't push me away a second time, I gripped his hand. It was ice cold. He had lost his gloves when he had tried to help Billy. "Did what again?"

"Paralyzed someone."

I shook my head. "No. Is that what the EMTs said?"

"They don't have to."

Five burly EMTs carefully rolled Billy onto his back. After strapping him into place, they lifted him onto their shoulders and slowly picked their way over the littered floor and out of the factory.

Chapter Twenty-Two

Still inside of the factory, I waited a few feet away from Timothy as he recited his statement to Officer Nottingham. Over and over again he said that it was his fault, that he should be held responsible.

His determination to take the blame for Billy's accident was tied to the guilt he felt for the fall that paralyzed Aaron from the waist down. Anytime Aaron joked about being confined to his wheelchair, sadness washed over Timothy's face. Aaron forgave his best friend years ago, but I didn't believe that Timothy ever forgave himself for what happened. The two had been working on a carpentry project on an upper floor balcony. Timothy, who was the expert carpenter of the two, told Aaron he had built the balcony wrong and that it would not hold. Aaron would not agree, and the two argued. The argument ended when Timothy dared Aaron to jump on the balcony to prove its sturdiness. Aaron did and fell twelve feet to the hard ground breaking his back.

Timothy wasn't the only one unable to forgive himself over the accident. Deacon Sutter, Aaron's father, was unable to forgive

Timothy as well. Timothy believed all of the deacon's animosity toward the Troyer family could be tied back to this one event. Billy's fall packed more guilt onto his shoulders.

The ambulance—with sirens blaring, lights flashing, and Billy secured inside—was on its way to the community hospital in Mount Vernon. If it turned out that Billy's injuries were more serious, like the broken back Timothy believed, he would be transported to a hospital in Columbus.

Officer Nottingham replaced the cap of his ballpoint pen. "Okay. I think that's all I need to write the report."

"Chief Rose doesn't want to talk to us again?" My voice was hopeful. I didn't want to be on the police chief's bad side.

Nottingham pursed his lips as he glanced over to Chief Rose who picked through the scene with a metal rod. "No. And my advice would be to leave her be for a few days. She's not happy with either of you."

We found Danny outside of the factory holding onto Mabel's leash. He handed it to Timothy. "I thought she should move around a bit. She was barking her head off when the cops arrived."

Mabel leaned her body against Timothy's leg as if she knew her master needed comforting. "Thanks," Timothy said to Danny. "I'll see you back at the house after I take Chloe home."

We rode in silence back to Young's so I could collect my car. Every time I opened my mouth to ask Timothy how he was, I thought better of it.

He turned into the parking lot, and all the lights were on inside the restaurant.

"Do you want to come over for dinner? We have a ton of food left from Becky's Christmas party," I said.

He shook his head.

"Okay. Good night."

He reached across the bench seat and squeezed my wrist. "You know I'm not mad at you, don't you?"

"Yes," I said, knowing my lack of conviction would leave him unconvinced. Timothy smiled a little. He heard the doubt in my voice too.

"Seeing Billy fall like that brought back a lot of bad memories. Memories I thought that I had already dealt with."

"You know Aaron doesn't blame you for what happened."

"Yes, I know, but I do." He squeezed my wrist again. "That's something I need to work out with *Gott*."

Timothy's comment made me think of my own personal demons: my mother's death and my relationship with my father. If I didn't deal with them, would they floor me like Timothy's seemed to do? "I wish I could help you."

"You already have. More than you'll ever know."

I kissed his cheek and patted Mabel good-bye before climbing out of the truck.

When I turned the Bug in the Quills' driveway, I saw Becky and Tanisha move back and forth in front of the windows. Grandfather Zook must have brought Tanisha home from the Troyer farm. I was relieved. I didn't want to go to the farm and answer the many questions the family must have.

In the living room, I found Tanisha and Becky twirling around the room to "Rockin' Around the Christmas Tree." Apparently, neither of them cared that Christmas was technically over.

Tanisha stopped. "Chloe, you're home. Finally. What took so long?"

Becky's straight white-blonde hair swung around her face as she spun around the couch. It had been cut to shoulder length.

"Becky, what happened to your hair?" I demanded.

She froze. "You don't like it?" She touched the back of her head self-consciously.

"I—I—you cut your hair."

Becky dropped her hand. "I told you that I wanted to. You said I should."

I shook my head. "I didn't say that you *should.* I said that it was up to you."

She placed her hands on her hips. "So I made my decision. I told Tanisha about it, and she volunteered to do it."

Tee's brow furrowed. "What's the big deal? She already wears jeans and makeup."

"I know, but this is permanent. What will your parents say?"

Becky face flushed red. "It doesn't matter what my parents think. This is *my* hair."

"But you can't take it back," I said.

She stared me down. "Who says that I want to? Do you want me to go back to the Amish?"

"No, of course not."

Becky crossed her arms in front of her. "Then what does it matter?"

I felt sick. "What about Aaron?"

Becky's mouth fell open. "What about him?"

I removed my coat. "I thought you cared for him."

"I do," she said slowly. "More than you know."

"He will have to leave the Amish to be with you. He will be shunned."

"Chloe, you don't have to tell *me* how the Amish world works. You think just because you're dating my brother—who's not even Amish anymore—makes you an expert."

"No, I didn't say that." Her words landed like a slap across my face.

She scowled at me. "You don't know how hard this is for me."

I placed a hand to my throbbing forehead. I was too tired for this conversation. I could barely think straight.

"I can't be who he needs me to be. I told you that." Her voice had pitched up an octave.

My heart ached when I thought about what Aaron would suffer. "You need to tell him."

"Don't tell me what to do. You're not my sister."

I lowered my voice. "I know that, Becky."

She dropped her arms by her side and looked away. "I'm going to bed. I have to be at the restaurant early tomorrow. It's my turn to bake the pies." Then she turned and stomped out of the room.

I fell onto the couch. It was the first fight that I'd had with Becky. After my emotional day with Timothy and Billy, this was the last thing I needed. I narrowed my eyes. "Tee, I can't believe that you cut her hair without checking with me first."

Tanisha reared back. "Asking you first? Why would I have to ask you first? She's an adult."

"You don't understand what a big deal this is for an Amish girl."

"And you do?" Tanisha folded her arm. "Chloe, it's just hair. Hair will grow back."

I thought of the young women who had their hair cut through the spree of Amish haircutting a month ago. It wasn't just hair to them. They would give anything for it to have never been cut in the first place. "You don't understand."

"Like you do? Chloe, I think Becky is right. You aren't an Amish expert."

I sucked in air. When I didn't respond, Tanisha said, "I'm going home tomorrow as planned. I will see you in the morning. I promise not to cut anymore hair while I'm here."

I let my head fall back onto the couch. "Tee, I'm sorry. I've had . . ." I let my voice trail off because I spoke to an empty room.

Chapter Twenty-Three

The phone rang before the sun rose the next morning. I grabbed for it on my nightstand. "Hello?" I croaked.

"Humphrey, good, you're awake," Chief Rose said. By her tone, I could tell that she was pleased with herself for waking me up.

I wished I had water for my dry mouth. "Is something wrong? Is Billy okay?"

"His name is not Billy. It's Walter."

I struggled to a seated position on the bed. "Fine. Is Walter okay?"

"That's why I'm calling. He's stable and sober. His leg is broken and the wound on his head is shallow. He's lucky to be alive. The doctors think the fact that he was dead drunk worked in his favor. He was completely limp when he fell. Had his body been able to tense up, his injuries may have been much worse."

I exhaled. "That's great news."

"Now that Walter is sober, he wants to talk to you and Troyer. He refuses to talk to me unless his lawyer is around."

I wasn't eager to see Billy again. "Tyler is his lawyer. I'm sure he will cooperate with you."

"You're not getting off that easy, Humphrey. He's willing to talk to both of you without Hart there. You will listen to what he says and report back to me. You're going to do this for me because you screwed up royally yesterday. Got it?"

"Got it." I punched my pillow. "Have you called Timothy to tell him?"

"No. Troyer is on my punk list at the moment. I will leave that up to you."

"How much longer do you plan to stay mad at him?"

"I haven't decided. I might make him sweat until next year."

"Next year is only five days away."

"Don't tell him that. Seriously, Humphrey, if anyone in this town should know the cost of a stunt like that, he should have. Give him the message." She hung up.

"He knows," I whispered. I called Timothy's number from my cell phone. No answer. I repeated the message that Chief Rose gave me.

Gigabyte saw that I was awake and yowled into my face as if to say, *Since your eyes are open, you must be able to feed me.*

I rolled over on my side and covered my head with my pillow. "Go bother Becky," I said in a muffled voice. "You won't like what I give you anyway."

He pawed at the pillow and yowled again, closer to my ear. His best Siamese screeches could crack glass.

I groaned. "Fine, but as soon as I'm done, I'm coming right back to bed."

He gave me a pleasant *meow* and hopped to the floor. I swore the cat understood English.

Tanisha was in the kitchen drinking coffee. She gave me a small smile. "I guess I'm not totally accustomed to the trans-Atlantic time change yet. I'm sure I will be just in time to fly back to Italy."

"Probably so." I removed Gig's cat food from the cupboard. The tawny-colored animal wove in and around my ankles, purring as if two of his feline lives depended on it.

"Chloe, I just want to apologize for last night. I didn't know you would be so upset or that it was such a big deal. I gave Becky the haircut she wanted. I didn't know there was anything more to it than that."

"I know. It's as much Becky's fault. She knows what a haircut meant for her."

"Can she really not go back to the Amish?"

"I don't know. I know that she doesn't want to go back, but if she doesn't, Aaron will be the one who will have to make the tough choice about leaving." I sighed and set Gig's food dish on the floor and turned back to Tee. "I'm not upset that Becky cut her hair. If that's what she wanted to do or felt that she needed to do, I supported her all the way. I was upset because you did it." I smiled sheepishly. "And I might be a little jealous that I wasn't here."

"Ah," Tanisha said and pointed to a nine-by-twelve envelope on the table.

"What's that?" I asked.

"Becky's hair. She said that you thought she should donate it to charity, like Locks of Love."

I smiled. "I did. I'm glad she remembered. It will be a blessing to someone who needs it." I sat at the table and picked up the envelope. It was already sealed and addressed in Becky's handwriting. "Becky's so angry with me. I need to apologize, but I won't see her until she finishes work later this afternoon."

"We could go there and talk to her."

I shook my head. "Aaron will be there. I don't want to have the conversation in front of him."

Tanisha set a mug of coffee in front of me. "Extra milk, just how you like it."

"Thanks." I curved my cold hands around the ceramic surface.

"Enough about Becky and her hair." Tanisha grinned. "I have a few hours left here. What should we do?"

Chief Rose's instructions to visit Billy in the hospital came to mind, but it was too early in the morning to do that. "Are you up for some sleuthing?"

"Oh my, yes. I think that is just what the doctor ordered." Her brow wrinkled. "Why did you come home so late last night?"

I took a deep breath and told her about my near-death experience.

Her eyes widened. "Why didn't you tell me yesterday?"

"Because of everything that was happening with Becky. I didn't want to add to the drama."

Tanisha stirred a fourth spoonful of sugar into her coffee. "Are we going to talk to this Billy guy?"

"No, we're going grocery shopping."

Tanisha added a fifth scoop of sugar. She wasn't a big fan of coffee. "Groceries?"

I nodded. "To pay a visit to your good buddy, Jason Catcher."

Tee grimaced as she sipped from her mug and made a face. "Will I have to sit on him again?"

"Not this time," I promised.

Chapter Twenty-Four

Evergreens and plastic holly decorated the entrance to Appleseed Marketplace. Beside the collection of grocery carts, a pink tinseled Christmas tree stood crookedly in its stand. Tanisha pulled a cart from the line. "Is that a pink Christmas tree?"

"Yep."

"I love this place." She beamed. "I feel like we have suddenly walked back into the time of black-and-white television and rotary phones. I bet I could find some fun gifts here for my Italian friends. They will think it's a hoot."

The market smelled like over-ripe vegetables and dirt. I grabbed a second shopping cart from the stand. It was part of my cover.

The market was a no-frills experience in one large room. There was a deli counter in the back, a display of Amish-made products from pies to relishes next to that, and the rest of the space was dedicated to produce. Two checkout counters stood by the front door. A bored-looking woman in a jingle bell Christmas sweater rang up a customer. Christmas was over, but I guessed she wasn't ready to say good-bye to her holiday sweaters just yet.

I wondered if Jason would be at the market today. I didn't know his schedule, so we could have been wasting our time. My concerns flew away when I spied a tall, gawky kid with sandy-colored hair stacking oranges in the produce section.

"There he is," I whispered to Tanisha.

Tanisha held a jar of pickles in her hand. She glanced at Jason, then placed the jar in her shopping cart.

"What are they for? You aren't going to take them all the way back to Italy, are you?"

"Why not?"

The image of broken glass and pickles all over Tee's clothes in her checked luggage came to mind. "What if the jar breaks?"

"It won't break," she said confidently.

I shrugged. "If you say so."

She leaned close to me. "Do you think Katie dated this guy? I thought the Amish and English weren't allowed to do that."

"They're not. This could be a good motive for murder." I ducked behind a display of cookies. "He's not going to be happy to see us."

She pushed the shopping cart forward. "Then this should be fun." She rolled the cart and came to a stop beside Jason. "Jason, long time no see."

Jason froze, an orange in his hand suspended in the air over his pyramid. "You!"

Tanisha cocked her head. "Is that any way to greet an old friend?"

"What are you doing here?" he hissed.

"A little shopping. I live in Italy, so I'm looking for some unique gifts for my roommates. Do you have any suggestions?"

"Oranges?" he stuttered. "We're having a big sale. We have four varieties. All from Florida. This is the best time of the year for citrus."

"I don't think I can pass those through customs."

His face flushed. "Oh."

I gripped the handlebar of my grocery cart. "Jason, you have to know that we aren't here about oranges. We need to talk to you about yesterday—and about how Katie died."

Jason dropped the orange on top of the pyramid, and the stack cascaded to the floor in a citrus wave. Shoppers hopped out of the way as rolling oranges bounced off their carts' wheels. An elderly woman hit an orange so hard with her cane that it sent orange juice and pulp flying in all directions.

The bored cashier shook her head. "Catcher, if any those are ruined, they are coming out of your paycheck."

His shoulders drooped. "My boss is going to kill me. I'm already on notice."

I picked up an orange that came to rest by my foot. "Is the lady at the register your boss?"

"No, but Marlene thinks she is. She's like a hundred years old and has worked here since before my dad was born." He made a face. "I need to start cleaning up."

Tanisha picked up two of the rogue pieces of fruit. "We can help." She cocked her head. "Why are you already on notice?"

He held up his left hand and showed a huge bandage on his thumb. "They let me try working in the deli. It didn't go well."

I grimaced and made a mental note not to buy meat at the market. Ever.

"Catcher, stop talking and clean up that mess." Marlene's hoarse voice cracked. She turned to her customers. "I don't know what they teach these kids in school today. They can't do the simplest tasks."

Jason gathered oranges from the concrete floor and carefully placed them inside the bushel basket at his feet with a dramatic sigh. The pyramid would have to be started again from the beginning.

I grabbed a shopping basket from the end of the lettuce counter and start collecting some in there.

"You don't have to help me," he said as he dropped five oranges into the basket.

I added three more oranges into mine. "We want to help."

When my basket was full of oranges, I grabbed a second one. Tanisha finished filling one as well. Jason got a mop and bucket and cleaned up the orange pulverized by the lady's cane. When that was done, he began reassembling the pyramid.

Tanisha set her basket of oranges by mine on the floor. "Maybe I shouldn't have startled you like that."

"Yeah," Jason agreed. "You tackling me yesterday wasn't cool either."

"Sorry," Tanisha said but could not hide the humor in her voice. "Now about Katie—"

"I don't want to talk about Katie," he said through gritted teeth.

"Okay," I said. "Then tell me how you know Billy Thorpe."

"Who's that?" He placed three more oranges on the pyramid.

I folded my arms. "Come on, Jason. Uncle Billy of Uncle Billy's Budget Autos? You know it."

He lowered his head and hid his eyes behind his hair. "Sure I know of that shop. Billy is the only mechanic in town."

"You know Billy better than that or you wouldn't have been at the Gundy barn yesterday."

"I—I don't know what you're talking about."

Tanisha was losing patience. "If you didn't know him, why did you dig that hole?"

"I . . ."

"Come on, Jason," I said. "I know that Chief Rose already asked you all of these questions. She would not have let you go if she hadn't felt like she'd gotten good answers from you. How do you know Billy?"

"Sometimes I work at the shop. Nothing official."

"What do you do there?"

"Just odd jobs when he needs help. I like working on cars."

Tanisha cocked an eyebrow. "Does he pay you under the table?"

Jason ignored the question and concentrated on his oranges with renewed interest.

I took the orange from his hand. "Did Billy call you about a job?"

His shoulders sagged. "Yes. On Christmas, he called me. He wanted me to go to the Gundy's old barn and dig up a box for him. He wanted me to go right then, but I couldn't. It was Christmas. My mom would freak if I left the house, especially with my grandparents there. It's my job to keep Grandma and Grandpa out of Mom's kitchen on holidays."

Tanisha pursed her lips. I knew that look. She was trying not to laugh.

"Did he tell you why he wanted you to dig up the box?" I asked.

Jason's forehead crinkled. "He said that he was out of town and couldn't get there, but he needed the box to be moved because there was important stuff inside."

"Did you ask him what that important stuff was?"

"No." He turned the color of a blood orange. "But I planned to open the box when I found it. I almost had it out, and then you two showed up."

"Sorry to ruin your party," Tanisha said.

I wasn't sure what to believe about Jason's story. Did he trust Billy enough to follow his directions without questioning him? Tanisha must have been thinking along the same lines because she asked, "How much was Billy going to pay you for this little errand?"

The pyramid of oranges was halfway back to its original height. "He didn't pay me anything."

Tanisha placed her hand on one hip and looked like a model with an attitude. "We know he didn't pay you anything because you didn't finish the job, but how much did he offer to pay you? You didn't trudge across the snowy tundra and dig a hole into the frozen ground for free."

Jason's lips quivered. "He promised me five hundred dollars."

Tanisha whistled. "I'd dig a hole for five hundred dollars. Where do I sign up?"

I elbowed her. "How were you going to deliver it to him?"

Jason sighed. "I was supposed to meet him at the wildlife reserve off of Route 13."

That wasn't too far from the factory where Billy had been hiding out. "Did you know where he was staying?"

Jason shook his head. When I talked to Billy later that day, I would see if Jason's story held up. Hopefully, their stories would match. I moved on. "How did you know Katie?"

He set four oranges in a line. "We were friends."

I folded my arms. "That's pretty unusual for an Amish girl to be friends with an English boy, isn't it?"

He shrugged a second time. "I guess."

"How did you meet?"

He scowled. "None of your business."

Tanisha gave him one of her most dazzling smiles. "Come on, Jason, we were doing so well. What difference does it make if you answer our questions about Katie now?"

He seemed to consider her question.

Tanisha repeated my question. "How did you and Katie meet?"

He straightened an orange on the pyramid. "She used to work at the cheese shop on the square and I saw her walk home every day from work. My family lives a couple of miles down the road from the Lambright farm, so one day it was raining really hard and I offered her a ride."

"She accepted a ride from a stranger?"

Jason glared at Tee. "I wasn't a stranger; I was her neighbor. We'd seen each other lots of times growing up."

"Were your families friendly then?" I asked.

Jason flicked his dark eyes in my direction. "No. Her parents didn't have much use for *Englischers*," he said, mocking the Pennsylvania Dutch word for non-Amish.

"When did you offer her that first ride?" Tanisha asked.

His pushed his glasses up the bridge of his nose with his thumb. "About two years ago. We chatted on the way home. She was really funny and friendly. Not like other Amish girls I've met or even most regular American girls. She was the first girl to take an interest in me."

Tanisha pounced on that comment. "An interest in you? Like as a boyfriend?"

He fingered combed his hair over his glasses. "No. Katie would never have thought of me in that way. I wasn't Amish." His voice was laced with bitterness. He added two more oranges to his structure. "We were friends. That was it. After that first one, I gave her rides home a lot. We could talk about things, like what we both really wanted. Katie and I understood each other."

"How did her family feel about you giving her rides if they didn't like non-Amish people?" Tanisha asked.

He picked up the shopping basket I filled with oranges and began setting them one by one back into place. His Adam's apple bobbed. "They didn't know. Katie always had me drop her off out of sight of the farm even when the weather was really bad. Her dad is a tyrant and her stepmother is a terror. They would have never allowed Katie to ride in my car." He frowned. "They'd rather she'd freeze to death on the side of the road."

Tanisha moved her basket of oranges closer to Jason. "Do you think her parents would become angry enough to hurt her?"

"I—I don't know."

I shifted my feet. "How well do you know Caleb King?"

His eyes flashed as he straightened up. "He's a jerk. I told Katie to break up with him. I knew if she married him, she'd be sorry. He's just like her father."

"What do you mean?" Tanisha asked.

Jason ignored her question. "Nathan was better for her."

"You know Nathan?" I asked.

"No. I know what she told me."

"What did she tell you about Caleb?"

He turned to me with eyes shining with tears. "What does it matter now? She's dead."

"Jason, that's exactly why it matters."

The woman at the cash register snapped her gum and glared at us. "Catcher, you think you're on break or something? Stop flirting and get back to work."

Jason's face turned red. "I can't talk to you anymore about this."

I leaned forward so the clerk couldn't hear me. "Can we talk another time?"

"No."

"What about Anna?"

He stared at me. "Katie's little sister?"

"Don't you want to help her? She wants to know what happened to Katie. She asked me for help. What was Katie's relationship with Anna?"

His mouth turned downward. "She loved Anna. Her sister was her whole world and the only reason she stayed in that awful house." He shuddered. "The last thing Katie would have wanted would be to leave Anna alone with no one to protect her."

"Protect her from whom?" Tanisha asked.

The cashier's glare dug into the back of my neck.

Jason's eyes flicked toward the cashier. "I'm done with my shift at three. If you want to meet me in the parking lot then, I'll talk to you."

"Thank you, Jason." I pulled on Tanisha's arm. It was time to go before Jason changed his mind.

Tanisha pulled a plastic bag from the turnstile and placed five oranges inside. "I'm ready to go." She walked to the cashier to check out.

The cashier snapped her gum. "What are two pretty girls like you doing talking to that screw-up? He's never had a girl look at him in his life." She said this loud enough for everyone in the small market, including Jason, to hear.

Tanisha gave her one of her more brilliant smiles. "I think he's cute." She slapped a five on the counter. "That should cover the ruined oranges."

Hiding a smile, I followed my best friend out into the parking lot.

Tee snorted as she zipped up her coat just outside of the automatic doors. "That woman was awful. I don't know how Jason can work with her all day long."

"He probably doesn't have much of a choice. There aren't many non-Amish jobs in Appleseed Creek."

"That stinks that he can't talk until three. I promised my mom that I would be on my way home by then. I'm kind of getting into this sleuthing thing."

"We can make one more stop for you to exercise your detective skills on."

She rubbed her hands together. "Are we going to question the boyfriend? He's usually the main suspect."

I shook my head. "We're going to buy some cheese."

Chapter Twenty-Five

Tanisha inhaled the earthy scent of the cheese shop. "I must buy some for my mom. She loves Amish cheese. It might make up for me coming down here and not spending every waking minute with the fam." She picked up a basket and fell into line with the other English shoppers taste-testing the cheeses from the room-long, open-air coolers. "Horseradish." She popped it into her mouth. "Wow, that has a kick." She scooted closer to me. "Who are we looking for?"

"The girl stocking the mustard display."

Tee whipped her head around and examined Debbie Stutzman, a tall and thin Amish girl with a slightly slumped posture, the kind often found in girls who wished they were shorter.

I poked her. "Can you be a little more subtle?"

"No need to be subtle. She already knows you're here. She's glaring at you. What did you do for her to dislike you so much?"

I sighed. "Got her arrested."

"What?" Tee yelped.

"Shh, it's a long story, and I'm not going to tell it to you here," I hissed.

"Fair enough." Tee started in Debbie's direction. "I think Mom would like some Amish mustard too."

I suppressed a groan and followed her.

Debbie crossed her bony arms. "What do you want?"

I wasn't surprised by the cold reception, considering that the last time I saw Debbie she was being handcuffed and read her rights by Chief Rose.

When I didn't answer right away, she said, "I know you're not here to buy cheese."

Tanisha shook her head. "We are. I'm making a gift basket for my mother. A belated Christmas gift. I have horseradish in here. What mustard do you recommend to go with that?"

Debbie appraised Tee with her small eyes. "I wouldn't put any mustard with it. It has enough bite on its own."

"You're right about that," Tanisha agreed.

"I see you have Amish Swiss in your basket. Our natural mustard will go well with that." Debbie, now more relaxed, removed a four-ounce jar from the shelf.

"That's not much," Tee said.

"It will last you a long time. It's not like mustard from the supermarket where you have to slather it on to taste it." She opened the taster jar, dipped a tiny white plastic spoon into it, and then handed the spoon to Tanisha. "Try it."

Tee placed the spoon in her mouth and her eyes watered. "Wow! Now that's a kick." Tee put two jars into her basket.

"Debbie, Tanisha is here to shop, but I want to talk to you about Katie Lambright."

Debbie fixed a hair pin that was falling out of her prayer cap. "Are you wearing a wire today?"

I cringed. "No."

"Is that police chief with you?"

I shook my head. "We heard that Katie worked here."

Debbie's expression was hooded. "She did, but she quit almost six months ago."

Six month ago. Why hadn't Jason mentioned that?

"Was she a friend of yours?" Tanisha asked while adding a jar of corn relish to her basket. At this rate her mother, who could not cook to save her life, would have a full Amish pantry.

Debbie glanced at her. She seemed more open to talk to Tee, and that was fine with me. I understood her hesitation around me. "We were friendly, but we weren't close friends. Katie was always more interested in boys than in girlfriends. There was also a new Amish boy coming around the shop hoping to court her. She was a very pretty girl, so it's no surprise. When word got around the county she had broken up with Caleb King, it was the worst. There wasn't a moment of peace in the shop with all the hopeful young men dropping by. It didn't last long though. She moved on to Nathan Garner within a few weeks."

"Why did she quit?" Tanisha asked, taking the lead in questioning.

She shrugged. "I don't know. I told you we didn't talk much unless it was about work, and there is only so much you can say about cheese. She worked here a long time, nearly five years." She pushed her cart away from the mustard display and in front of the Colby and cheddar cheeses.

Tanisha sniffed a wedge of white cheddar. "Did she find another job?"

"I don't know." She stacked Colby cheese in a pile on a bed of plastic grass. "I always thought she left because of that *Englischer* who hung around the shop. He seemed to make her nervous."

Jason.

"What was his name?" I asked.

Debbie shot me a dirty look. "I heard her call him Jason once."

Tanisha added a small round of Colby to her basket. "Did she ever say anything about him?"

Debbie shook her head. "*Nee,* but most days when it was near to closing time, he waited for her outside in his car. She was always extra nervous when the *Englischer* was around. She became clumsy, dropping jars and baskets or tripping over her own two feet when he was outside."

"Would she have confided in anyone here at the shop about him?"

She shook her head. "Like I said, she didn't really talk to any of the ladies. She was quiet."

Debbie straightened the cheddar on the bed of artificial grass. "Mr. Umble, who owns the cheese shop, got tired of the *Englischer* standing around outside of his shop. One day last summer he went out to confront the boy. He told him that he wasn't allowed to park in front of the cheese shop anymore. Didn't make much of a difference. The *Englischer* just moved his car to a spot by the square where he could continue to watch the store. It was unnerving. I didn't like to go out there by myself when he was watching. Katie quit a week after that."

Debbie peered into Tanisha's basket. "You have some good stuff there, but have you tried the mint-chocolate cheese?"

Tanisha's eyes glowed. "Mint-chocolate cheese? Tell me more."

"Follow me." Debbie led Tee across the room to the specialty sweet cheeses.

I stayed by the mustard. Debbie's account of Jason wasn't meshing with the awkward teen that Tanisha and I questioned at the market. Was he a goofy kid head over heels in love with an Amish girl? Or a crazy stalker? Had I been wrong about him? I hurried over to Debbie and Tanisha, my friend's basket so full of cheese and other Amish foods she could barely lift it. Debbie grinned ear to ear as she rung up the sale.

We loaded all the cheese Tanisha bought into my car. "I kind of feel bad that your visit has turned into a murder investigation."

Tanisha shrugged. "I don't mind."

"Well, I do. Can you stay an hour longer than planned?"

"Maybe," she said with a grin. "What are we going to do?"

"It's a surprise. First we need to go back to the house and change into warmer clothes, and then we pick up the Troyer kids."

Chapter Twenty-Six

Thomas and Naomi squealed with delight as they sledded down the hill on a toboggan at the back end of Harshberger's campus.

"You're next," I told Tanisha, who sat on a second toboggan. I gave her a running start. Her scream was three times louder than the children's.

Thomas and Naomi waited for her at the bottom of the hill, jumping up and down. "Tee! Tee!"

I smiled. My nickname for Tanisha was much easier for them to pronounce than her given name.

The trio climbed back up the hill, which wasn't particularly high compared to the hills that Tanisha and I had sledded down as children. Knox County was much flatter than our hometown in Cuyahoga County. The only thing that would have made the afternoon better was if Ruth had agreed to come with us.

"It's your turn," Thomas shouted and handed me the string of the toboggan.

I took it. "Okay. Who wants to ride with me?"

Naomi waved her hand in the air.

"Let's do it." I positioned the toboggan to face downhill and sat on it. Naomi snuggled in front of my lap.

"I'll give you a push." Thomas's mittened hands dug into the upper part of my back.

"Not too hard," I told him. "Naomi is riding with me."

"*Ya*, not too hard," Thomas assured me.

I knew that Thomas had every intention of sending us catapulting down the hill. I wrapped my arms around Naomi. "Okay, go!"

I could no longer feel Thomas's hands on my back as we flew down the hill. Naomi squealed with delight. I heard myself squeal too. Faintly, I recognized the shouts of Tanisha and Thomas at the top of the hill, cheering us on.

At the bottom, Naomi and I rolled off the sled in a heap. I tickled her and she giggled. We struggled to our feet and waved to Tee and Thomas above. My wave froze. Behind Tanisha, a man stood watching us—and it looked like Curt. "Tee!" I cried.

She laughed and waved, but missed the urgency in my voice.

Naomi clung to my arm. I picked up the rope to the toboggan, and we made our way up the hill. Because of the angle, I could no longer see Curt anymore. "Tee, there's someone up there with you."

This time she heard me and glanced behind her. She looked back at me and held her hands aloft.

Naomi and I reached the top of the hill, but Curt was nowhere to be seen.

"I saw him too," Naomi whispered.

"Tee, can you keep sledding here with the kids? I thought I saw someone. I'm just going to go check to see if I can find him."

Thomas was already on the next toboggan cruising down the hill.

Tanisha's forehead crinkled. "Okay."

Curt's footprints were easy to follow in the snow. The sledding hill stood behind the gym, and his footprints stopped at the edge of a large parking lot. Curt's beat-up green pickup sat near the curb in front of the gymnasium doors. The sight of it made me sick to my stomach.

I ducked behind the side of the building. Should I stay or should I go? I peeked around the corner. Brock, Curt's best friend, leaned against the hood of the truck and his voice carried across the still winter air. "If I hear one more thing about that girl I'm going to puke. Seriously man, I can hardly stand you anymore."

That girl? Katie? Did Brock and Curt have something to do with her death?

Curt stuck his hands deep into his jeans pockets. "I think she might be doing something right."

Brock sneered, an expression I found disconcerting on his smooth features, "'Course she is. Red is a goody two-shoes. Is that what you want to be too?"

I took in a sharp breath. *Red?* They weren't talking about Katie . . . they were talking about me.

Curt winced. "If I could talk to her—"

"That would take guts to go up and talk to her, and you surely haven't shown any of those lately. I don't even understand you anymore, man."

Curt opened the door to the truck's cab. "I need time to think."

Brock pointed a finger at him. "That right there is your problem."

"Let's just leave, okay?" Curt said.

"Fine by me," Brock replied. He stomped around the vehicle to the passenger side of the truck and got in.

Curt gunned the engine, and the duo peeled away—thankfully in the opposite direction of my hiding place.

When I could no longer hear the truck, I ran back to Tee and the children.

"Everything okay?" Tanisha asked when I made it back.

I nodded, but some of the joy of the day had vanished.

After we dropped off the children, I drove us back to the house so that Tanisha could pack for Cleveland. Inside the guest room, I felt an ache in my chest as I watched my friend gather her clothes. Even though she had only stayed with Becky and me for two days, her possessions were strewn all over the room. I smiled as I wondered how her roommates in Italy dealt with her messy habits. That was the only thing I didn't miss about living with Tanisha.

Tanisha chewed on her lower lip. "Chloe, after hearing what Debbie had to say, I don't know if you should talk to Jason alone. He seemed harmless in person, but she made him out to be a nutcase."

"I won't talk to him alone," I promised. "I'll ask Timothy if he will go with me." *If I can find him,* I mentally added. I hadn't heard from Timothy since he dropped me off at the house last night. I called and texted. No answer.

Tanisha wadded up a T-shirt and threw it into her overnight bag. "What's that face for?"

I blinked. "What face?"

She placed her hands on her hips. "Please. I've known you my entire life. When you said Timothy's name, your face pinched. Is something wrong in paradise?"

"No. Nothing is wrong. At least I don't think so. He was just really shook up about what happened in the factory yesterday."

"Anyone would be."

"It's more personal for Timothy." I told her about Aaron's accident.

Her brow shot up. "This is the same Aaron that you were all upset about Becky cutting her hair over yesterday?"

I nodded.

She gave me a reassuring smile. "I have something to cheer you up—your Christmas gift," Tanisha said.

I smoothed the comforter on the bed. "If I'd known you were coming, I would have had something for you too."

She placed a hand on her hip. "Please. Those iTunes credits you e-mailed me were perfect. You don't know how starved I am for music over there." She rooted through her bag and removed a crumpled business-size envelope and handed it to me. "Merry Christmas."

I turned the envelope over in my hand. "*This* is my gift?"

"Ignore the presentation. It's the contents that count. Oh, and the gift is from my parents and me. It was my idea, but their money."

Now I was really curious. I opened the envelope and removed a hot pink sheet of paper, which read, "Merry Christmas. This document entitles you to one round-trip airfare to Milan, Italy, at a date of your choosing. With love, The Greens."

I let the page float to my lap. "I . . . I . . ."

Tanisha jumped up and down. "You're coming to Italy." She squealed so loud she sounded much like Naomi on the toboggan.

I didn't say anything but read the paper over again just to make sure I understood it correctly.

"You will come, won't you? I've seen your new world, now I want you to see mine. This summer will be perfect. I will be off from teaching, and college here won't be busy." She stopped bouncing. "Why aren't you saying anything?"

"Tee, your family has already done so much for me. How can I accept this?"

She sat next to me on the bed. "Because you have to. It's a rule. You have to accept Christmas gifts. I read it somewhere."

I read the paper again and grinned. "Okay, I accept."

"Eeee!" She squished me against her in a mammoth hug. "I can't wait for you to come. We will have so much fun. We can go to Venice and Rome. It will be amazing."

"It sounds amazing," I agreed.

She hopped off the bed and started to cram everything she had taken out of her bag in search of my gift back into it. "I wish I could stay longer, but I promised Mom that I'd come back home today. I fly back to Italy on New Year's Eve." She rolled her eyes. "What a fun way to spend a holiday—in an airport. Mom wants you to come up and spend my last couple of days with us. You should. You don't have to work."

"I can't. I need to be here for—"

She grinned. "For Timothy. I get it. Just promise to spend your honeymoon in Italy, and I won't gripe about not having more time to spend with you."

I snorted. "Honeymoon?"

She smiled knowingly. "Cole never looked at me the way Timothy looks at you, and I never looked at him the way you look at Timothy. That engagement was doomed. We just fell into it because it was the logical next step after dating for such a long time. With you and Timothy it will be different." She jabbed her fists into her hips. "I'd better be your maid of honor."

I leaned forward and hugged her. "I promise that if I ever get married, you will be my maid of honor."

"Excellent. I'm going to start dress shopping in Milan. They have some gorgeous options there."

"Way out of your price range." I pointed at her basket. "Especially now that you spent half of your salary on cheese."

She pulled a brightly colored stocking cap onto her head. "You can't buy just one." She picked up her overnight bag. "Tell Becky and Timothy I said good-bye, okay? And tell Grandfather Zook that I want him to adopt me."

I laughed. "I will."

"And I expect you to go find that handsome carpenter the moment I leave and give him a great big hug."

My smile wavered. "I'll try to do that too."

Chapter Twenty-Seven

After Tanisha was gone, I retrieved my cell phone from my purse and called Timothy again. No answer. I knew I shouldn't be too concerned. Many times when Timothy was on a job with all the power saws and nail guns going off, he didn't hear his cell phone ring. However after last night, a kernel of anxiety plagued the corner of my mind. Was he avoiding me? I left him a voice mail early that morning telling him Chief Rose wanted us to visit Billy at the Mount Vernon hospital, but had he gotten the message?

I shook it off. If I couldn't reach Timothy, Chief Rose was the next best option. After the factory disaster, I planned to keep the chief abreast of all my movements.

"Chief Rose," her sharp voice barked into my ear. It lacked all of its typical humor. She was still angry and wanted me to know it.

"I have some information for you," I said, keeping my voice businesslike.

"What is it, Humphrey?"

"I spoke to Jason Catcher today."

"Did you sit on him?" Sarcasm leaked into her voice.

"No, and neither did Tanisha."

"Good to know. I had him down at the station for a couple of hours yesterday. I assume he told you about how Billy a.k.a. *Walter* was going to pay him for his trouble over the box."

"He did. Do you believe his story?"

"I don't see any reason not to as long as Walter corroborates it. I've seen folks do a lot worse things for five hundred bucks."

I was sure she had. "He also told me that he and Katie Lambright were friends, so much so that he gave her a ride home from the cheese shop on the square several times a week."

"Interesting," she said, her voice holding a friendlier quality. "What else you got?"

"He also alluded that the Lambrights' home life wasn't good."

"Abuse?" The sound of her voice had turned sharp again.

"Maybe. I'm going to talk to Anna again about it."

"Be careful. If the girls were being abused, too many questions will make her clam up. I will say that when Troyer and I left the Lambrights' house after delivering the news about Katie, I was happy to go. It was a cold place."

I shivered. "After talking to Jason, we stopped by the cheese shop." I went on to tell her what Debbie said.

She grunted. "I'm glad Debbie talked to you. Your old Amish whisperer tricks are back."

Debbie had talked more to Tanisha, but I didn't bother to correct her.

She continued. "That's interesting, though, Debbie's take on Jason Catcher. I will stop by the shop later and talk to Mr. Umble about him."

"I didn't talk to Jason as long as I would've liked. His coworker thought he was slacking, so he said he would talk to me again after he got off work. I promised to meet him in the market's parking lot at three."

"Whoa, Humphrey, you are telling me about this *before* it happens?" Her voice grew stronger, bolder. "To what do I owe this honor?"

I frowned. "Do you want to go with me to talk to him?"

I heard tapping, as if the police chief drummed her fingers on a table. "If I show up, he won't say a word. I have to admit, Humphrey, you got some good information here. As much as you and Troyer annoy me, I'm impressed with your ability to convince the Amish to trust you. Something, I've unfortunately never been able to do." She paused. "Is your friend Tanisha going with you? If this Jason kid really is a nut job, you shouldn't be alone with him."

"Tanisha went back home. If you won't go, I plan to ask Timothy to come with me."

"Good. Hold on a minute."

I heard the clicking of computer keys.

"Catcher has a speeding ticket from two years ago. Other than that he has nothing on his record. That doesn't mean he's innocent. I don't trust everything Debbie Stutzman says. As we both know she can lie with the best of them, but I don't see why she would bother to make this up unless it's to aggravate you. It is partly your fault that she spent those few days in jail, so I wouldn't doubt that she holds a nasty grudge against you."

I opened my mouth to protest, but she kept talking.

"I'll head over to the cheese shop now and talk to Umble. If he corroborates Debbie's story, I have no reason to doubt it. I will call you right away after I talk to him. Either way, I want you to keep your appointment with Jason, and we will see how it plays out. This is the best lead that I have. Other than Walter/Billy strung up at the hospital. I haven't ruled him out as the killer yet."

"Strung up?"

"You'll understand when you see him. You do still plan to visit the hospital, don't you?"

"Yes."

"Good." Chief Rose sighed as if the weight of the world rested on her shoulders—or at least the weight of the tiny community of Appleseed Creek. "If Katie felt she was being stalked as Debbie Stutzman described, why didn't anyone tell the police? If she lived in an abusive home, why didn't anyone report it?"

"Because—"

"Don't answer that, Humphrey, it was a rhetorical question. Yes, I know it was because they're Amish." She cleared her throat. "There would be a lot less crime in this town if folks were willing to talk to the authorities. Unfortunately, I'm not going to be the one who breaks a two-hundred-year history of silence."

I didn't know what to say.

"I'll have Nottingham stationed across the street from the market in the gas station's parking lot. That way he can swoop in and save you if things go bad. I don't expect any problems if Troyer is with you, though. He's twice Jason's size. Find out why someone may think he stalked Katie."

"I'll do my best."

"Do better than your best, Humphrey, you owe me. Now, call Timothy and get him on board." She hung up.

I called Timothy's cell again. Still no answer. I dialed the main office at Young's. Ellie's son, Uriah, picked up on the first ring. "I don't know where he is, Chloe. He called and said that he couldn't make it today."

"Is he sick?"

"He didn't seem sick. I figured that he was doing something with you or his family. It was pretty unusual. Timothy comes in no matter what, even when he's deathly ill. If he can't make it, I don't question him. I knew it must be important."

I thanked Uriah and ended the call. A knot tightened in the middle of my stomach as I called Danny's cell.

"Yo," Danny said in my ear.

"Do you know where Timothy is? He called off work today."

"Timothy didn't go to Young's?"

"I just spoke to Uri. He's not there. Do you know where he is?"

Horses whinnied in the background. "What? I can't hear you." In addition to driving a delivery truck, Danny was a horse trainer at a large English farm in the next county. "Timothy is usually at Young's by now. You should try there."

I didn't bother to repeat that I already had.

It was close to one. I needed to find Timothy soon if he was going to make the interview with Jason and me. I hopped into my car and drove the twenty minutes to the rented house where Timothy and Danny lived near the square.

Timothy's truck was gone. I removed my key from my pocket, happy that Timothy had given me a spare. Mostly it was to let Mabel in and out of the house if he was out of town.

Frantic barking came from inside of the house. Timothy left Mabel behind? He never left Mabel behind. With shaky hands, I turned the key in the lock. The fluffy brown and black dog launched herself onto me like she had just escaped from the kennel. I managed to keep my balance. "Settle girl. Settle."

She dropped her front paws to the porch floor. I stepped in the house. Everything looked just as it did that last time I was there. Baskets of clean laundry from the laundromat sat in the middle of the living room in the perfect location for someone to trip over. A pizza box sat on the coffee table. The place wasn't a pigsty, but it wasn't neat as a pin either. It was clear a couple of guys lived there alone. Guilt itched the back of my head. I felt like I was intruding onto Timothy's personal space. Was barging into his house a sign that I didn't trust him? I shook worry from my head. It wasn't lack of trust—I was afraid for Timothy.

A notepad sat on the kitchen counter with *Knox Room 211* scrawled across it in Timothy's handwriting.

The light dawned. "He means Knox Community Hospital room 211," I told the dog. "He went to see Billy after all."

Before I left, I let Mabel into the backyard for a potty break. She wasn't happy when I locked her back inside the house.

Since I had moved to Appleseed Creek, I had seen more than my fair share of the community hospital in Mount Vernon. I wasn't at all surprised when the nurse at the receptionist's desk recognized me with a smile.

"I'm looking for Timothy," I told her. "I think he's in room 211."

She pointed in the direction of the elevators. I nodded to the young doctor as I stepped into the elevator. The hospital in Mount Vernon was much smaller than the one my mother had been in after her accident in Cleveland, but the antiseptic, sterile smell was the same. The scent always took me back to the memory of my mother's accident, of my father picking me up from the sleepover when I expected to see my mother, of him not talking to me while we drove to the hospital, of a doctor I never saw before and would never see again telling us my mother was dead. I closed my eyes as the elevator rose to the second floor, willing the memories to recede just like the first floor of the hospital.

"Afraid of elevators?" The young doctor asked.

I gave him a weak smile. To my relief the elevator doors opened, and I stepped out. A few feet away, Timothy sat in the hallway in one of the plastic molded chairs, his head bent in prayer. My mother's death was forgotten for the moment. There was an empty seat next to him, and I took it without a word. He didn't look up, but quietly reached across my lap and took my hand.

Chapter Twenty-Eight

Timothy's voice cracked. "Billy put me down as his emergency contact. I got a call from the hospital last night. He asked them to call me. He wanted to see me."

"You've been here since last night?" My voice rose.

He nodded, his blue eyes bloodshot.

"Why didn't you call me?" I tried to keep the hurt out of my voice. "I would have come with you."

"I know, but it's something that I had to do alone."

I left it at that. "What did the doctors say? Is he going to be okay?"

"Yes, the prognosis is the same that Chief Rose gave you over the phone. A broken leg is the worst of his injuries. He's very lucky," Timothy added in a whisper.

"If he's going to be okay, why are you so upset?"

"Because I was careless just like before. I was overconfident. I thought I could talk Billy into doing the right thing without Greta's help. I didn't know that I was that person again. I reminded myself of my younger self, who I didn't like very much. Because of it, Billy was hurt just like Aaron."

Becky's short hair came to mind. That would be more pain for Aaron to deal with. Timothy didn't know about it yet, and I didn't have the heart to tell him there in the hospital. I needed to tell him soon, though. He should be warned before he saw his sister. "You can't take all the blame. I won't let you. We both made a mistake." I touched his cheek, turning his head so that he looked me in the eye. "And Billy made a mistake too. No one is innocent in this situation."

His eyes filled with tears. "Something could have happened to you. You could have been killed. I could never have lived with myself."

"I'm here. I'm fine. God protected us."

"Even though I didn't deserve it."

"God's protection is not about what's deserved. If that were the case, no one on earth would have it."

He took both of my hands in his. "Chloe, I—"

The hospital room door opened, and Becky's lawyer, Tyler Hart—who was also Billy's lawyer—stepped into the hallway.

Timothy dropped my hands like they burned his fingers.

I swallowed my hurt, knowing he hadn't meant to wound me.

By the sour expression on his face, Tyler didn't miss the hand holding. "Timothy, Billy wants to see you again before you leave."

Timothy stood. "All right."

I stood too. "Can I come with you?"

Timothy put his hand on my back. "Let me talk to Billy a minute alone first."

"All right," I whispered.

Tyler raised an eyebrow at me after Timothy slipped into Billy's hospital room. "He is beating himself up over Billy's accident."

I nodded.

"I expect that you told him it wasn't his fault."

"I did."

He cracked his knuckles, the sound of it like a gunshot in the sterile white hallway. "Good. Both Billy and I told him the same thing. I don't think he believed either of us though."

I frowned. "Can you tell me why Billy kept you as his lawyer now?"

Tyler chuckled. "You never give up. I'll say this—Billy's run-ins with the law have never resulted in his arrest. He's received some strong warnings, but never been fingerprinted or booked. His problems were violations pertaining to his business, like where he parked the unregistered vehicles he was revamping or what machinery he had in his shop. He's paid some hefty fines over the years to avoid arrests. I thought it was just because he didn't want to spend a night in jail. Now I know the real reason. Had he been fingerprinted, the truth would have come out a lot sooner."

"I still don't understand how he was able to change his identity like that. Aren't there checks for that sort of identity theft?"

"Sure there are if anyone is watching or cares. Billy had some powerful friends in the Detroit crime circuit who owed him some favors. They got him the new identity and were almost able to erase the real Billy Thorpe—who had no family or connections who would have noticed someone using his identity."

"Wouldn't the computer system have blocked them from doing that?"

"We're talking over twelve years ago. Computer security wasn't even close to what it is today. The really good Internet hackers were three steps ahead of the police. Some of them still are ahead of law enforcement, but nothing like back then. The Detroit PD may have been able to track it down if they had been so inclined to pursue Billy, but they had bigger problems right in front of them, like gangs and organized crime. So they just let it go."

I adjusted my purse strap on my shoulder. "What will happen to Billy now?"

Tyler sighed. "That depends if Chief Rose charges him with Katie Lambright's murder or not."

"Will she?"

"Don't know. She's pretty steamed over the whole incident in the factory."

"Trust me. I know that." I winced, thinking of Chief Rose's icy tone over the phone. "Do you think Billy killed the girl?"

Tyler shook his head. "No. As far as I can tell, the first time he ever laid eyes on her was when he found her behind the barn. He made a mistake. He should have called the police, or at least given an anonymous tip. The girl was there for a couple of days before you and Timothy came along."

"But the family didn't report her missing," I said barely above a whisper.

"Greta said that. I wonder why not. She's legally an adult, but that seems harsh."

"They thought she ran away and became English."

Tyler, whose grandfather left the Amish way for the English life, nodded. "Ah."

The hospital door opened, and Timothy stepped out. His movements appeared lighter and the color had returned to his permanently tan cheeks. "Chloe, Billy wants to talk to you alone."

I frowned. I knew the chief wanted me to talk to Billy, but I'd thought that Timothy would be at my side during the conversation. I wasn't eager to see the three-hundred-pound mechanic on my own. However, Timothy looked so much happier than when I first saw him in the hospital's hallway. I didn't want to ask him to join me in Billy's hospital room and possibly upset him again.

Timothy placed an arm around my shoulder, not caring that Tyler was standing right there. "It's okay. He needs to talk to you."

I nodded, told Tyler good-bye, and then stepped into the room. An IV was attached to Billy's arm. White gauze wrapped his head like a turban, and his badly broken leg was elevated. Chief Rose's joke about Billy being strung up at the hospital finally made sense. Billy's eyes were closed, as if he were sleeping. I didn't think that I could sleep if my leg were suspended like that.

"Thank you for coming, Chloe," Billy said, his voice, hoarse and gravelly, maybe from all the yelling he did before his fall.

I inched toward the bed, but left four feet between the two of us. "How are you feeling?"

He half-laughed, half-coughed. "I've been better."

I folded my arms. "I'm sure you have."

"I've been telling the nurse how they could make some improvements around here with duct tape. I see a lot of potential."

"If you're giving duct taping advice, that's a very good sign."

His smile dissolved into a cough. "I'm sorry. The doctor says I have a respiratory infection from living in the factory."

"Probably not the healthiest place to be hiding." My voice was sharp.

"No." He grimaced. "I've done nothing but make wrong decisions since I saw that girl outside of the Gundy barn. I don't know what came over me. I panicked. I should have called for help. I should have thought of someone other than myself. All I could see was my life in Appleseed Creek falling away." He turned his head and rested his cheek on his white pillow. "Chloe, I'm so sorry. I don't remember much of what happened yesterday, but Chief Rose and Tyler filled me in on a lot of it. Not that it's an excuse, but I had been drinking. Please know that I would have never put you in harm's way like that had I been in my right mind."

"I know, Billy. Both Timothy and I know that." I said it like I almost believed it.

He closed his eyes for a brief second. "Timothy thinks that this is somehow his fault. It's not. It's my fault, and I gladly take the blame."

"I know he appreciates that."

He held out his meaty hand. I stared at it but didn't take it. My boots rooted into the linoleum flooring. His face fell as he folded the arm back onto his chest. "I understand if you can't forgive me for what I've done."

I stood perfectly still.

He turned to gaze straight ahead. "I don't blame you."

"Billy, I know you weren't yourself yesterday. I forgive you. I just need a little time before I trust you again."

A tear slid down his cheek. "That's fair."

Guilt coursed through my body, but I didn't move any closer to him. I cleared my throat. "Tell me about Jason Catcher."

He raised his head from the pillow. "Jason? Why do you want to know about him?"

"You tell me."

"A 2007 Chevy Cavalier."

"What?" I asked.

"That's the car I sold him two years ago. I may forget a person, but I never forget a car."

"Did you know him before the car sale?"

"No. I'm the first person all the young guys in Appleseed Creek come to for a car. My stuff is reliable, and more importantly, it's cheap. Most of my customers are young guys. I sold Timothy his first truck."

"I know. But you know Jason better than that, don't you?"

Billy rested his cheek on his pillow again. "He works for me around the shop when I need extra help." His tone was evasive.

Was he protecting Jason or himself?

"And?"

He turned his head away.

"Billy, if you want me to trust you again, you have to earn that trust. Right now, I don't think it's possible."

He still said nothing.

I clenched my jaw. "What about the box at the Gundy barn? Will you tell me about that?"

Billy whipped his head back so fast in my direction that it must have pained the injuries from his fall. "How do you know about that?"

"Jason was caught red-handed with it." I didn't add that Tanisha and I were the ones who caught him.

Billy gasped, which turned into a cough. "Where is he?"

"He is at the police station being interrogated by Chief Rose."

He continued to cough, shaking his head. "Jason doesn't deserve that. He was doing me a favor."

"What kind of favor?" I knew, but I had to hear it from Billy to make sure his and Jason's stories matched.

Billy licked his dry, cracked lips. "I asked him to go to the Gundy barn and dig up a metal safe-deposit box I buried there years ago. It held photos and mementoes from my past—things I couldn't have with me, but that I couldn't part with either. And it held escape money in case anyone in Appleseed Creek learned about my past. When I found the dead girl, I was too terrified to dig it up myself." His watery eyes bore into me. "I'm telling you, Jason was only doing me a favor. He is innocent in all this. He is a good kid."

"A favor that you were going to pay him five hundred dollars for."

His head dropped back onto the pillow. "Yes." He closed his eyes for a minute. "I was so furious when Jason didn't come with the box at the time we agreed on. That's when I thought it was all over and started drinking."

"And then Timothy and I showed up."

He gave the slightest of nods.

"What do you know about Jason's relationship with Katie Lambright?"

His eyes flashed. "Jason worked for me, and I did ask him to bring that box to me. He had nothing to do with the girl."

"How do you know? Were the two of you close? Did he talk to you about his friends and girlfriends?"

His mouth fell open, and then he clamped it shut. "I did know that there was a particular girl he liked. He talked about her all the time, but he never told me her name and I never asked."

"What did he tell you about her?"

"Oh, that she was very pretty. All boys think that the girls they like are the prettiest girls in the world. She worked at the cheese shop on the square." Billy must have noticed the change in my expression. "What?"

I shook my head. "Anything else?"

"He hated her parents and said they are the reason he and this girl could never be together." He sighed. "I thought it was normal teenage boy hormones, so I let him talk about it at my shop to blow off some steam."

"Did he say anything in particular about the girl's parents?"

"Just that they were really strict." He licked his lips again. "Jason thought the dad might have hit the girl before."

I closed my eyes for a moment. "And you didn't tell anyone about this?"

"How could I? I would risk—"

"Revealing your own secret," I finished for him.

Billy's face flushed as red as his beard.

"Did you suggest to Jason to tell the police about the possible abuse?"

"Yes, but he said the girl would be angry with him if he did."

I turned to go. "I hope you feel better, Billy. I really do, and

I hope for Timothy's sake you can put your life back together. He cares about you."

His eyes watered. "I know. He's one of the good guys. Don't ever forget that."

"I won't," I promised, and took the two steps to the door.

"I need to tell you one more thing."

I placed my hand on the doorknob and half-turned his direction. "What's that?"

"I'm not a natural redhead."

"I already know that." I gave him a small smile. "Even if it's not natural, we are still the only two bright redheads in town."

"Thank you," he whispered. Another tear slid down his cheek.

When I stepped out of Billy's room, Tyler Hart was gone. Timothy sat in a plastic chair, his head against his hands. It was the same posture I'd found him in an hour before. I held out my hand to him. "Come on. The best way to help Billy is to find out who really killed Katie Lambright. We have a meeting."

He titled his head up and took my hand. "With who?"

"The orange kid," I replied.

Timothy's brow furrowed. "Orange kid?"

I looped my arm through his. "I'll explain in the car."

Chapter Twenty-Nine

Since the Quills' home was on the way to Appleseed Marketplace, Timothy and I drove separately to drop off my car. In the driveway, I hopped out of my Bug and climbed into Timothy's truck. As we drove the twenty minutes into town I filled him in on the morning's events.

Timothy took his eyes off the road for a second. "It seems like you had quite a busy day while I was at the hospital. How did you know where to find me?"

I blushed.

He shot a glance over at me again. "What?"

"I used my key and went into your house. I'm sorry. I was worried when I called Uriah and Danny and neither one knew where you were. How did Danny not know that you didn't spend the night at your house?"

"He got home late from the stables. He probably thought I was asleep in my room." He tapped the steering wheel. "So you broke into my house to look for me?"

Heat rushed to my face. "I . . . you gave me a key for emergencies. I didn't know where you were. No one did. I'm sorry." I clenched my hands in my lap. "It won't happen again."

He smiled. "Chloe, don't apologize. Actually, I'm flattered that you were that worried about me."

I gave a sigh of relief.

"I've never had anyone care about me as much as you do. It's one of the reasons that I love you," he said simply.

There they were—the three little words that could change a person's life. He said them so effortlessly as we drove down the snow-covered country road. *I love you.* That was it. My automatic response should have been to say, *I love you too.*" But I didn't. The words caught in my throat.

Then again, Timothy had said, *It's one of the reasons that I love you.* Was that the same as *I love you*? I worried my lip because I wasn't sure. I could say that sunshine was one of the reasons I loved summer, but I wasn't *in love* with summer. Was Timothy lumping me in with love of summer? Timothy didn't seem to expect or want a response, and I didn't know if I should feel relieved by this or concerned. I worried about this the rest of the short ride to the market.

As promised, Officer Nottingham's patrol car was parked off to the side of the gas station across the street. Nottingham wasn't inside, but close by and watching our every move. I pointed him out to Timothy.

He nodded. "That was a good idea to call Greta and give her a heads-up."

"I think we both learned our lesson when it comes to what to tell and what not to tell Chief Rose."

Timothy grimaced. "Right."

A snow-covered picnic table sat at one end of the market only a few feet from the dumpsters. In the warmer weather, market employees could take their smoking breaks there. Was it worth the smoke to have to stand by a dumpster to enjoy it? Jason stood nearby, fidgeting. He wore a brown, shapeless coat and gray gloves. Despite the cold, he didn't wear a hat.

"That's him," I said.

"He doesn't look like he could hurt anyone," Timothy commented.

"That's what I thought until I talked to Debbie."

Timothy parked the pickup a few feet away from where Jason stood. Both of us got out. Jason scowled. "Who's this? Where's your friend?"

"Tanisha had to go home. This is Timothy."

"I didn't know a guy was coming."

"Is that a problem?" I asked.

Jason shrugged. "It doesn't matter to me."

I folded my arms. "Jason, we need your help in finding Katie's killer."

"I told you in the market. I don't know anything. If I did, I would have told the police. Katie was my friend, and I miss her every day." His eyes teared up. "I still can't believe she's gone."

I adjusted my gloves on my wrists. "Katie never turned you down for a ride home?"

His brow creased. "N-no, she didn't."

His hesitation told me he was lying.

"What did Mr. Umble say to you when he asked you to stop hanging around the store?"

The stock boy appeared stricken. "I don't know what you're talking about."

"One of Katie's coworkers at the cheese shop said you were stalking Katie, and Mr. Umble asked you to stay away from the shop. Is that true?"

"No, I mean, yes, I mean, no." He raised his hands. "I wasn't stalking Katie. Mr. Umble did ask me to stay away from the shop.

He's a grouchy, old Amish man. He thought I was distracting her from her work."

"I believe that. But Katie's coworkers said that she acted afraid when you were around."

"That's what the Amish are saying?" His face turned an impossible shade of red. "All they wanted to do was to keep Katie and me apart. They didn't understand our friendship." His eyes pleaded with me. "I did not stalk her."

"She quit her job there to avoid you."

He balled his fists and got into my face. "That's not true. If this is what I stayed after work to talk to you about, I'm out of here. I don't have to take this."

Timothy stepped between us. "You might want to think twice before you do something you will regret."

"What do you know about it?"

Timothy stared him down. "A lot more than you do."

"Katie stopped working at the cheese shop over six months ago, but you never mentioned that. If she stopped, did the rides home stop too?" I asked.

Jason's shoulders sagged. "I didn't mean to scare her like that, but I wasn't stalking her. I was guarding her."

"Guarding her from what?" Timothy asked.

Jason examined his boots.

"Jason," I said in a gentler tone. "If you believe that Katie needed protecting from someone, we need to know who that he or she is. That person is most likely the one who killed her."

He brought his head back up, and he whisked the tears away from his eyes, streaking the lens of his glasses in the process. "I watched her whenever I could to make sure that the guy was never around." His face flushed. "She should have been grateful I took such good care of her. Instead she put herself within his reach. Now she's dead."

I felt cold, and it wasn't from the freezing air temperatures. "Who?"

"Caleb King, her ex-boyfriend. If you are looking for the killer, look at him. The guy was awful to her. Treated her more like property than a person. He hit her once, right in front of me because she accepted a ride and he was mad about it." His head dropped to look at his shoes again. "I just stood there and didn't do a thing about it. She broke up with him the next day. I vowed I would never let him hurt her again, but I failed. I wouldn't have treated her like that. That may be the Amish way, but it's not the right away."

Timothy balled his fists at his sides. "It is *not* the Amish way."

Jason shook his head as if Timothy had no idea what he was talking about. Obviously, Jason didn't know that Timothy grew up Amish.

"What did you mean when you said she ran right into his reach?" I asked.

"She left the cheese shop to take an office job at Garner Dutch Furniture Warehouse. That's where Caleb works."

"Did she tell you why she took that job?"

He turned up his collar. "No. We weren't speaking then."

"Why not?"

"She said that she and Nathan were planning to marry and it was her time to be baptized. She had to give up the things of her *rumspringa*, including our friendship, and be more Amish." He snorted.

Behind Jason, I saw Officer Nottingham casually making his way across the parking lot. Timothy saw him too.

"Katie left the cheese shop six months ago. You haven't spoken to her since then?"

He dug the toe of his boot into a small pile of gray slush. "No."

I tried to gauge if Jason was lying to me again.

"Mr. Catcher," Nottingham's voice interrupted our conversation.

Jason jumped, startled when he heard the officer's voice only a few feet behind him.

Nottingham rested his right hand on the butt of his gun. "I hope you're keeping yourself out of trouble."

Jason dug his hands deeper into his jeans pockets. "What are you doing here?"

"We'd like to ask you a few more questions about what you were doing at the Gundy barn. Can you come with me?" Nottingham asked.

Jason lunged at me. "You set me up!"

I jerked back. "I didn't. I didn't know that the police wanted to talk to you again."

Timothy stepped in front of me, and Nottingham clamped a hand onto Jason's shoulder. "It's just a few questions, Jason. You're not under arrest, but if you keep up that attitude toward Ms. Humphrey, you will be."

"Fine, I'll go." Jason shot me one more parting glare as he followed Nottingham across the street to his squad car.

"That went well," I said as Timothy and I walked back to his truck. It was only four o'clock, but already nearing dusk. I reminded myself that the winter solstice was over and the days grew longer with an upward march to summer.

Timothy just shook his head. "Do you think he did it?"

I frowned. "I don't know, but I do think that we need to talk to Nathan and Caleb again."

"Agreed. If Caleb is as awful as Jason says he is, I want to be there when you talk to him."

I cocked my head. "What do you know about him?"

Timothy shrugged. "I saw him at church when I was Amish and also around town. He always seemed to have a lot of other Amish guys around him who followed his lead. There is too much of a gap in our ages for us to overlap in school much. He couldn't have been more than eight when I finished eighth grade."

"And Nathan?"

"I know him just as well. He was always in the gang of Amish guys with Caleb."

At the truck, I placed a hand on Timothy's arm. "The day we found Katie, Caleb and Nathan were at your farm."

Timothy shrank back. "You never told me that before. Why were they there?"

"They were there with Nathan's father."

"Levi?"

"That's right. Levi took some of Grandfather Zook's woodworking projects on consignment to sell at the warehouse. The warehouse's wagon was loaded with furniture made by craftsmen from all over the district, and Levi said something that I just remembered."

Timothy leaned forward. "What?"

His closeness distracted me for a second. "He said, 'They are in an awful fight over a girl.'"

"Katie?"

I nodded.

He opened the passenger door to the pickup for me. "I guess we need to find out how bad that fight became."

I climbed inside. "And if Katie was a victim of being caught in the middle."

Chapter Thirty

I wrapped my hand around the shoulder strap of my seat belt. "Becky went into work early this morning. She's home by now." I bit my lip, wondering if she was still mad at me for overreacting about her hair.

"Great. We need a break. Why don't I go pick up Aaron and we can go get ice cream with him and Becky."

I shivered. "We just spent a half hour standing outside, freezing to death. It's too cold for ice cream."

"It's never too cold for ice cream," Timothy assured me. "But we can go to Rita's Coffee Haus in Mount Vernon, and you can have hot cocoa."

"It sounds nice, but there's something I need to tell you about your sister."

He glanced at me. "I don't like the sound of that. Is there something wrong with her community service or her probation?"

"No. She's doing great in both. Her last report was excellent."

"Then, what is it?"

I swallowed. "She cut her hair."

His face fell. "Oh."

"She's not Amish anymore," I said in Becky's defense. "And there's no reason she shouldn't cut her hair."

"She wouldn't cut it if she thought she'd go back," he said. "Have my parents seen her?"

"I don't think so."

"*Daed* is not going to be happy. I know he wants Becky to return home and be Amish." He shot a glance at me. "He wants that for both of us."

I pulled on my seat belt's shoulder strap again, holding it away from my neck. "I know."

"Since so much time has passed for me, he has accepted my decision as permanent. I left the Amish way nearly eight years ago. Becky isn't so far removed from it that she couldn't go back. By cutting her hair, though, she is telling the whole world her decision is final."

The whole world, including Aaron, I thought.

As if he could read my mind, Timothy asked, "Does Aaron know?"

"I don't know. He might have seen her at Young's today. I don't know if he was working."

"He wasn't. He told me he had the day off."

"That's a relief. I would hate for him to learn about Becky's haircut at work. He's bound to have a reaction."

Timothy wrung his hands on the steering wheel. "He needs to know. It's a statement as much to him as it is to my father."

"I know."

Timothy sighed. "I told him something like this might happen. That my sister is young and doesn't know what she wants out of her life."

"Becky is in another place than Aaron is. He's ready to marry. Clearly, she is not." I let go of the shoulder strap and it snapped back into place against my heavy winter coat.

Timothy frowned. "She needs to be the one who tells him, and she needs to be clear. I won't deliver the message. I don't want to be trapped between my sister and my best friend."

"I know she cares about him but maybe not as much as he cares about her."

Timothy parked the truck in my driveway. "That's what I'm afraid of."

I placed a hand on his arm. "Are you mad at her?"

He shifted the truck into park. "No. How could I be? I left too. More than anyone I know what a difficult transition this has been for Becky. You being here made it easier for her. I cringe to think where she might have ended up if you hadn't come along last summer and saved her from Brock and Curt. The moment you took her in, I knew you weren't like most *Englisch* girls. You weren't like most girls period." He laughed. "I fell in love with you the moment I saw you pinch your finger while trying to put your bed frame together when you first moved to Appleseed Creek. You were so cute trying to line up the bars and then insisting that you could do it yourself when I offered to help."

"I eventually did put it together," I said while thoughts ran through my head. *I fell in love with you.* There was no question there. There was no way my brain could twist that phrase into meaning less, into something it was not.

I love you too, I wanted to say, but something held me back.

Timothy smiled and leaned over and kissed me, erasing all the thoughts racing through my head. He touched my face. "Okay if we do hot cocoa another night?"

"Of course."

Timothy nodded. "Let's go inside. I want to see my sister's new hairdo."

"Okay," I said a little breathless.

I opened the front door and found Becky on the couch examining her appearance in a hand mirror. Her white-blonde hair fell straight and smooth to the shoulder and side-swept bangs crossed her forehead. In her jeans and teal, cable knit sweater, no one would ever know that she spent most of her life wearing plain dresses and a prayer cap. She dropped the mirror into her lap. "You're home! I was wondering where you were. Did Tanisha leave?"

I removed my coat and hung it on the hall tree by the door. "She had to go back to Cleveland to spend some time with her family before returning to Italy."

Timothy stepped through the door.

Automatically, Becky's hand flew to her hair. "I didn't know Timothy was coming over."

He stepped out of winter boots. "Chloe warned me about your hair."

Her eyes flitted in my direction. "You still don't approve?"

I sat on the couch next to her. "Becky, if this is the right decision for you and it makes you happy, I don't see anything wrong with it."

She squinted at me. "Then, why were you all upset last night?"

"I'd had a long day." I shot a look at Timothy. "And I was caught by surprise. I thought you would tell me before you cut your hair. I'm sorry I overreacted."

Becky bumped my shoulder. "It's okay. I'm sorry that I didn't wait until you got home. I told Tanisha about it, she was so excited, and I guess I just got swept away in her enthusiasm." She squeezed my hand. "I shouldn't have snapped at you. I knew you were just concerned."

"It's okay. Trust me, I've been swept up in Tee's enthusiasm more than once."

Becky looked to her brother.

He frowned. "You need to tell Aaron."

Becky made a face. "I'll see him at work tomorrow."

Timothy folded his arms. "He needs to know *before* he sees you."

"Why's that?"

"You know why."

Becky's lip quivered. "I'm afraid. I don't want to hurt him."

Her brother's eyes softened. "Becky, he's going to be hurt. There is no way around that, but he deserves the truth."

"I know," she whispered. "I need to stop putting the conversation off."

"How about this?" I asked. "I'll drive Becky to work early tomorrow and that will give her and Aaron time to talk. Ellie won't mind."

Timothy nodded. "Sounds like a good plan."

Becky shuddered. "Okay."

THE NEXT MORNING BECKY shifted side to side in the front seat of my car.

"Nervous?" I asked.

She nodded. "I thought about it last night, and I don't know what I'm going to say to him."

"Just be honest with him."

She looked at me. "Have you ever dumped anyone?"

"First of all, you're not dumping Aaron because the two of you never dated. Second of all, yes, I have broken up with someone. It's not fun."

"Why did you break up with him?"

"He talked really loud. His voice drove me crazy." I joked, but I knew this situation was so much different. My ex-boyfriend and I didn't care about each other as much as Aaron and Becky did.

Becky laughed, and I was happy to make her smile.

We entered Young's through the employee entrance. Ellie was in the kitchen instructing her cooks how she wanted them to make her famous breakfast casserole. Apparently, one of the cooks had started experimenting and Ellie wasn't having it. The argument ceased when Becky stepped into the kitchen after me. A collective gasp went up in the room.

Under her winter coat, Becky wore the same plain blue dress as the others did and the white apron with "Young's Family Kitchen" stitched on the pocket. However, the prayer cap she typically wore to work was missing, and her white-blonde hair fell to the shoulder.

Ellie placed a metal spatula on the counter. "So you cut your hair."

Becky pursed her lips and nodded.

Ellie gave a single nod. "Good. It's better to pick a room than to stand in the middle of a doorway."

Becky's shoulders relaxed.

Ellie picked up the spatula again and waved it at her Amish cooks. "What are you all looking at? Back to work. Breakfast service starts in thirty minutes." She handed the spatula to her head cook and placed her arm around Becky, leading her out of the kitchen. I followed them.

The main lights in the dining room were just coming on as waitresses and busboys set the tables for breakfast. They only set tables in one-third of the dining room because breakfast attracted the smallest crowd at Young's.

Ellie watched her staff closely. "I thought I had you scheduled to come in at ten today. It's not even eight yet."

Becky swallowed. "You did, but I want to talk to Aaron."

"Ah," the older Amish woman said. "*Ya*, he is the opening host today. I think he is in the break room. He should be out here any moment."

"Becky, let's go talk to him back there," I said.

Amish women continued to bustle through their breakfast preparations, ignoring us this time when we stepped into the stainless steel, professional grade kitchen. Off to the side of the kitchen a swinging door led into the staff break room. Becky stared at it.

"It's better if you just get it over with," I whispered.

She nodded and pushed her way through the door. I didn't follow her, so she stopped and looked over her shoulder. "Aren't you coming with me?"

"I—"

She grabbed my arm and pulled me into the room. We both froze. Aaron sat in his wheelchair. His mouth fell open. "Becky?"

"Aaron . . ."

"You cut your hair." His tone was sharp.

"Yes."

"You aren't going back to the Amish way?" His voice was tight.

"No." A large tear rolled down her cheek. "I can't be Amish."

He gripped the arms of his wheelchair. "If you want to be an *Englischer*, that's fine. You can do that." He drew in a harsh breath. "I can do it too."

She licked her lips. "I can't ask you to do that."

"I want to. If that's how we can be together."

I shouldn't be here for this conversation. It was too personal. I inched toward the door, but Becky held my arm in a vise-like grip. "You should leave if it's your choice to leave," she said to Aaron. "Not because it's what I decided to do. You're happy being Amish, and I am not. I'm not going to take you away from a life you love."

"I love you more than how I live," he told her.

She shook her head. "Please, Aaron, try to understand. You wouldn't be happy. I want you to be happy for the rest of your life, even if it makes us both miserable for right now."

He steadied his gaze on her. "Is it because of my chair?" His question hung in the air for a long, painful minute.

"No." Becky said, her voice strangled. I felt a bruise forming on my arm as she squeezed it that much more tightly. "It's *not* because of your chair. It's because of who we are. We want different things. It would never work. You think being *Englisch* will be all right now, but what will happen when you are shunned?"

"You can do what you want and be Amish." His voice was choked. "Look at Ellie."

She took a step toward him, pulling me with her. "You may think you love me, but I'm nothing like what you need. You need a stable Amish girl like Sadie Hooley. Someone who is content in the Amish way. I was never content there. I'm not even content in the place I am now."

"We can find the right place together."

She shook her head. "No. I'm sorry."

She finally let go of my arm, and blood rushed into my veins.

Realization dawned on his face. "Oh." He released the brakes on his wheelchair. "I need to get to work." He rolled across the floor, and I hopped out of the way. When he was gone, whispers could be heard through the open door leading to the kitchen.

Becky fell onto the couch. "They are talking about me."

I rubbed my arm. "Let them talk."

She buried her face into her hands and began to cry. "I feel awful. How could I treat him so badly? He is a good man and deserves someone who will love him and enjoy the life he wants to lead."

I perched next to her on the couch and rubbed her back. "I think you did the right thing."

Her head whipped around. "You do?"

I nodded. "Aaron is happy being Amish. No matter how much he loves you, he would be heartbroken if the district shunned him."

She fingered her short hair and whispered something under her breath that I couldn't make out.

I leaned closer. "What?"

She cleared her throat. "I didn't do this because of his chair." She dropped her head. "I hate that he thinks that."

"I know you didn't."

She lifted her head. "He won't be the only one who will think that, will he?"

"Probably not. You can't worry what others will think. You did what was best for yourself." I paused. "And for Aaron. Focus on that."

"What am I supposed to do now?"

"Take it one day at a time. You are only nineteen. You don't have to figure it all out today. God has a plan for your life."

"Do you think me leaving home was part of that plan?" she whispered.

I swiped her bangs out of her eyes. "I do. This wasn't a moral decision of right or wrong. There is no correct answer. You chose to let Aaron live the life he was most suited for. There is nothing wrong with that."

"Then why do I feel so awful?"

I gave her a sad smile. "Because Aaron wanted you to make a different choice and you feel guilty. I have my black belt in guilt. I recognize it when I see it."

She wiped at her cheeks. "This is something I should have done months ago. I knew this before he got so attached to me. I saw him seek me out each day here at the restaurant. I know he started working here to be closer to me. I ignored the warning bells in my head because I've had a crush on him since I was a schoolgirl and he was my brother's friend. He is so strong and solid—how could I not fall in love with him?" She paused. "Despite everything that has happened to him, he is happy. I couldn't be the cause of his unhappiness, but it seems I am that anyway."

I patted her arm. "He will recover."

"But will I?" She rubbed her eyes with the heels of her hands and stood. A sigh escaped her. "I should help in the kitchen. I hope you're right about Aaron." Then she left the room.

My cell phone rang. Chief Rose's number came up on the readout. "We let Catcher go. He's still a person of interest and had a seriously unhealthy obsession with Katie Lambright, but I don't believe he's the one who did it."

"Why not?"

"I asked him to describe what he knew about the scene of Katie's death, and he got it completely wrong. He said she was inside the barn under a car battery. He probably heard that theory while working in the market. There is a lot of gossip floating around. Sadly, lots of them are even more morbid."

I grimaced. The scene Timothy and I found was bad enough. "Because he didn't know, you concluded he wasn't there."

"It's an old cop trick."

"Could he have been playing dumb?"

"It's always possible, but I don't think he's smart enough to play dumb that well." She clicked her tongue. "I will keep my eye on him though. I have a feeling that I'm going to have trouble from that boy in the future. Sometimes you have a feeling that a person isn't thinking just right."

I shivered.

"What else do you have as far as leads go?"

"There are still the two Amish suitors. Jason seemed to think that Caleb King did it. He said that Katie was in an abusive relationship with Caleb until she dumped him for Nathan . . ."

"He told us that same thing and he might be right. Talk to both of them and report to me."

"You want me back on the case?"

"I've decided to forgive you."

"Um, thanks."

"Don't make me regret it, Humphrey." And she hung up.

Chapter Thirty-One

Before I spoke with Katie's suitors, I wanted to talk to Anna again to see what she knew about them. Timothy texted that he was going to Newark to pick up a part for the pavilion and wouldn't be back until late afternoon. I smiled. Apparently he remembered how scared I was when I couldn't find him, so he decided to keep me in the loop. A blush rose on my cheeks as I remembered him saying that he was in love with me. The happy tickle in my heart was followed by a thud of guilt as I remembered how I had not been able to say the words back to Timothy. As I had told Becky, I had my black belt in guilt.

Although it wasn't even eight in the morning yet, I knew everyone in the Troyer household had been up for hours. As I drove down the country road to the family's farm, I was reminded of the first time I visited there a few short months ago. The family didn't know what to make of me then, and I thought Mr. Troyer still wondered—although he had come a long way in accepting me. The person that welcomed me immediately was Grandfather Zook, and I would always be grateful to the elderly man for that.

When I pulled into the driveway, Thomas was clearing freshly fallen snow from the doorway to the house. His face broke into a grin, and he dropped his shovel. Thomas had found any excuse to abandon his chores. "Chloe! What are you doing here? Is Timothy coming?"

"Not today. He had to run to Newark for a part for the pavilion."

"I can't wait until the pavilion is done. I'm telling everyone at school that my *bruder* made it. They are jealous they don't have such important *bruders*."

"Your father would say that was boasting."

He puffed out his chest. "I am not boasting about myself! It is about my *bruder*, so that is much different."

I patted the stocking cap on top of his head. "I agree. You don't have school today?"

"*Nee*. It is still the Christmas holiday. *Grossdaddi* said teacher gave us the whole week off because I wear her out."

I chuckled. Thomas wore out just about everyone, me included.

"We had breakfast ages ago, but *Mamm* will make you something if you are hungry."

"Maybe later. Where's Ruth?"

"Ruth is in the barn. Do you want to come inside?"

"I will in a minute. I want to talk to Ruth first."

"Okay!" The seven-year-old ran into the house to announce my arrival as I followed the hard-packed snow path to the large barn behind the house.

Although snow covered the ground, most of the Troyers' cows were in the field. A large metal container held a fresh hay bale, and the cows gathered around it, removing pieces with their blunt, square teeth. They then ground them with their molars over and over again.

When I entered the barn, Sparky kicked the dirt floor of his stall. "I'm sorry, Spark, I didn't bring any carrots for you today."

His ears pointed down in disgust. A barn cat balanced on the stall door and strolled by Sparky, wiggling her tail in his face.

Ruth was in the barn shoveling feed into the cows' troughs. "Miss Kitty, don't tease Sparky like that." She shook her head at me. "She is determined to drive him crazy."

Sparky snapped at the cat's tail, but she flicked it away in the nick of time with a devilish grin on her face.

"It seems to be working. I've seen her expression on Gig's face more times than I can count."

"She's not as bad as your cat is. He's the one ruling your house."

I didn't argue with her because it was true.

"Need some help?" I asked.

She nodded.

I picked up the second bucket of feed. "How much in each trough?" I started at the other end of the troughs, so that we would meet in the middle.

"Three big scoops. Does my family know that you are here?"

I smiled. "I'm sure they know by now. Thomas saw me arrive."

"Then they know. There is no way to keep secrets in this family with Thomas around. He is a blabbermouth."

"Blabbermouth?"

"I heard Becky say it about him once."

I grinned. "I'm sure she learned it from television."

Ruth nodded.

I bit the inside of my cheek wondering if I should tell Ruth about Becky's hair. I decided against it. Just as it was Becky's place to tell Aaron about her hair, it was also her place to tell her family. I winced thinking of her father's reaction and hoped he wouldn't blame me.

"You are here to talk about Katie?"

"Yes. Have you seen Anna lately?"

"*Nee.* Her father won't let her out of his sight." Her voice was sad. "I took a basket *Mamm* made up as a gift, and he wouldn't even accept it. I left it on the family's porch, but I wouldn't be surprised if he threw it away right after I left."

"I'm sorry, Ruth."

"I'm afraid he won't let Anna come back to school when the new term begins."

"Has he ever done that before?"

"*Nee.* But this is so much worse than anything else that has ever happened to the family."

I had to agree with her there. "Anna mentioned him at the holiday program. Do you know the English boy named Jason Catcher at all? Did you ever see him with Katie?"

"*Nee.* Is he the one?"

I shook my head. "Chief Rose doesn't think so, but he was definitely infatuated with Katie."

"Infatuwhat?"

"Infatuated. It means that he really liked her."

The thirteen-year-old shivered. "I never saw him. If it's not him, who can it be?" She added another scoop of feed to the trough in front of her.

"Do you think I will be able to talk to Anna again?"

Ruth chewed on her lip. "I don't know. I wasn't even able to talk to her when I took that basket over."

I added two more scoops to the trough in front of me and moved to the next one. "You know my friend, Tanisha?"

"*Ya. Grossdaddi* brought her to the farm. She was so loud she scared the dairy cows. She's funny."

I smiled. "She is, and she went home yesterday. Tee and I grew up together, and she's been my friend since we were about Thomas's age. Any time we wanted to see each other we had a code or signal to meet at a certain place. Do you and Anna have something like that?"

Ruth dropped her pail of cow feed onto the floor. "How did you know?"

"I was a little girl once with a best friend who I wasn't allowed to see."

"Tanisha's parents wouldn't let you see her?"

"No. Tanisha's parents are wonderful people. In fact, when my father and his new wife moved to California, her family invited me to live with them."

She picked up her pail. "I didn't know that."

I smiled. "My father was the one who wanted to keep Tanisha and me apart."

"Why?"

That was a loaded question, and one I wasn't completely certain that I could answer. Because Ruth needed an answer to help her understand Mr. Lambright, I tried. "He was scared, overprotective. He lost my mother and was afraid he would lose me too."

"Then, why did he leave you behind when he moved to California?"

The question hung in the air because it's one that I had asked myself a thousand times over the last ten years. Didn't my father want me? Why didn't he ask me to go with them? Shouldn't I, as his child, have been more important to him than his new wife? "I don't know."

"Did you ever ask him? Did you ask if you could go with him?"

I loosened my grip on the full feed scoop in my hand and all the grain poured out onto the dirt floor.

"Chloe, did I say something wrong?"

To cover my expression, I bent over to pick up the scoop. "What a mess."

"I'll grab a rake and pan to clean it up." She hurried to Mr. Troyer's workshop to collect a dustpan.

"But I wasted all of the cow food."

She pulled a metal waste can over to the mess and lifted a rake that hung from the wall. "It's no trouble. It was an accident." She made short work of raking the feed into the pan that I held. As I dumped the pan into the waste pail, I admitted to myself for the first time that I never asked. I never asked my father why he made that decision, why he didn't argue with Sabrina more to let me be a part of the family. It would have been hard to move to California and leave my friends, especially Tanisha, but how different would my life look? Would I have a father now? Would I know who my half brother and half sister really were instead of just reading about them in e-mail updates that Sabrina sent just to remind me how superior her children were to me? I could give myself a pass and say that I didn't ask then because I was a hurt child who still grieved for her mother, but what about now?

Ruth hung the rake back onto the wall. "You can't tell anyone, even Timothy."

I blinked at her, preoccupied in my own family drama that was a decade old. "What?"

She examined my face. "Where Anna and I meet. You can't tell anyone."

"I won't tell," I said quickly.

She picked up her bonnet from the hay bale and twirled the black ribbon around her index finger. The barn cat, which pestered Sparky, appeared on top of the hay and watched Ruth twirl and untwirl the ribbon with studied fascination. "If I want to see Anna I tie a green ribbon on a spruce tree in the woods behind her house. She goes out often enough to look for the ribbon."

"A green ribbon? Isn't that hard to spy in the tree?"

She dropped the bonnet on the hay bale and the cat dashed

away. "That's the idea. You can only see it if you know what you are looking for. The last thing we want is her *daed* or stepmother finding it." She picked up her feed bucket and scooped again. "Then I hide a note that says the date and time to meet. Not every time, but most of the time she is able to slip away and meet me there. When she doesn't make it, I know that she has tried."

I picked up my feed pail. My wrist gave a little under its weight. How could such a small girl like Ruth move such a heavy pail around the barn so easily? There wasn't a bit of strain in her demeanor. "Where is your meeting spot?"

Ruth looked away and filled two more troughs with grain.

The metal pail handle dug into my curled fingers. I set it down. "Ruth?"

"We meet at the old Gundy barn," she said barely above a whisper.

There was no need for her to add *the spot where Katie was killed*, because that was something I already knew.

Chapter Thirty-Two

Ruth added another scoop to the trough in front of her. It was almost overflowing.

"I think there's enough in that one," I said.

She glanced down at the trough and blushed. "Oh, what am I thinking?" She scooped some of the surplus feed into her pail. The cow that was already eating from the trough mooed at her. "It's my mistake, Maisy. You can't have that much to eat. It's not good for you."

Moo.

I watched her. "Why didn't you mention before that you and Anna use the Gundy barn as your meeting spot?"

"It has nothing to do with what happened to Katie, if that's what you think." She stuck the scoop into the pail of feed. It stood straight up like a shovel in a snow bank.

"It doesn't?" My voice dripped with doubt.

She lifted her chin. "No, it doesn't, and I couldn't tell anyone because if her parents found out about it, they would put a stop to it. If they had their way, I would never see Anna at all."

"Did Katie know that's where the two of you met?"

"*Ya*. Katie knew. Last summer she caught Anna taking my note from the hollow in the tree. She promised that she wouldn't tell, and she never did. Katie was a good sister to Anna." Tears gathered in Ruth's blue eyes that looked so much like her older brother's.

"Are you sure that Katie never told anyone?"

"*Ya*. She promised."

Katie's promise made to Anna and Ruth months ago may have been enough to reassure the two thirteen-year-old girls, but I wasn't so easily convinced. It was too coincidental that Timothy and I found Katie's body in that same location. It seemed to me that the old Gundy barn saw a lot more action than anyone in Appleseed Creek knew about. Billy used it for storage, Anna and Ruth used it for a secret meeting place . . . Katie's killer used it for murder.

Instinctively my hand rose to the place where the necklace Timothy had given me lay hidden beneath my coat and shirt. The necklace was another event at the Gundy barn. Would I ever be able to separate it from Katie Lambright's death? Or would one always remind me of the other?

"Do you know who Billy Thorpe is?" I asked.

Ruth picked lint from her mittens. "Who?"

"He's a big guy with bright red hair like mine. He owns a mechanic shop in town. Have you seen him before?"

Her eyes were wide. "*Ya*. I've seen him at the Gundy barn. He unloaded boxes from a truck and put them inside."

"Did he see you or Anna?"

"*Nee*. I was the only one there. It was one of the days that Anna couldn't come. She told me later that her stepmother had been angry because Anna burned the breakfast rolls that morning. She made Anna scrub out all the cupboards in the kitchen as punishment."

The image of an Amish Cinderella on her hands and knees

scrubbing the kitchen floor boards came to my mind, but unlike the Disney version there were no singing mice to take away the sting of the work. Also unlike the fairy tale, Anna's father was very much alive:

"Is the tree far?" I asked.

"No. It's maybe a half mile into the woods. On a good day, I run there and back while on my chores."

"Let's go now and leave a note asking her to meet both of us at the barn."

Her forehead bunched. "*Mamm* and *Daed* will wonder what's taking me so long to feed the cows."

"They know I'm here. I'm sure Thomas told them. They will think I am keeping you."

She cocked an eyebrow at me. "Which is true."

I smiled to see a bit of her teenaged spunk back. "I need to talk to Anna again."

"Why?"

I bit my lip. *Should I tell her that there were rumors of abuse in the Lambright family?* Surely, Ruth would have told someone if she knew her best friend was in danger. If Tanisha had ever been at risk, I'd have told everyone who would listen. Then again, I wasn't raised Amish, and what the Amish see fit to tell and what the English see fit to tell were much different. In the short time I had lived in Appleseed Creek, I learned many of the secrets in the closed-off community, but I knew there must be that many more buried.

"I need to talk to her about her family," I said. "It might help me understand what happened to her sister. Also, I have more questions about Katie that only Anna can answer."

Ruth chewed on her lips some more, and then she crossed the barn floor to the wooden ladder that led into the hayloft. She started up the ladder and disappeared over the ledge.

I looked up. "What are you doing?"

Her hand appeared, waving a bright green Christmas ribbon back and forth. "I had to find the ribbon." She slid down the ladder in a practiced manner that led me to believe she had done this countless times before. "We must be quick."

We exited through the back door of the barn. A large field separated us from the woods beyond, and our boots crunched on the snow-covered ground. Ruth lifted her skirts to keep them out of the worst of the snow drifts. In the woods, the snow wasn't nearly as deep because the trees had sheltered the forest floor from the worst of the storms that had raked across the Ohio countryside.

Ruth moved among the trees with ease. She made barely a sound as if instinctively knowing where the broken limbs had fallen and how to avoid them. I, on the other hand, made noises like Big Foot running loose in the forest as I stepped, tripped over, and knocked into anything that made noise.

Ruth's head snapped around when I stepped onto yet another loud twig underneath the snow. "You don't go hiking much, do you?"

"You forget that before I moved here, I spent most of my time in front of a computer screen."

Ruth shook her head as if she couldn't understand such an existence. Now, in the middle of the frozen woods I had to agree. I may know how to build my own computer motherboard or read computer code like another person reads a book, but how did that compare to this?

"How far are we from the Lambright farm?" I asked, slightly breathless. I told myself it was from breathing in the cold air, not from being out of shape.

She slowed down, so I could match her pace. She was only thirteen but nearly as tall as me. I knew she would pass me up all together in a few years and be as tall as Becky, who was five nine. "If you go by buggy, the Lambright farm is three miles away, but through the woods, it is only a mile. The spruce where we hide the ribbon is right at the halfway point between the two farms."

"And the Gundy barn? Where is it in relation to your farms?"

She pointed west. "It's over in that direction almost two miles from the spruce."

"Your meeting point is over two miles from your home?"

"It's not far."

I smiled at another way Amish and English differ. Back in Cleveland, a two-mile journey would require a car. In Appleseed Creek, it was a leisurely stroll.

"We are almost to the tree." Ruth pointed to another tree, a skeleton-like sycamore in the middle of the woods. Its leaves, ranging from the size of a toddler's fist to a full-grown man's splayed hand, had fallen and were most likely buried in deep layers of snow. There was a hollow knoll just above my head in the tree.

She removed a scrap of paper and pencil from her coat pocket.

"Ask her to meet us at the barn today," I said.

She held her pencil over the scrap of paper. "When?"

"How is three o'clock?" I hoped Timothy would be home by then.

Ruth scribbled away, then stuck her note inside of the knoll. She stepped back from the sycamore, removed the bright green ribbon from her other coat pocket, then walked about twelve feet away to where a spruce stood. There Ruth buried the ribbon inside the spruce's branches. I could see the ribbon because I knew what I was looking for. A passerby would never have noticed the green ribbon among the evergreen needles. "Why don't you tie it on the same tree?

"Because if someone searches this tree because of the ribbon, that person might take the note." She blushed. "We learned our lesson. That's how Katie found out about our meeting spot. We used to hide the note and ribbon in the same tree."

I looked down at our boot prints in the snow. "Don't your footprints give away which trees you are walking up to, especially in the snow or in rainy weather?"

Ruth began stomping a zigzag pattern into the snow. I joined her. "This distracts them and makes it impossible for them to follow our trail."

Clearly, the girls had considered all contingencies.

Ruth had us stomp a random path every which way through the forest for a few more minutes until she said, "Done. Let's go back. *Daed* will be coming to the barn soon if we don't show up in the kitchen."

The walk back to the Troyer farm was quiet as we were both preoccupied with our own thoughts. In the forefront of my mind were questions about Katie. What was her home life like? Had Caleb hurt her? Or her father? Jason accused both men of abuse, but was he a trustworthy source? I thought of the old spiral fracture of her index finger and winced. To me, that injury was more telling than her actual murder.

The moment we stepped into the farmhouse, Ruth disappeared upstairs. Mrs. Troyer insisted on making me a full breakfast even though the family had eaten hours ago. "I know Becky cooks at your home, but you need a solid Amish breakfast, not one of those fancy recipes that she sees on the television." Mrs. Troyer scrambled farm fresh eggs on the stovetop. I didn't think this was the best time to tell Mrs. Troyer about Becky's hair.

Grandfather Zook sat at the kitchen table drinking coffee from a white ceramic mug. "Where are you off to today, Chloe?"

"I . . ." I searched my brain for a something to say that wouldn't worry the family. They wouldn't be happy to learn that Timothy and I were involved in another murder investigation.

A knowing grin crossed the older man's face. "Because I could use a ride. I have a whole new mess of items—napkin, paper towel, and letter holders—to deliver to the Garner's furniture warehouse. I could wait for the next pick up, but that won't be for a few more weeks. I'd rather drop them off at the store today. In the winter time, the family could always use a little bit more spending money."

Mrs. Troyer flipped the eggs onto a plate along with a hot biscuit and a ham slice and slid it in front of me. "*Daed*, you make it sound like we are in a hardship. We are doing fine. That's the fact of farm life. There are fat times and there are lean times." She pointed at him with her wooden spoon. "It is a *gut* thing that Simon is at the auction house today. He wouldn't like hearing you say that about money."

Grandfather Zook snorted. "Bah! My son-in-law doesn't like most of what I say, but he puts up with me."

Mrs. Troyer shook her head. "I don't know if I want you to go out today. The temperature is supposed to drop this afternoon, and I'm afraid that you will catch a cold. Remember that awful case of pneumonia you had two years ago? You scared me to death."

My eyes widened. "I don't want you to become ill."

Grandfather Zook reached his wrinkled hand across the table and squeezed mine. "Don't mind my Martha, she worries too much. Besides, we won't take Old Spark and the buggy to the store. We'll go in Chloe's car." He wiggled his eyebrows at me. "What do you call it? Your cockroach?"

I nearly choked on my biscuit and took a big gulp of milk. "It's a VW Beetle, but mostly I call it a Bug."

He tsked. "Beetle, cockroach? What's the difference? You still name your vehicle after a pest. You *Englischers* surely choose the strangest names for things." Grandfather Zook held up his coffee mug to his daughter, who refilled it without a word. "Since we'll be in Chloe's Bug machine, she will have the heater on. That will keep me warm and the pneumonia away."

"I'll have it on full blast," I promised between bites of egg.

He grinned. "See? I will be nice and toasty."

I promised Timothy that I wouldn't go to the warehouse without him, but because Grandfather Zook had a believable reason for being there, my appearance would be far less suspicious. The Garners met me on the Troyer farm and knew I was close to the family. It wouldn't be too much of a surprise to them if I drove Grandfather Zook around town on errands.

Thomas bounced into the room. "Can I go to the furniture store too?"

The child must have overheard our conversation from the living room.

"*Nee*," Grandfather Zook said sharply, and then he smiled to take some of the bite out of his words.

Too late. Thomas stumbled back. "I-I thought I could help you, *Grossdaddi*."

Grandfather Zook held out one arm to his youngest grandson. "I'm sorry to have snapped at you, *kinner*. There is no need for you to come because I will have Chloe with me to help."

"Oh," Thomas said, still unsure. He allowed his grandfather to squeeze him in a bear hug, and by the end of it, he was squealing to be let go. Next Naomi ran into the room, demanding a hug of her own.

Thomas may have been taken aback by Grandfather Zook's reaction, but it convinced me that the elderly man knew exactly why I wanted to visit the Garners' business—and that it had nothing to do with furniture.

Chapter Thirty-Three

I turned my car onto the Appleseed Creek square. "Do you care if we make a stop before going straight to the warehouse?"

Grandfather Zook yanked on the seat belt, holding it away from his neck. He wasn't happy when I insisted that he wear it while inside my car. "Where would you like to stop?"

"The cheese shop. I want to talk to Mr. Umble."

He laughed. "You have a cheese emergency. Does Becky need some exotic flavor for one of her recipes?"

"Not that I know of." I tapped the steering wheel. "Katie Lambright worked at the cheese shop until six months ago."

"Ahh." Grandfather Zook nodded. "I could use some gouda."

I laughed.

It was still early morning and the bakery next door to the cheese shop was doing a brisk business, so all the parking spots in front were full. "It's not even ten yet. The cheese shop may not be open."

Grandfather Zook waved away my concern. "Amos Umble will open his door to me. Drop me here."

I frowned at the frozen-over slush clinging to the curb. "Do you need any help reaching the door?"

"*Nee*. I may move slowly, but I will get there eventually."

I gnawed on my lip as I watched him shuffle over the slush. A car behind me honked its horn, but I ignored it until Grandfather Zook was safely onto the salted sidewalk.

I parked on the square, and when I reached the shop's glass door, I saw that Grandfather Zook sat on a barstool across from the cash register where a chubby Amish man, who looked to be in his sixties, smoothed dollar bills on the counter with sausage-like fingers.

I tried the door and it was locked. The man tucked the bills back into the drawer, then approached the door and let me inside. "You must be Chloe. Joseph was telling me all about you."

The bells on the glass door chimed as it slammed shut behind me.

I scraped the snow from my boot on the bristle mat by the door. "I'm sorry that we intruded on you so early."

"No need to apologize. If you want to talk to me, this is the best time. When the shop opens and the tour buses start rolling in, it becomes hectic. Winter is a slower time for us, but it is still close enough to Christmas that the *Englischers* are in a buying mood. Now in January, *that's* when business will slow down."

Grandfather Zook straightened his braces against the counter so they wouldn't topple over. "It is the same for the farm. The deep winter is the quietest time of year and makes you eager for the planting season. My son-in-law can barely stand it. He has his cows to tend to, of course, but the worst punishment for him is being forced to be idle."

Amos laughed. The large Amish man sat on a rickety old bar stool behind the cash register. "Simon Troyer is one of the hardest working men in the county. Chloe, why don't you sit too? There is another stool over by the mustard counter."

I unzipped my winter coat and stuffed my hat into the coat's deep pocket before collecting the stool. I placed it next to Grandfather Zook, then perched on the seat.

Amos opened the cash register drawer again. He stuck his meaty hand inside and scooped out a fistful of quarters. He set the quarters on the worn wooden counter and began organizing them in stacks of ten. Paper coin rolls sat on the counter waiting to be filled. "Joseph tells me that you are here to talk to me about Katie."

I shifted on the stool and it squeaked. "I heard that she worked here a long time."

"She did—almost five years. I was sorry to see her go." The smile fell from his face. "Her funeral is tomorrow."

"Oh, I didn't know that," I said.

Grandfather Zook's forehead wrinkled so much that it reminded me of a basset hound. "I didn't know that either."

The shopkeeper pushed the quarters down farther into the paper tube with his pinkie. "The deacon came in yesterday to pick up a selection of cheddars for a casserole his wife is making for the Lambrights and told me. I'm not surprised that you don't know about it. The Lambrights are private folks, even by Amish standards. Many customers have come into the shop and mentioned that they were turned away by the family when they stopped by their farm to bring food or offer help with chores."

Grandfather Zook braced his hands on his knees. "That is the Amish way—to offer help in time of loss. The community is supposed to come together and support them."

So it wasn't just the Troyers' gift basket that was turned away. I didn't know if I should be relieved or depressed by this news. I was sort of relieved because now I knew that the Troyers weren't being singled out by the Lambrights, but at the same time, I was depressed thinking of Anna trapped in that house with no support. "Why do you think they've shut everyone out?" I asked.

"When Jeb's first wife died, he became despondent and refused to see anyone. I was afraid for him and the girls. I thought when he married Sally he would be his old self, but she only seemed to pull him further away from the community." Amos wrinkled his nose as if he smelled something sour. "Except for business and Sunday church, the family rarely leaves their land."

I leaned forward and the stool squeaked again. "Sally has two sons from her first husband."

Amos nodded. "*Ya.* I don't know them well. They never lived on the Lambright farm, but I know that they have visited a few times, never for a long while. They own their father's farm up a little bit north of here in Ashland."

I wasn't sure if the cheese shop owner would answer my next question, but I had to ask it. "Did Jeb ever hurt the girls?"

Amos looked up sharply from his coins, and Grandfather Zook watched me. Amos set the roll of quarters on the counter. "Why would you ask such a terrible thing?"

My cheeks felt hot. "Chief Rose said that there were signs of old injuries on Katie's body. The injuries were consistent with abuse. One in particular—a broken finger—concerned her. Chief Rose said that break indicated that someone had twisted it."

He frowned and his eyes drooped. "I know about Katie's broken finger. She came into work that very day with her hand in a makeshift bandage. It pained her. She said that it got caught and that she twisted it while trying to climb over a fence on the farm. She refused to go to the hospital, even when I offered to take her." Slowly he shook his head. "I knew I should have insisted."

"But you don't think the injury came from her father." I watched his face for any sign of doubt.

Amos began stacking quarters again. "*Nee.* I can't believe that about my old friend. Jeb is a cold man, but he would never physically hurt either of his girls."

I wanted to ask him how, if Jeb Lambright discarded their friendship after the death of his first wife, he could be so certain.

Mr. Umble seemed to sense my doubt. "If anyone hurt Katie, it would have been one of her young men."

"One of her young men? Were there many?"

He set five rolls of quarters to the side and returned to the cash register where he scooped out the dimes. The coins clattered onto the counter. "I never cared much for Caleb King. He is a tough young man, too harsh for someone as sweet as Katie. I told her so many times. It was a *gut* thing when she let Nathan Garner court her."

"When was that?"

"Not long after her finger was broken."

Coincidence? I don't think so. "And Jason Catcher?"

He started to stack the dimes. "That *Englischer.*" He snorted. "He was always standing outside of the store, watching Katie. I knew it made her nervous, so I asked him to stop. Didn't do much good. He watched her from the square."

A dime rolled across the counter. I stopped it with my hand and slid it back to Amos. "Do you think he could have broken Katie's finger?"

"I don't know. He never struck me as the sort of guy who would do that, but she did seem wary of him after the break. Before that, she was perfectly normal around him." He dropped several dimes into the paper roll and used the eraser end of the pencil to push them to the bottom since his pinkie was too large for the dime roll. "I hired Katie because her *daed* was a *gut* friend of mine once upon a time, but she turned into one of my best employees."

My brow shot up. I had learned much about Katie over the last few days, but nothing about her work ethic.

Grandfather Zook shifted on his stool. "She was reliable."

"*Ya.* I hired Katie on like I do with most of the Amish girls who come into the shop looking for work as a stock girl, but I learned that she had a great head for figures. Within the first month, she balanced all of my accounts and organized my expenses and income in a way that I could understand. I was sorry to lose her. Now that she's gone, my ledgers are a mess. I'm considering hiring an *Englischer* accountant to straighten them out."

"Why did she quit?" I asked.

He placed a roll of coins beside the quarter rolls. "I wish I knew."

I had a feeling only Anna Lambright would be able to answer that question for me.

My phone rang in my purse, and my face turned beet red. "I'm so sorry." I grabbed the bag off the counter and searched for my cell to silence it. When I pulled the phone out, the readout displayed my dad's number. My hand shook and the phone kept ringing.

"Chloe?" Grandfather Zook's voice was heavy with concern.

I blinked. "Excuse me. I'll be right back." I hopped off the stool and slipped out the shop's front door, answering the call just before it went to voice mail. "Hello?"

"Hello, Chloe, this is your father."

As if I didn't recognize his voice. "Hi . . . Dad." My tongue tied.

"Sabrina told me that you phoned on Christmas. I'm sorry I missed your call," he said stiffly.

He was? "It's okay," I said, even though it wasn't.

"Did you have a nice Christmas?"

"Yes. Did you?"

"I did," he replied.

There was an awkward pause.

"I'm sorry that you couldn't come out for Thanksgiving," he said.

That I couldn't come out? Sabrina uninvited me to Thanksgiving. I bit my tongue to hold back a smart remark.

"But I was wondering if you could come out here for a few days sometime after New Year's."

A few days? I hadn't spent much more than forty-eight hours with my father since he had moved to California. "Well, I . . ."

"I know it's short notice, but I thought you would have the time since the college is closed."

He was right. I did have the time. Classes wouldn't resume until mid-January. One of my staffers, Miller, said that he would be back in town the day after Christmas. He could keep an eye on things while I was gone, but did I want to go?

My father was reaching out. This might be my only chance. If I didn't take it, somehow I knew there wouldn't be another. Timothy's face flashed in my head. He would understand why I needed to see my dad because he loved me. That gave me courage.

"Yes, I have the time," I said, hoping my voice didn't shake.

"Good," he clipped. "I will have my secretary book your flight and e-mail you the reservation."

"Thank you." I paused. "Does Sabrina know I'm coming?"

"Of course. She's looking forward to seeing you."

I'll bet.

I hung up as Grandfather Zook came out of the cheese shop. I hurried to his side.

"Who called you?" Grandfather Zook asked.

"My father," I said.

"Ahh," he murmured and left it at that. As we shuffled toward my Bug, I was grateful he didn't ask anything more about it.

Chapter Thirty-Four

Garner Dutch Furniture Warehouse was located on a lonely stretch of Route 13 between Mount Vernon and Appleseed Creek, not far from the wildlife preserve and the auto parts factory where Billy had been hiding out. The shop had just opened, and Grandfather Zook and I were the first customers of the day. I helped Grandfather out of my Bug and popped the trunk. Then I lifted the large plastic bin of Grandfather Zook's wooden wares from the trunk.

"Do you need help with that?" the old man asked, even though he surely knew that with his braces he could not offer me any assistance.

I adjusted my grip on the bin. "Nope. I got it." At the door, I balanced the bin on my knee and held it open for us both.

Inside the warehouse, the first detail that hit me was the smell, which had the hard bite of vinegar—Amish used it to polish furniture—and the earthiness of sawdust. Not that there was any sawdust on the floor. The simple concrete flooring was swept so clean

I wondered if the proverbial statement was true and if the Garners ever ate off of it.

Unlike those furniture showrooms that helped the shoppers imagine the pieces in his or her own home, the Garners displayed their wares in like groups. All the chests of drawers were in one corner, the end tables in another, the pie safes in another. Shoppers had to hunt for what they wanted, but discovering hidden gems instead of being coaxed into an impulse buy was part of the fun.

Levi Garner grinned ear to ear, showing off his dimple. "Joseph Zook, you came all this way to see me. To what do I owe this honor?"

Grandfather Zook knocked the snow off the end of his braces by the front door. "*Gude Mariye*, Levi."

Levi's eyes slid to me. "I remember you from our last visit to the Troyer farm."

"Chloe is driving me around on my errands today. I have some more items to sell to you."

The dimple appeared again. "*Gut*. The *Englischers* like your small woodworking projects. They feel like they can take a little bit of Amish country home with them." He pointed to a dining room table to the left of the door. "We can look at everything right here."

I set the bin on top of the table and stepped back. Levi peered inside and pulled out one of Grandfather's letter holders. It had a cardinal carved into the front of it that was so lifelike, I thought it might fly right off the piece of wood. The source of Becky's artistic talent was obvious. Levi placed two more letter holders next to the first, each one more beautiful than the last. "You do excellent work, Joseph."

Grandfather Zook lowered himself into one of the dining chairs and grinned. "It passes the time."

Levi ran his hand over one of the carvings. "I'll price these at thirty a piece. We will break the sale as always. Sixty, forty, in your favor."

Grandfather Zook scratched his chin. "Is that what you sell them for? Last time you said forty for each."

The warehouse owner folded his hands on the tabletop. "It's the time of year. We're entering January and February and there will be far less visitors to the county until the winter weather breaks. I have to consider space costs, because these will likely be in my warehouse at least until spring.

Grandfather Zook rubbed the short white beard on his chin. "Maybe I should hold them and come back and sell them to you in the spring then."

A knowing sparkle glinted into Levi's dark eyes. "Thirty-five it is. Let me grab my ledger and calculator."

Grandfather Zook chuckled. "You use an *Englischer*'s calculator to do your figures?"

Levi slipped behind the counter and waved the calculator at the older man. "Sure do. The district says we can if the calculations are work related. Trust me, it has come in handy recently."

Grandfather Zook leaned back against the straight back dining room chair. "I heard you had Katie Lambright working for you. Did she help you with the figures before?"

Levi's eyes narrowed. "Who told you that?"

Grandfather Zook's eyes widened innocently. "We were just over at Amos's cheese shop on the square, and he said that Katie helped him with his arithmetic before she quit and came to work here."

Levi snorted. "Amos Umble may need help with his facts and figures from a girl, but I do not."

Still standing, I held onto the back of one of the dining room chairs. "If Katie didn't help you in the office, what did she do here?"

His dark eyes flicked in my direction. Was I mistaken, or was there a bit of distrust in his expression? The warehouse owner cleared his throat. "I hired her as a favor to my son. He and Katie were to be married, and he wanted her to work here in the family business. She did help me in the office some with clerical work. Mostly, she worked the cash register or on the floor helping customers."

"That was nice of you to hire her for your son."

"He wanted to keep an eye on her. Apparently she was being stalked at the cheese shop by some *Englischer*."

Grandfather Zook's white bushy eyebrows knit together. "Must have been tense around here sometimes, seeing how Caleb courted Katie before."

Levi frowned. "Caleb knew Katie made her choice. He should have had more understanding for his friend."

Remembering the coldness between Caleb and Nathan on the Troyer farm days ago, I wasn't so sure that was possible.

Levi interlaced his fingers on the tabletop. "My son was never happier than when he and Katie talked of their plans to marry. It wounds me to see my son so distraught over her death. It's a terrible, terrible act, and the person responsible will be punished, if not by the world, by *Gott*."

"It is terrible, but perhaps there can be forgiveness too," Grandfather Zook said.

"*Nee*," Levi said. "Not for this." He cleared his throat. "Now, let me count all these pieces and tally up the total for you, so you can be on your way."

"Mind if I look around?" I asked. "Where I'm living now is fully furnished, but I'm hoping to move to a new place soon and put my own pieces in it."

Levi showed me his dimple. "By all means then, see what we have. If there's anything that catches your eye, we can hold it for you until you move."

I thanked him and wandered around the maze of furniture. Before long, I could no longer see Grandfather Zook and Levi, but their voices echoed through the expansive building. Along a back wall of the second cavernous room, I found Grandfather's napkin holders for sale. I smiled as I straightened them on the shelf. If I were a tourist shopping in the warehouse, I certainly would be tempted to buy one of them. I picked one up, a buggy carved into the front of it, and flipped it over. The small sticker on the bottom said that napkin holder was seventy dollars. My forehead crinkled. Hadn't he told Grandfather Zook he priced them at thirty-five? Why were these different? Did Levi think someone would pay seventy dollars for a napkin holder? Either he was confident in Grandfather Zook's craftsmanship or delusional about what an English person would spend.

I turned to find my way back to the front of the store, but the muffled sound of angry voices stopped me. I walked along the back wall of the warehouse and discovered an entrance to yet another room. How big was this building? They could house the Goodyear blimp in here.

Sunshine flowed into the room through an open bay. An Amish wagon, the one I had seen at the Troyers' home, stood right outside of the bay, and Caleb and Nathan glared at each other near the open bay doors. They held either end of a dresser. I couldn't tell if they planned to load it onto the wagon or take it off.

Caleb gripped his end of the dresser until his fingers turned white. "She loved me!"

Nathan glared at him. "If that is true, why did she leave you?"

"I will tell you why—because you are going to inherit the furniture warehouse. *You* will be able to provide a good living and life for her and . . ." He gave a strangled breath, "her children. After the childhood that she had, that's all she ever wanted." He dropped his end of the dresser with a resounding thud, and it echoed through the warehouse.

Nathan stumbled back but was able to keep hold of his end of the dresser. He carefully set his end down and examined the piece. "Look what you have done. We just got it from a craftsman and you ruined it."

"Maybe your father will sell it for a fair price, then?"

Nathan launched himself at his former best friend, and the two Amish young men crashed to the concrete floor. Caleb, clearly the stronger of the two, pinned Nathan to the ground in seconds. He wiped blood from his lip.

Nathan kicked at him, but Caleb easily stayed out of the way of the wayward boots.

"What are you going to do? Strangle me like you did Katie?" Nathan cried. "You could have hit her dozens of times, and she would have never said a word. It won't be that way for me. You're fired. You will never work in this county again. I will ruin you. *Ruin* you."

Caleb laughed. "You can't fire me. You can't do anything to me."

"Yes, I can. Have you read the sign on the warehouse? It says *Garner.*" He spat the words out. "King is the name of a *grunt.*"

Caleb straddled Nathan's back and pulled his friend's hand backward, twisting his index finger. The crack and pop of Nathan's finger breaking went off like a gunshot in the enormous room, echoing off the bare walls and rafters.

I gasped and covered my mouth, my stomach roiling. In my mind's eye, I saw him breaking—not Nathan's finger—but Katie's. I had little doubt that Caleb was the one behind the old wounds on Katie's body.

My gasp caught Caleb's attention and he jumped off Nathan—but it was too late. I had seen everything and he knew it. I stumbled backward and the corner of a desk stabbed my hip.

"What are you doing?" Caleb bellowed.

Writhing in pain, Nathan rolled back and forth on the concrete floor, holding his broken finger.

I turned and ran.

"Stop!" Caleb cried.

I was lost. The maze of furniture had me confused. It was all the same color, the pieces blending together. I turned a corner and smacked into Levi Garner's chest.

He pushed me back, holding me at arm's length.

I gulped air. "Caleb broke Nathan's finger like he did Katie's."

"Where are you?" Caleb cried.

Levi's eyes narrowed, and he pushed me aside. Caleb appeared in the aisle and saw Levi's fury. It was his turn to run. He spun on his heels, dashing back the way he came when a silver brace spilled quietly into the aisle. Caleb never saw it and landed face down on the floor.

Levi reached Caleb in four strides, lifting the young Amish man off the ground by his shirt as if he weighed no more than Naomi's favorite doll. "What did you do to my son?"

Caleb cowered.

Grandfather Zook appeared in the aisle and waved one of his arm braces at me. "That worked like a charm."

I dialed 911, followed by Chief Rose's direct number.

Chapter Thirty-Five

Emergency lights from the ambulances and police cars reflected off the snow and through the windows into the warehouse. Grandfather Zook and I sat at the dining room table where he and Levi had negotiated prices for Grandfather's woodworking projects.

A few feet away, an EMT wrapped Nathan's broken finger. "That should hold for the ride to the hospital."

"Can you fix it?" Nathan asked through a wince of pain. "Will it be the same as before?"

The EMT grimaced. "That's hard to say. It's a pretty bad break. The doctor will look at it and give you a better idea. Hopefully, you won't have to see a hand specialist."

Nathan held his injured hand to his chest. Levi glared at Caleb. His son's former friend stood in handcuffs, and Officer Nottingham had a firm grip on his upper arm. Caleb strained against the officer's hold. "I didn't kill Katie. I didn't. Just because I fought with Nathan, you think I killed someone." He spat those last words in Chief Rose's face.

The police chief removed a napkin from her pocket and wiped her cheek, but she held her ground. She nodded to Officer Nottingham. "I'm tired of looking at him. Take him to the sheriff's station. I don't even want him in my department."

Officer Nottingham pulled on Caleb's arm. "Let's go."

"Can we take Garner to the hospital?" the EMT asked the police chief.

She nodded. "I'll be there within the hour."

Officer Riley held the door as the EMT wheeled Nathan out in a wheelchair. Levi moved to follow him, but Chief Rose held up her hand. "I need to speak with you first."

"My son."

"I'll be brief," she said and led him to another part of the warehouse out of my earshot. I couldn't help but think that was on purpose.

"Are you all right?" I asked Grandfather Zook for the fifth time.

He squeezed my hand. "Chloe, I'm fine. I have told you this. I'm glad that Levi insisted that he go look for you when you didn't come back to the front of the store. He didn't want me to go with him, but I hobbled along anyway." He knocked on his braces leaning against the table. "Sometimes these come in handy."

I groaned. "Mr. Troyer is going to be angry when he finds out what happened."

The skin around Grandfather Zook's eyes crinkled at the corners. "Simon will recover. He always does."

"You think Caleb killed Katie?" I asked.

His bushy eyebrows shot up. "Don't you?"

"I still want to talk to Anna. Ruth and I plan to talk to her later this afternoon. I think she knows more about her sister's life than anyone." I frowned. "I just don't know if Caleb is the one who killed Katie."

"Why not?" The voice came from behind, startling me.

I jumped and found Levi Garner glaring at me, his dimple nowhere to be found. "Did you see what he did to my son? An Amish man with an injured hand is nothing! What work can he do if the doctor cannot mend it?"

"I—I don't know."

"Okay, okay, calm down, Garner." Chief Rose stepped between us. "Officer Riley here will take you to the hospital to see Nathan. Considering how he drives, you two might beat the ambulance there."

Riley adjusted his utility belt under his protruding belly. "I used to drag race back in the day."

Chief Rose shook her head.

Levi and Officer Riley started to leave.

"Wait," I said. "Levi, I noticed the prices for Grandfather Zook's woodworking pieces were higher than you quoted them to be."

Levi's mouth fell open. "You want to talk about that now? My son is in the hospital."

I dropped my head. "I just noticed that—"

Grandfather Zook waved my concern away. "I've sold my goods to Levi for years. There is nothing to worry about."

Levi shot me another glare before he followed Officer Riley out of the building.

Chief Rose pointed at me with her finger as if firing a gun. "I want to talk to you too, Humphrey, but first I need to take some more pictures of where the fight occurred. You and Mr. Zook hang tight here until I return." She opened a black crime scene kit on the tabletop and removed an SLR digital camera.

When the chief disappeared among the furniture aisle, I stood.

"Where are you going?" Grandfather Zook asked.

"I need to step outside for a second. I need some air."

Grandfather nodded. "Don't be gone long. I don't want to be in trouble with the lady copper."

I arched an eyebrow. "Copper?"

"It's another new *Englischer* word I learned. What do you think?"

"I wouldn't call Chief Rose that to her face."

As I stepped through the warehouse's front door, he laughed.

Just minutes ago, the warehouse's parking lot had been full of emergency vehicles, now all that remained was Chief Rose's cruiser and my Bug. I took a deep breath of air. Was I wrong? Was Caleb the killer like everyone believed? Why did I doubt it? If he could snap his girlfriend and best friend's fingers without thought, why couldn't he commit murder in the same cold manner? I placed a hand on the frigid side of the Bug to steady myself and shivered. This was Chief Rose's problem. If it turned out that I was right and Caleb did not commit the murder, I would help her find the killer—if she asked me to help. But no more volunteering. After seeing Nathan's mangled finger, I was out of that business.

A large hand wrapped around my wrist and spun me around. My back slammed against the car door, but the grip on my wrist tightened as I cried out in pain.

Brock Buckley leaned in. "I've been looking for you, Red. Lucky you have a unique girly car."

That's it. I would trade the Bug in and get something generic, like a Corolla.

He jerked my arm up. "Does that hurt?"

"Let me go," I shouted. Frantically I looked around for Curt. Until recently, the two were always together. "How stupid are you? Didn't you see Chief Rose's squad car? It's right over there. She's inside the warehouse."

He dropped my wrist and placed a tree-trunk thick arm on either side of my shoulders, pinning my arms to my sides and me to the car. "She can't hear you out here. That place is like an airplane hangar."

"Where's Curt?" I asked.

He snarled. "That's what I wanted to ask you."

"Ask me? Why? Why would I know where he is?" *If I screamed would Chief Rose hear me?*

"You're all he talks about lately. You and that church."

"Me?" My eyes darted around the parking lot. There was no one else there.

"Yes, you turned my best friend into a wimp. He'd rather spend time at church than with me."

"I don't see anything wrong with that."

He squeezed his arms more tightly. I felt like I was about to fold in half the long way.

"Help!" I cried.

Brock pressed his forearm up against my throat. I choked. "Don't think I won't finish you. I've had my eye on you since the moment you showed up in this town. I left you alone because of Curt, but his wish to keep you safe doesn't matter much to me anymore."

Spots flashed in front of my eyes. Curt protected me from Brock? How is that possible? I had always thought Curt was the instigator, and Brock was the one who followed his lead. Had it been the reverse all of this time?

He pressed down harder. "You cost me a best friend."

I gagged. My eyes felt like they might pop out of my head, and I shut them tight to hold them in place. Was this what Katie felt before she died? Had Brock—not Caleb—been behind her death? My vision blurred and in my mind, I could see Brock looming over Katie's body through the fog. I heard someone talking, but I couldn't understand the words. "Don't think I won't." I caught that phrase. *Don't think I won't what?* My thoughts swam in a gray mist. I couldn't take hold of any of them.

Then, the pressure was gone. I slid to the snow-covered gravel parking lot, holding my throat and gasping for air.

Brock stood three feet away from me with his hands in the air. Chief Rose had her handgun trained at his chest. "Lay on the ground with your arms stretched out in front of you!"

Brock glowered at her. "The ground is freezing."

"Ask me if I care," the police chief barked back. "Do it. Now."

Brock did as he was told.

"Get up, Humphrey," Chief Rose said to me. I struggled to my wobbly legs. The police chief handed me her gun. "If he tries anything while I'm cuffing him, shoot him."

The gun shook in my hand. My finger wasn't even on the trigger. Was she serious? Thankfully, I didn't have to answer that question because Brock let Chief Rose cuff him with little fuss. She yanked him to his feet. For a small woman, she was awfully strong.

"Thanks for cooperating, Buckley," the police chief said sarcastically. She walked him over to her cruiser and shoved him into the backseat behind the wire mesh. She slammed the door on him. "You okay, Humphrey? Do you need to be checked out?"

I rubbed my throat, wondering if I would have a bruise. "I'll be fine," I croaked. I didn't want to go back to the hospital. I had been there too many times before. If I weren't careful I would need to make a change of address with the post office to have my mail sent there. "Thank you for rescuing me."

"Okay then. If your sore throat doesn't go away by tomorrow morning, I want you to go to the hospital. I need to take charming Mr. Buckley here to jail. I'm sure the warden will be happy to see him again. They are old pals."

I nodded, because talking would take too much effort. All I wanted to do was go home and drink a big mug of lemon and honey tea.

The police chief opened her car door. "I'll have Officer Nottingham swing by your place tomorrow to record your statement for both incidents. Is there anyone else out to get you that I should know about, Humphrey? Being attacked twice in the span of three hours is a little much—even for you."

I wish I knew.

Chapter Thirty-Six

The three youngest Troyer children wandered aimlessly around the front yard. When my car shuddered to a stop on the Troyers' frozen drive, Thomas and Naomi came running. Thomas opened his grandfather's car door as I slipped out of the driver seat.

Naomi hugged my legs, and I squeezed her back.

Grandfather Zook adjusted his braces above his elbows while Thomas steadied him. "What are you all doing outside in the cold?"

"Becky is here," Thomas said in an unusually hushed voice. "Ellie Young dropped her off a little while ago."

Grandfather Zook cocked his head. "I'll bet Ellie was disappointed that I wasn't here."

Naomi giggled.

Her grandfather's grin turned to a frown. "That was nice of Ellie to give Becky a ride to the farm, but it still doesn't answer my question as to why you are moping outside."

Ruth joined us and kicked off snow that gathered on the toe of her boot. "Daed said we had to go outside so he and *Maam* could talk to her."

My stomach clenched. I knew why.

"Hair," Naomi whispered.

Grandfather's bushy eyebrows fused together. "Hair?"

"Becky cut her hair," Thomas whispered. "Like an *Englischer.*"

Grandfather Zook sighed. "I see." He hobbled toward the house.

The children and I followed. Even before we reached the screened-in front porch, we heard the angry timbre of raised voices. Grandfather Zook didn't hesitate and went inside. Through the opening, I saw Becky and her parents in the living room. Mrs. Troyer sat on the couch. Her hands covered her face and her body shook as silent sobs rolled through her.

Mr. Troyer stood across from his eldest daughter, his face bright red as if he had scrubbed it hard with a bristle brush. Becky stood defiantly across from him with her arms folded across her chest. "I told you that I wasn't coming back. You knew that. I don't know why cutting my hair makes any difference."

Mr. Troyer responded in Pennsylvania Dutch. Even though I couldn't understand the words, I knew by the way Becky sucked in air that his comments bit. "So you care what Deacon Sutter says now?" Becky asked.

Mr. Troyer opened his mouth again, but Grandfather Zook stamped one of his braces on one of the wide floor boards. "What is going on?"

I hovered in the doorway, but the three younger Troyer children dashed back into the yard. Should I run too?

Mr. Troyer spun around and faced his father-in-law. He said something in their language.

"*Ya,* I see that she has cut her hair."

Mr. Troyer responded again in their language.

Grandfather Zook sniffed. "Speak *Englisch.* Chloe is here."

Duly outed, I stepped forward.

Mrs. Troyer dropped her hands from her face and stared at me through her tears. Her expression was pointed, accusatory. I glanced at Mr. Troyer and saw the same look on his face. Behind me, cold wind sliced into my back through the open door. Did I leave it open as a means of escape?

Mr. Troyer's eyes narrowed. "You did this to her."

"I—I didn't."

"Your *Englisch* friend did."

I licked my lips. "Becky asked her to."

Becky took a step closer to her father. "*Daed*, Chloe had nothing to do with this. Cutting my hair was my decision."

I stepped forward. "Becky didn't take the decision lightly. I know she's thought about it for a long time."

Mr. Troyer turned to me as if seeing me for the first time and he did not like what he found. "You knew she would do this?"

"I . . ."

Mrs. Troyer covered her face again as if she couldn't look at me.

Mr. Troyer pointed at the open door. "Chloe, please leave. This is a conversation for the family."

His words cut, but they were true. I shouldn't be there. I wasn't family, and if Mr. Troyer's thunderous expression was any indication, they didn't want me to be.

I stumbled back. "Oh, right, I'm so sorry."

"Close the door when you leave," Becky's father added.

"Chloe, wait," Grandfather Zook said.

I shook my head. "I should go." I backed out onto the front porch and shut the door behind me. I hurried down the steps, waving at the children, but avoiding eye contact because more than anything I didn't want them to see me cry. Naomi and Thomas were making snow angels. "Bye," I choked out. "Gotta run."

My hands shook as I opened my car door.

"Chloe," Ruth called from behind me.

I closed my eyes for a moment because I didn't want her to see how much her father's words affected me. I inhaled slowly and turned.

"What's happened? Are you all right?"

"I'll be fine." I gave her a weak smile. "I have to go to work and check on some things."

She placed a hand on my sleeve. "You will come back later, won't you? To come with me to see Anna? We have to go. She will be waiting for us."

I blew out a breath, and a white cloud blurred my sight. "I'll come back. Can you meet me here? In the driveway?"

Confusion crossed over her expression. "*Ya*, if that's what you want."

"See you then," I said and jumped into the car.

THE HARSHBERGER COLLEGE CAMPUS was like a graveyard, which wasn't the best analogy to think of while still reeling from the morning's events. I parked as close to the front entrance as possible and made sure I had my keys to the Dennis academic building where the computer service department was located. Inside, the building was still and quiet. It was hard to believe that in a few short weeks, the campus would be buzzing again with students and faculty.

I hurried to the server room and unlocked the doors to the racks. All of the machines blinked happy green lights at me. I fired up the laptop and ran a few small tests on the system. Everything pinged back with no complaints. My shoulders sagged with relief as I turned the laptop off again and locked the door.

I ran up the stairs and was outside of the building on the way to my car within five minutes. I cleared my throat and felt the scratchiness from Brock's attack. I wished for some of Mrs. Troyer's honey lemon tea, but considering what had just happened, would I ever be invited to drink it again?

The parking lot outside of Dennis overlooked a small pond on the campus, and I made the mistake of glancing in its direction as I made my way to my car. A figure sat on one of the park benches beside the pond. *Curt Fanning.* He sat bent at the waist with his face buried in his hands. I hesitated. Even though I was over a hundred feet away, he must have sensed me because he lifted his head in my direction. His sad expression didn't change when he saw that it was me.

I bit my lip. *I should leave.* Something told me that I needed to see if Curt was okay.

Was he *okay*? That wasn't my problem. How many times over the last few months had he and Brock gone out of their way to make the Troyers' lives and mine miserable? Too many to count. Yet again, I felt the nudge toward him. He looked like he needed someone to talk to. I glanced around the campus grounds. I was the only one there. Despite everything, how could I ignore him now?

I groaned. I would check to see if he needed any help, but then I was out of there. I wasn't going to be stupid about it though. I unlocked my car and tucked my purse under the passenger seat after slipping my cell phone into my coat pocket. I pushed the front seat forward and grabbed my ice scraper from the back. If Curt tried anything, I'd whack him one. I relocked the car and put the key into my other pocket. Slowly I made my way down the icy steps that led to the pond.

Curt was alone. The geese and ducks that called the pond home during the warm months had gone for the winter to points south. A fresh pile of snow lay on the ground next to Curt's feet. He held his father's army dog tags in his hands and caressed them with his thumbs as if they were some type of talisman.

I held my snow scraper in front of me.

"Is this how you're going to approach me from now on?" Curt asked hoarsely. When I had seen him on campus earlier in the week, I had been brandishing the same scraper. It almost came as a relief to hear some of the characteristic sarcasm in his voice.

"Better safe than sorry," I replied and lowered the scraper just a hair.

His eyes grew sad. "I don't blame you. I would be nervous around me too, if I were you."

I took another step forward, but still left over twenty feet between us, having no desire to move any closer than that.

"I heard what Brock did." Curt's voice sounded gravelly. "Are you all right?"

Reflexively, my free hand went to my throat and touched the sore spot. "I will be okay. Brock is a strong guy and he was very angry at me."

Curt turned his gaze back to the frozen pond. "Because of me."

"That's what he said."

He made eye contact with me again. "He doesn't like how I have changed since meeting you."

"How is that?"

He sighed. "I've started asking questions, wondering if there is something more to life than causing trouble and just getting by."

"Is there?" My voice was barely above a whisper.

"In your life there is. In my own life, I wasn't so sure. Over the last couple of weeks I've been thinking how you saved Brock last month. You could have left him to die in that freezing pond and gotten away from us, but you stayed and helped." Curt's shoulders rolled forward. "I would have never done it. I wanted to know what could possibly make you do that. Brock wasn't curious about it at all."

I took two small steps forward. "What did you do?"

"I knew you were a Christian, so I wanted to see what all the fuss was about. I found my dad's old Bible in his knapsack from the war. Mom never even bothered to unpack the bag when the army sent it home. The Bible was dog-eared and written all over, like my dad spent hours and hours studying it." His eyes glistened as he looked at me. "Do you think that means he was a Christian when he was killed?"

My heart thundered in my chest. How could I possibly answer that? How could I answer that question for anyone other than myself? And yet, for some reason, I believed I knew the answer. "I do," I said.

His shoulders relaxed. "I read the part my dad underlined and that made sense when I thought of you and how you react to things like people being hurt or when Brock was in trouble."

"Then what happened?"

He laughed softly. "You saw me at the Christmas Eve service. I have to say the look on your face when I sat next to you was priceless." His tone became serious. "But you didn't run away when I sat down. It meant a lot to me."

He had no idea how close I had been to bolting out of that pew.

"I went back to the church the day after Christmas and spoke to the pastor. I asked him what I had to do to be like you. He told me, and we prayed together."

"And then?" I asked, choking back the emotion bubbling in my throat.

"I waited and nothing happened. I thought it might feel like being struck by lightning or being filled with the force. I thought something big would happen, but nothing did."

I smiled. "I don't think believing is like being struck by lightning. And having the force would certainly be nice sometimes, but that's only a George Lucas fairy tale. Faith is a choice, and making that choice is more powerful than lightning. In your case, it is your choice to change your life." I touched my throat again. "Considering how upset Brock was about it, I'd say that you changed a lot."

"I'm not like you, though. You would never turn your back on someone. You always reach out to help." He lowered his voice to a whisper. "I want to be the same way."

The truth was—I wasn't as perfect as Curt made me out to be. I didn't always reach out to help. I *did* turn my back on others. My father's face dominated my mind. When he rejected me, I rejected him right back. I never gave my best effort to fix our relationship. My father wasn't the only one. Even Billy had reached out to me to make peace, but I hadn't been able to trust him again completely.

Curt's face flushed red. "Will you pray with me again? I know that I already prayed with the pastor, but I want to make sure it sticks."

"You don't have to keep praying the sinner's prayer over and over again. When you do it once, it sticks, but I'm happy to pray with you if it will bring you comfort."

He gave me a crooked grin. "I just think that considering my checkered past, better safe than sorry, you know?"

I smiled. "Okay." I sat on the bench next to him and bowed my head, gripping the snow scraper the entire time.

Chapter Thirty-Seven

I was an emotional mess when I arrived at the Troyer farm a half hour later. Thoughts of Curt, my father, Sabrina, Becky, and the Troyers mixed with my fears of Brock and Caleb. I called Timothy on the way to his parents' farm. "Are you home yet?"

He laughed. "Miss me?"

The sound of his laughter put me immediately at ease. There was so much to tell him. How would I begin? "You have no idea."

"I like the sound of that. I'm turning into your driveway now."

"I'm not at home. I'm on my way to your parents' farm to meet Ruth." I went on to tell him that Ruth and I were meeting Anna at the Gundy barn. Ruth wouldn't be happy about this because she made me promise not to tell anyone about her and Anna's secret meeting place, but after the day I had, I felt a whole lot better with someone knowing where we were.

"You think Anna knows who did it?"

"Maybe, but Chief Rose already made an arrest." I related my adventure with Grandfather Zook at the warehouse. I left out the part about Brock. I wanted to tell him about my encounters with Brock, and later with Curt, face-to-face.

"You promised not to go to the warehouse without me." Timothy's voice took on an edge to it.

Another promise I'd broken that day. Not a great track record. "I know, but Grandfather Zook had a great excuse to go there. I thought it would be a lot more believable than if you and I showed up and randomly started asking questions. Can you meet Ruth and me on the side of the road closest to the barn?"

"You want me to go with you to talk to Anna?"

I turned into the Troyers' driveway. "Yes."

"Ruth won't like that."

He knew his sister well. "I know, but I need you to be there. I'm at your parents' house." I couldn't tell him about his parents' reaction to Becky's hair. I decided to wait until after we spoke with Anna.

"I'll see you outside the Gundy barn," he said and disconnected.

Ruth waited for me outside of the Troyers' barn. "Where have you been?" She jumped into my car. "We are going to be late. The walk from the road is only a quarter mile, but it's still going to take some time in this deep snow."

I shifted the car into reverse. "Where did you tell your mother we were going?"

She lifted her chin. "I told her the truth. I said that you promised to drive me to see Anna because it was too cold to walk there."

"Ah," I said. Apparently, Ruth had already mastered the tried and true teenager trick of telling a half-truth. I backed onto the Troyers' country road. "And she didn't mind, considering what's going on with Becky?"

"She said it was nice, but not to be surprised if Anna's parents turned us away." Ruth wrinkled her nose. "She didn't say I couldn't go."

That wasn't exactly the same thing as not minding.

We drove in silence the rest of the way and stopped at the farthest spot where we could leave my car. I had beat Timothy to the meeting spot.

Ruth unbuckled her seat belt. "Turn off the car and let's go."

I pulled on my gloves and removed my cell phone from my purse, sticking it in my pocket. "We can wait for a minute."

"Wait for what? I'm sure Anna's already there. She is going to think I'm not coming. I can't do that to her."

I sighed. "We are going to wait until Timothy shows up, and we will all go see Anna together."

"Timothy?" she yelped. "You told *Timothy* about mine and Anna's meeting place?"

"Not exactly. I told him that we were meeting Anna at the Gundy barn. I didn't tell him that you and Anna have met there before."

"What's the difference? He will know and then so will everyone."

"Timothy won't tell," I said.

"Like you didn't?" She glared at me and threw open her door.

I yanked the keys from the ignition and jumped out of the car. "Where are you going?"

Tears rolled down her pale cheeks. "Where does it look like I'm going?"

"You can't go alone. It's not safe."

"What do you know about it? I've come here every time by myself. This is the first time that I've brought anyone, and you betrayed me."

I locked my car with the key fob and jogged after her. "Ruth, I'm just being cautious."

She kept going, refusing to even look at me.

We were still close enough to the road for my cell phone to have good reception. Timothy picked up on the first ring. "How far away are you?"

"Ten minutes. Why?"

"Your sister already took off for the barn, and I'm following her."

Timothy groaned. "I'll be there as soon as I can. You'd better stick with her."

"I plan to," I said and hung up. I tucked my cell back into my pocket.

Ruth gave me a dirty look. "Were you calling your boyfriend?"

"As a matter of fact, I was," I replied. I wondered what her parents would think if they had heard me. If Becky's haircut could derail their opinion of me so quickly, maybe they weren't as at ease with Timothy courting me as I had thought.

We walked the rest of the way in silence. Before long, the familiar stand of evergreen trees came into view and just behind them, the Gundy barn.

A small figure stepped out from behind the Gundy's barn. Ruth lifted her heavy winter skirts and broke into a run when she saw her friend. I followed at a much slower pace, the events of the day weighing heavily on me. The sun was low in the sky behind the Gundy barn, throwing shadows toward us. I wrinkled my forehead. Another shadow seemed to peek out from behind the barn, but it didn't belong to Anna.

"Ruth! Wait!" I cried and ran after her.

The shadow moved. Levi Garner emerged from around the corner of the barn, his arms gripping Anna. He held a woodworker's chisel under the young girl's chin.

Ruth froze as if she had smacked into an invisible wall. I sprinted to Ruth's side and grabbed her arm. The cold air pumping into my mouth made my sore throat hurt that much more.

Levi Garner's lip curled. "I *knew* you would come back here. It's where it all started, isn't it? I knew the moment you said that you didn't think Caleb was the killer that I would have to do something about you. Imagine my pleasure when I found this little girl waiting patiently for you." He bent Anna's arm behind her back, and she cried out in pain.

I released Ruth's arm. "Let her go. If I'm the one you've been waiting here for, then fine. The girls have nothing to do with this."

Despite the cold, sweat glistened on Levi's forehead. He wasn't wearing a hat. I hoped that he would catch a cold.

"Ruth," I whispered. "I want you to take my cell phone and keys and run back to the car."

Ruth began to sob. "I can't. I can't leave you and Anna."

"Listen to me. It is Anna's best chance if you run back to the car, lock yourself inside of it, and call for help."

"I don't know how to use your phone."

How did I give an Amish girl a crash course in smartphone use without attracting Levi's attention?

"What are you two talking about?" Levi's voice thundered. "You better not think about leaving. The moment one of you is out of my sight, I stab her in the throat."

Ruth crumbled to the ground in tears.

Okay, plan B. "Levi, you don't want the girls. You can have me. Let Anna go, and you can hold the chisel to my throat. Isn't that what you really want to do?"

He relaxed some.

I took three tentative steps toward him, and his hold on Anna tensed up again. I froze and looked Levi straight in the eyes. I needed to attract his attention away from Anna and onto me. If he became distracted enough, then maybe she would be able to wriggle away from him. It wasn't a great plan, but it was the best I had until Timothy showed up. *Where was he?*

"You killed Katie because she figured out that you were cheating the Amish craftsmen out of their fair share of their woodworking sales. You made a deal with them that they would receive sixty percent of the sale of their items, but you lied to them about the prices the items sold for and pocketed the difference." My voice shook with anger as I spoke because I knew Grandfather Zook was also a victim. "How did she find out?"

He closed his eyes for a moment. "All I had her do was file some of the receipts, and she started asking questions. I told her that she wasn't supposed to be reading the receipts, just filing them. Later I caught her digging through the drawers as if she were looking for something. I would have strangled her right at that very moment if Nathan hadn't stepped into the office."

Tears rolled down Anna cheeks as she listened to Levi give his reason for killing her sister as if it made perfect sense. *Keep it together, Anna,* I whispered in my head. *Keep it together. We can still get out of this. Don't give up.*

"I knew I shouldn't have hired her, but my son begged me to. He said she wanted to leave the cheese shop because some *Englischer* wouldn't leave her alone there. He knew the *Englischer* would never come to our warehouse."

"She told Nathan, didn't she? She told your son that his father cheated the families in the district."

Levi dropped the chisel two inches from Anna's throat. "*Ya*. The stupid girl. My son did the right thing, told her that she must be wrong, that I would never do anything like that. After talking sense into her, he told me. I denied it and told him that Katie must be confused. Before he left, I saw the glimmer of doubt in his eye, and I knew it was all over. I had no choice. I had to get rid of the girl before she made it even worse. What if she reported me to the deacon? Or to the police? I couldn't have that."

A new shadow appeared on the side of the barn, and it was

moving. I blinked, wondering what I was seeing. *Was it Timothy? Had he heard us and snuck around the other side of the barn?*

Jeb Lambright appeared behind Levi holding a tire iron. *What is he doing here? How did he know to come here? Did Levi tell him?* I shivered as I remembered the abuse accusations Jason made against Jeb.

Jeb took two long strides behind Levi Garner and hit the man on the head with the tire iron.

Anna screamed as Levi fell forward and knocked her to the ground, landing on top of her. Jeb dropped the tire iron onto the ground and shoved the unconscious man off his daughter. Anna scrambled to her feet. Ruth ran to her friend and the two girls clung to each other as Jeb stood still as a statue, as if in a stupor.

Timothy burst out of the stand of evergreen trees and took in the scene. "I heard shouting and ran here as fast as I could." He blinked. "What happened?"

I gave him an abbreviated version.

"We need something to tie him up before he comes to," Timothy panted.

"I know just the thing." I ran into the Gundy barn and removed a roll of duct tape from Billy's backup stash. I handed it to Timothy.

"Silver." He smiled at me. "Because Billy is a purist."

"Right."

Timothy kneeled in the snow and pulled Levi's wrists together behind his back and secured them with a long strip of duct tape. He then moved to Levi's ankles. Then, Timothy stood back and admired his handiwork. "It's not that much different than tying up a cow."

A few feet away and with tears in his eyes, Jeb Lambright folded his surviving daughter into a hug. He said something to her in their language.

Anna held onto him for dear life.

I looked at Timothy.

He swallowed. "He promised that their life would be different now, and he said that he loved her."

I watched a father and daughter reunite. It was something I longed for too. Was it possible for me? Would my father risk his life to save mine? I didn't know. Shouldn't that be something children should know about their parents?

"Will you call Greta?" Timothy asked, shaking me from my black thoughts.

I gave him a lopsided grin. "Don't I always?"

Twenty minutes later the sound of snowmobiles broke into the quiet of the winter-washed fields. Chief Rose and her team appeared over the horizon and came to a stop a few yards from us.

The police chief climbed off her snowmobile and removed her helmet. Her brown poodle curls sprang perfectly into place. "Humphrey, when I asked you earlier today if there was anyone else out to get you, you didn't need to go find someone."

I didn't bother to respond to that.

She poked Levi's side with the toe of her snow boot. "Duct tape. How appropriate."

"In Billy's honor," I said.

The Appleseed Creek police chief snorted. "You're welcome to keep helping me sort out cases like this, Humphrey, but let me make it very clear, you will never be on my payroll."

"Understood." I watched Jeb wrap his arm around his daughter's shoulder. "I don't do it for the payroll."

"Neither do I," the chief murmured, before looking over her shoulder at her crew. "Nottingham, strap this turkey to the back of one of the snowmobiles, and do me a favor. Make sure he is strapped in good and tight. I don't want him rolling off and suing the department for his injuries."

Nottingham nodded, and he and Officer Riley rolled the still unconscious Levi onto the sled that would hook to the back of one of the snowmobiles.

"If you hit a few ruts making your way to the road, that's okay," the chief said. "Got that, guys?"

"We got it, Chief," Nottingham said with a wicked smile.

Chief Rose squinted at me. Her silver eyeliner caught the light of the setting sun. "You didn't hear that, Humphrey. Okay?"

"Hear what?" I asked with a grin.

Epilogue

A few days later, Timothy waited with me just a few feet away from the security checkpoint at the Columbus airport. I adjusted my carry-on, hoping that I remembered to pack everything I would need. The last thing I wanted to do when I got to California was ask Sabrina for a toothbrush.

My feet rooted to the linoleum. I stalled. "Have you heard from Billy?" I asked.

"You mean Walter?" he asked bitterly.

"Is that what we're calling him now?" I asked. A woman with a hot pink animal carrier walked by with a dog yapping from inside. If they were on my plane, it was going to be a long flight to LA.

Timothy shifted his feet. "I don't know what to call him. He's still in the hospital. When he can be moved, Chief Rose will ship him off to Michigan."

"What can we do for him?"

"We can pray. He's on the church's prayer list." He paused. "Nathan Garner is too. He's in Columbus. Surgery is scheduled for tomorrow on his finger."

I winced. "Poor guy. His girlfriend is murdered, and he learns his father is the killer. Plus, his best friend attacks him."

"With Levi and Caleb out of the picture, it looks like he will be running the warehouse all by himself—if he can figure out how to pay back everyone his father swindled over the last twenty years."

"Tell your family, I said good-bye." I bit the inside of my lip. "I mean, if you think that they want to hear it." I hadn't been back to the farm since Mr. Troyer asked me to leave, and neither had Becky.

Timothy faced me and squeezed my hands. "Chloe, my parents are just upset right now over Becky's hair. You know that they were hoping she would go back to being Amish. They know it was her decision and that what Becky does is not your fault."

I wasn't sure his parents would agree with him. I'd gotten the impression that they thought it was *all* my fault because I was an intruder, an outsider. I changed the subject. "Has Ruth been able to see Anna more often?"

Timothy nodded. "*Grossdaddi* told me that Anna was over at our farm all day yesterday."

"I'm glad. Anna deserves happiness and a father who loves her."

"Everyone does," Timothy said. "Including you."

A TSA agent barked just a few feet away. "Have your IDs and ticket out. Any liquids? Laptops need to go in trays. Those shoes must come off."

I shivered. "I should get in line."

"Are you sure you don't want me to come with you? I can buy a ticket right now. The pavilions will be fine without me. It's too cold to work on them anyway."

I gave him a smile and squeezed his forearm. "Thank you, but I need to do this by myself."

He folded his hands over mine. "Remember that I'm proud of you."

"You might not be so proud of me when I throw up on you in a few minutes. I'm so nervous."

Timothy laughed. "You can face down a killer, Chloe. A few days with your dad will be a piece of cake."

My dad, maybe. Sabrina, not so much.

He grew serious. "Whatever happens with your dad and Sabrina, remember you tried. If they don't accept you after that, then that's their monumental loss."

Comments like this made what I was about to tell Timothy even more true. "Before I go I need to tell you something."

His eyes twinkled. "What?"

I looked him dead in the eye. "I love you."

He grinned and leaned forward to kiss me. When he pulled away, he said, "Now, go. You have a plane to catch."

I filed into the slow-moving security line. Timothy stood there, watching me until I crossed through the security scanner.

On the plane, I lifted my small overnight bag into the bin above my seat, when my cell phone in my pocket beeped, telling me I had a new text message. I fell into my seat next to the woman with the hot pink dog carrier. A Bichon Frise's head popped out of the top opening.

I smiled at the woman. "He's cute."

"Don't pet him." She sniffed. "He bites."

"Oh." I scooted over in my seat as far as I could without actually hanging into the aisle, then I removed my cell phone from my coat pocket. The text was from Timothy. *Focus on your family now. Don't worry about mine. We'll all be family someday.*

I stared at Timothy's text until the flight attendant announced it was time to put away all electronic devices. And the weight of the worries I had carried onto the plane with me blew away like a breeze across the Troyer farm.

Dear Reader Letter

Dear Reader,

I knew the moment I added Billy from Uncle Billy's Budget Autos to *A Plain Death*, the first Appleseed Creek Mystery, he would have a larger role in a future book in the series. I didn't know he would have a dark past and be a murder suspect. Characters doing the unexpected is one the great delights of writing, and the characters in *A Plain Disappearance* are no exception. All the characters have astonished me in some way, even my protagonist, Chloe Humphrey. When they surprise me, that's when I learn the most about them as characters and when I learn the most about myself as a writer.

However, even though I typically write without an outline, I know where some key characters will end up. One example is Curt Fanning. I hope he surprised readers in this novel, but I knew the position he would be in by the end of this book before I finished writing *A Plain Death*. I hope you agree with me that it's the place he needs to be.

In interviews, I am consistently asked what the theme is in my writing. I answer this question with "I don't write to themes. I don't have a theme in mind." This is true. My goal as a writer is to tell a story. That is all. There is no big message I am trying to express to the reader. However, when I finished *A Plain Disappearance*, I surprised myself yet again because I realized I wrote a theme into this series even if it was unintentional. The series' theme is forgiveness. The forgiveness is between the English and Amish in Appleseed Creek, between the Troyers and their children who left the Amish way, between Timothy Troyer and his past, between Becky Troyer and her ambitions, between criminals and their victims, and we hope between Chloe and her father. Only future novels will tell how the story ends for Chloe and her father.

May the characters make you smile, the mystery raise your suspicions, and the romance touch your heart.

Blessings and Happy Reading!

Amanda Flower

Discussion Questions

1. What was your favorite part of the novel? Why?

2. Which character did you identify with the most? Why?

3. The Amish in the novel celebrate Christmas. How is their celebration similar to yours? How is it different?

4. How is Chloe's relationship with her father similar to Lambright girls' relationship with their father?

5. Who is your favorite character and why?

6. What's your take on Billy from Uncle Billy's Budget Autos?

7. Of the antagonists in the novel, which did you dislike the most? Why?

8. Did you learn anything new about Amish culture from reading this novel?

9. In this novel, you finally meet Chloe's best friend Tanisha. What does Tanisha bring to the story?

10. Before the end of the novel, who did you think the murderer was? Were you right?

11. What are your thoughts on Becky and Aaron's relationship?

12. What are your thoughts about Curt Fanning and Brock Buckley after reading the third book in the series?

13. What do you hope for Chloe in the future?

14. What do you hope for Becky in the future?

15. What plotline would you write if you were writing an Amish mystery?